Also by James A. Lyons

*"A" Different Kind of Superpower*

# Out in Greenwood

James A. Lyons

SRL PUBLISHING

SRL Publishing Ltd
London

www.srlpublishing.co.uk

First published worldwide by SRL Publishing in 2025

# SRL PUBLISHING

THINKING DIFFERENTLY, DELIVERING CHANGE



ISBN: 978-1915073-40-2

1 3 5 7 9 10 8 6 4 2



A CIP catalogue record for this book is available from the British Library

SRL Publishing is a climate positive publisher offsetting more  carbon emissions than it emits.

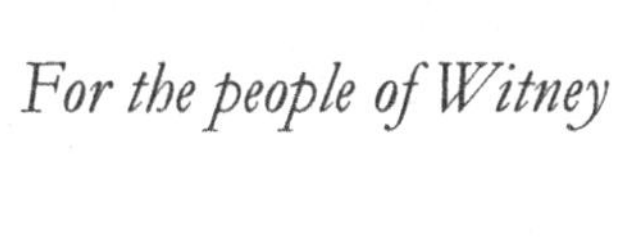

*For the people of Witney*

# One

## *Sunday*

**Hey. When are you back home? We need to talk. Johann x**

Tim Johnson was not an expert on relationships by any length, however even he knew getting the dreaded '*we need to talk*' message was the great big shiny number one in the 1,000 Texts That You Don't Want To Receive From Your Almost-Boyfriend homosexual dating guidebook.

Now, coming out as gay is often romanticised in films, books, and on television as if going from monochrome to technicolour. A character's grey backstory is suddenly replaced by a brilliant rainbow-filled life, with them being thrown into a world of partying, confetti cannons, and newly found confidence. The reality is, if you are gay, you spend just as much time being stuck in the mundane as everyone else.

Tim's current version of the mundane found him sat waiting for his family on the edge of an endless field of fruit, the smell of freshly spread manure invading his nostrils. Maybe strawberry fields were forever after all.

**Is everything okay? I will be home in thirty. T x**

He re-read Johann's message after firing off his

response, slumping at the base of a solid oak tree at Mr Murray's Park 'n' Pick farm. There was something ominous about Johann's tone, especially the harrowing second half. Each word felt like a pair of hands squeezing his temples together. He grabbed at his hair, trying to break their grip. His muscles were stiff after a long car journey back from the family holiday in Clacton. He needed to be anywhere else but right here, right now.

He gazed across the fields, bleached gold by the August sunshine, at the heads of his parents and brother, who were still shoulder deep in fruit plants. Tim had enjoyed the holiday on the Essex coast, despite getting soaked to the skin for most of it. It had rained heavily for five days out of seven at the Eternal Sunshine Holiday Park. Having left their caravan at just before midday, Tim could have been on his way to meet Johann at least an hour ago. According to the Sat-Nav, the drive in the family Volvo would have been just over three hours (or three-and-a-half with a toilet break added in).

Trouble started not long after handing in the keys to the park reception. Firstly, they had got stuck behind a dawdling tractor on a single-track road for forty-five minutes, and then some sheep had got loose as they passed through Heynsham, which caused yet another tailback. On top of that, a milk spillage across the main road close to Greenwood had finally stopped them from completing their journey altogether. The smell of evaporating milk in the heat was vile, and Tim had resorted to burying his head into the neck of his t-shirt, trying to mask the scent with the Lynx he had liberally sprayed over himself that morning.

All these incidents came before it was decided they would swing off the road altogether to be dragged into Mr Murray's. At present, Tim decided he hated farms, farmers, and anything related to either. After all, they were only here to collect berries so his mum could make some fruit pies for the upcoming fete.

The Greenwood Secondary School Fete was always the key event in the summer calendar. This years would act as a fundraiser in order to afford much needed building repairs, such as fixing the windows in the English block which either didn't open (awful in summer) or wouldn't shut (freezing in winter). Tim's mum had been obsessed with the Bake Off element since it was announced a few weeks ago, even though she was someone who constantly burnt microwave meals.

Tim laid back on the cool grass and closed his eyes, taking in the sound of a light aircraft passing overhead. The peace was broken quickly when his mobile rang. He jumped up, ready to speak to Johann. His heart sank a little when he saw it was just Leo's name on the screen.

"Alright, Leo?" Tim answered.

"Hey. Where are you at?"

"I'm at Murray's. You?"

"Home. I'm bored," Leo said. "Mum has got me helping to plan the Christmas arrangements."

"Already?"

"I know, it's ridiculous. We've got most of the Caribbean side of the family coming over though so apparently this takes a military operation to organise."

"Can always come to mine on Christmas afternoon if you need to escape."

"Ha. Ha. Ha. I would take you up on that, but there would be no way my mum would let me. You know how full-on a Gardener family party is. When are you home this evening, anyway?"

"No idea," sighed Tim, looking back across the fields. "Hopefully before six. My parents are so slow at picking," he added, gesturing towards his parents before realising Leo couldn't see them over the phone. "Leo, can we hang out tomorrow?"

"Yeah, for sure. Lydia is having a buffet thing if you want to come?"

"I guess that works," Tim replied.

Leo was quiet for a moment. "What's wrong?"

"Nothing."

"Tim?"

Tim let out a sigh, realising Leo knew him too well for him to be able to hide his emotions. "Johann just messaged me."

"Why's that bad?"

"He said we need to talk."

"Ah, shit," Leo replied, matter-of-factly.

"Shit, indeed," Tim agreed. "And he forgot to send me a goodnight message on Instagram on Monday *and* Wednesday.

"That sucks, mate, sorry."

"I was kinda planning on asking him to be my boyfriend properly, too."

"You still can."

"He's going to break up with me, isn't he?" said Tim. Saying it out loud made it all far too real.

"No, course not. He probably wants to catch up. Anyway, you don't need to make all this boyfriend stuff official, as it pretty much is anyway." A newly irregular breathing pattern stopped Tim from replying. "Trust me, Tim, it'll all be fine. Look, I gotta go. Mums come back with more post-it notes and pins. Keep me updated won't you, just stop thinking about Johann and you'll feel better. If you need back-up, gimme a shout. Laters."

The screen went blank. Zero new notifications in the last five minutes. Since the Sunday four weeks ago when he had first met Johann, Tim's life had revolved around him. Seeing Johann, thinking about Johann, learning about Johann's Swedish childhood, messaging Johann, everything Johann. Them holding hands in the park for the first time had made all these feelings multiply by approximately ten billion percent. The fear of losing that made Tim decide there was no time to lose. He would need to make Operation Boyfriend a reality!

He opened the notes app to start a plan. His fingers hovered over the keyboard, but his mind was blank. As he was still coming to terms with accepting his sexuality, a real date terrified Tim. How could he publicly date another boy (even if it was an extremely, breathtakingly, annoyingly hot one) when only Leo, Lydia, and his brother knew he was gay? With school starting again soon, being out would make Year Eleven extra crappy. If homophobia was an arrow, Tim would be a bullseye. He had two weeks to sort out this mess.

He checked his messages again. Still no new notifications. Would double-messaging Johann be too keen? By this point, Tim didn't care.

***Yo J! Just near Greenwood still. I am stuck fruit picking. Please come and rescue me lol x***

As soon as he hit send, the voice of an announcer on his dad's portable radio drifted across on the warm breeze. He quickly buried the phone in his shorts pocket.

"…and the time is now coming up to a quarter to six. I will be back with the birthday shout-outs and then a lovely cheesecake recipe sent in by Sandra from Northlee, shortly after a travel update from Rob in the FoxyCopter"

"…Yes, thank you, Judith, the traffic is currently still looking very heavy after the earlier milk spillage on the Greenwood slip road. I can see the services down there now trying to fix the issue. The temporary traffic lights are still in place by the Tesco store so there are some blockages in that area also, making progress slow in both directions, and—"

"Please can you turn that off or change the station or anything? I can't listen to more of the same news and boring recipes on loop all day!" Tim said, picking at some loose rubber on the side of his Converse.

"The radio stays on," replied his mum as she took a seat on a nearby picnic table, rearranging one of her new oversized kaftans she had suddenly started wearing literally everywhere she went. "Your dad wants to hear the football report." She turned her attention to a crossword in the latest edition of her *Live Your Life* magazine, slowly tapping at her front teeth with a blue ballpoint, before adding, "We are nearly ready to go home now, anyway, so just sit and wait."

"We've been nearly going home for an hour now," Tim responded.

"Well, I wasn't the one who poured a load of milk on the road, was I?" said his dad, placing two baskets laden with fruit down next to him.

"Nor was I!" Tim replied, as he started punching his thighs with clenched fists.

His brother, Marty, stood a few metres away, messaging on his phone with blackberry-stained fingertips, headphones on full volume. His dad took a seat at the table, leaning forward on his elbows, checking out his t-shirt suntan in the small make-up mirror from his wife's handbag. Most of his tan had come from his time on a boat in the Pacific during the few months he had spent there as part of his latest Navy expedition. As it had rained in Clacton, it can't have been from catching the rays of the sun this week. Tim looked down at his own forearms, noticing his own tan was closer to a ghost than one of the Strictly Come Dancing celebrities.

Tim stared into the distance. He was certain he could see the roof of his house in Oak Tree Crescent if he squinted enough through the heat-haze. "Can I just walk home from here?" he asked.

"Absolutely not!" replied his dad.

"Why not?"

"Ha!" exclaimed his mum. "You would have to cross the main road. You'll get yourself killed."

"How? No one has moved on there for yonks. It just said on the radio. I won't get run over."

"A no is a no," she said again firmly, turning the volume up to drown out the moaning from behind her. She had given up on the crossword already and had tucked the pen behind her ear, under her short platinum-dyed hair. He was desperate to get home he even thought about calling Pat and Pet, who lived next door, asking them to drive up and collect him. The radio was tinny and on the verge of giving Tim a headache. The slight wind made it harder to hear, which was good, but this didn't stop him learning all about Sandra's stupid cheesecake.

"What's with that face?" Marty said as he moved closer, his phone camera pointing towards his younger brother, oblivious to the argument. He sat down next to Tim, slipping his headphones off and nudging his brother's foot with his own. He pulled at his black band t-shirt to cool off.

"Stop taking photos of me," Tim said, pushing Marty's phone away. "And there's nothing wrong with my face. I just wanna be home."

"I didn't mean your face, but never mind. Hey, hopefully we'll be home by half six," Marty said. "Got any plans?"

"Nothing concrete, nah, but I need to see Johann. I also need to do some reading on diving techniques too because I missed my last lesson and can't fall further behind."

Marty shuffled closer and put his headphones into

Tim's bag. "Enjoy the holiday, though?" he asked, offering Tim a Malteser from a share-sized bag.

"Yeah, it was okay," Tim replied, taking four.

"What was your fave bit?"

"I'unno, maybe the amusements?"

"Not Harry in the café?"

"Shut up!" Tim whisper-shouted. "We can't let them know I'm G-A-Y," he added, nodding in their parents' direction.

"Spelling it out hardly helps, mate. They're not dogs."

Right, okay, so yes, the café was Tim's favourite bit of the holiday. It was called "Creams" (bad name) and sat just on the edge of the holiday park near an algae-strewn (and criminally underused) boating lake. Tim had been to the café every day, sometimes twice, to read. The holiday park coffee may have been the best Tim had ever tasted, apart from the ones he used to get at The Lucky Coffee Café in Greenwood, which had sadly gone bankrupt.

Harry the barista was the second most attractive person Tim had ever seen in his life (after Johann, obviously). His perfectly formed sharp jawline drew you up to his rich, dark eyes. He always wore a sky-blue polo shirt, which allowed toned, tanned arms, to bulge out in all the right places. Looking at him was enough to make Tim lose his place in his book multiple times. Harry inspired Tim to make more effort in gym classes at school, rather than just at his weekly diving lessons. Tim was thin and spindly in comparison, like if you stood a tomato plant next to a cactus.

Anytime Tim got caught staring, he would feel his cheeks turn crimson within milliseconds. He would have put Harry at about twenty-one years old, so too old for a relationship, discounting the fact he himself already had a boyfriend (sort of, but not officially). Harry probably wasn't even his name. They didn't wear name badges frustratingly, but to Tim he looked like a Harry. If he were to build a Harry he would have surfer-style blonde hair, Cadbury's-chocolate-coloured eyes, and perfectly shaped biceps. Therefore, this was a Harry.

Tim had found the café on Instagram and painfully scrolled through all two thousand, three hundred and twenty-six followers they had, but alas, had no luck in finding a personal account. On the penultimate day, Marty had come to the café and quickly realised Tim was besotted. Since that moment, Marty had teased his brother about it, which had made Tim feel guilty for looking at other boys. He did know Marty had kissed a girl from a caravan placed seven berths down from their own, though, so he had some comebacks, except Marty knew this girl's name (Moesha), and they had swapped numbers AND social media handles. She lived in Scotland, though, so it was unlikely their relationship would blossom, or even produce a tiny green sprout of romance.

Thinking about the previous week, and aside from Harry and his biceps, Tim decided the only other part of the holiday he had enjoyed was the amusements. (Obviously. Who *doesn't* like a seaside amusement arcade?)

There was something about their nostalgic faded glory that appealed to him. He had spent around £15 on the two-pence sliding machines alone. It was worth it as he had come home four rubber Stegosaurus keyrings richer. He planned to give one each to Johann, Lydia, and Leo. He and Marty had also challenged each other on a basketball game named *Slam Dunkers*, which Marty won (three times in a row), a confusing one called *Polybius* which wasn't there on the second visit, and they had fought on some retro arcade machine called *Street Fighter II*, which seemed to revolve around smashing any of the available buttons and hoping for the best. Marty also won that.

"Still got your keyring?" Marty asked, continuing the conversation in the shade of the tree.

Tim waved it at him and smiled, before looking back across the fields. He could see there were no other fifteen-year-olds stuck out here on a Sunday afternoon. They would all be out with friends or seeing their own almost-boyfriends. His mind wandered back to Operation Boyfriend. *We need to talk.* Why had Johann gone and said that? Tim could feel sweat forming under his armpits again, so he sat up, putting his weight on his knees, before reaching out and grabbing some strawberries. He stuffed them in a napkin and buried them in his pocket.

"What are you doing with them?" asked Marty, spotting the theft.

"Gonna give them to Johann," he replied.

"You could at least rinse them in water first. They're covered in mud. What if he's a germaphobe?"

Tim shook his head. "Nah, he isn't. He said he wants to go to Berlin on holiday next year." His mouth became dry again. "Marty, speaking of Johann, can I ask you something?"

Marty moved to sit close to him. "What is it?" he whispered.

Tim pulled out his phone and showed the message. "What do you think this means?"

His brother took the phone and started scrolling. Tim wished everyone would be so cool with him being gay. Marty had been protective from the moment he had seen Tim's secret in a notebook that he had foolishly left on his bedroom desk. However, not being out to his parents or any adult at all in Greenwood made Tim paranoid he was being silently judged. Whenever he was asked if he had a girlfriend by anyone, he would go silent and fidgety. It felt as if he was walking round with a megaphone on his head screaming the word GAY back at them. The thought of actually telling the truth scared him more than heights or even spiders.

He wanted his own coming out to be perfect. In his head he had played through around a million scenarios, ranging from leaving them a letter and running away for a weekend, to hosting a gigantic coming out party in their front garden with balloons and party bags. Maybe the latter was slightly too over the top, though. Anyway, he'd never be able to afford that on his paper boy wages, even after scrapping the idea of having a marching brass band introduce him to the guests.

Marty handed the phone back to Tim. "Johann just wants to talk to you," he said dryly.

"I know that, but this is bad, ain't it?" Tim replied, begging for some useful guidance.

"Not always, he might just have missed you as much as you have missed him, as unlikely as that is," Marty said, making sure their parents were out of earshot.

The holiday was the longest he and Johann had been apart since meeting. Tim knew he would miss Johann, but he didn't realise just how much. It wasn't just the holding hands part (they had done that a few times secretly, but not in town), or the kissing part (they hadn't technically done this yet, but Tim thought they would have if he didn't have to go to the other side of England to stay in a caravan). He just missed being around Johann. The holiday had been made slightly worse when Johann had forgotten to send his usual goodnight "X" Instagram DM on two occasions (Monday and Friday).

The more he thought about it, the more he convinced himself Johann had changed his mind about their relationship (if he could call it that). It was making him feel ill, and he even did a small sick-burp. He went back to Instagram and replied to Johann's latest story. He didn't care how desperate the triple-messaging looked, because it was far less desperate than he actually was.

Johann appeared online, but then disappeared again without even beginning to type. Tim threw the phone into his bag and leant back against the bark again, staring blankly at the clouds. He tried to focus on something positive. He was looking forward to restarting his paper round at Patterson's Papers on Tuesday. Mr Patterson was good at providing advice to Tim, even if he couldn't tell his manager exactly what was troubling him just yet.

Operation Boyfriend would mean, eventually, Tim would have to be courageous enough to go on his first ever real-life gay date. That would be a key part of the mission before school restarted. Leaving things in limbo always led to uncertainty, and the stomach cramps he was experiencing about being summoned to talk were too painful to continue like this. Tim wasn't Johann's first boyfriend, so he had some catching up to do. He needed to act like a Very Normal Human Being™ when in his presence, rather than a bumbling bag of jelly-like stress.

So far, the couple had mainly gone to Freddie's Diner for chips. Normally he wouldn't think twice about heading in and getting a table, but with Johann he questioned every single moment.

Have I picked the best table?

Am I sat on the chair correctly?

Am I being boring?

Would ordering chips with ketchup AND mayonnaise be weird?

Am I talking enough?

Am I talking too much?

Tim wished he was more like Leo, who had taken his own bisexuality in his stride and never had mini panic attacks when talking about it. The difference was, though, Leo wasn't not-dating someone.

"Next weekend we should head into town," said his mum, breaking Tim from his thoughts. She switched off the radio. His dad's team had been beaten heavily. "You need new shoes and trousers for school so we better head down to Keates' and get them before they sell out of your size."

"Can I have a new jumper as well?" asked Tim.

"Yours still fits. And you only need it for one more year, anyway."

"But Mum, it's already quite faded. It's not a nice blue anymore." Tim was at the age now where he wanted to fit in more. He had started becoming more self-conscious at the end of the previous schoolyear and had dabbled with skinny jeans, eyeliner, and pretending to like rock bands rather than his secret pop star favourite, *Saint Monique*. Even if it was just a mask, he needed to keep his new cool persona going. Having a cheap, tired looking jumper would ruin that impression on day one of Year Eleven.

"We will see. I might have Marty's old one in the loft somewhere which could do the job."

"Nope," Marty responded. "I used it last year at Halloween when we all dressed as zombies. I mean, I think I still have it, but it's got holes ripped into it and it's covered in fake blood."

"Katherine, buy the boy a jumper," said his dad, looking again at his tan.

"But they are forty pounds," she replied.

"Forty quid? It's just a jumper with a logo stuck on. Can't he get away with just a blue one from Primark or something?"

"He probably could, Cameron, but he thinks he is above that now."

"Can you stop talking like I'm not here?" questioned Tim.

"I am just saying a blue jumper is a blue jumper," his mum responded.

"Even so, I don't want to look cheap."

"We have to be careful with money, darling," she sighed.

"But Dad must have earned a bit from his last tour?"

His parents didn't respond but looked at each other silently. His mum didn't push the matter, instead turning back to the table as she ate Jelly Babies, using a copy of Slimming World as a makeshift plate.

Thinking about going to back to school agitated Tim, even more so on top of the Johann silent treatment situation. There was the unstoppable GCSE exam stress, and he would need to join a new committee, too. He didn't want to get involved with the School Disco Committee again, after lasting less than two months on it last year. Maybe he would try again with forming a Diving Club. If it turned out just to be him and Leo, it would be a start. Of course, without Greenwood Secondary having a pool, let alone a diving board, there wouldn't be much they could do in this club aside from watching videos of divers on YouTube.

Campbell from Year 11 Jupiter had asked Tim just before summer if he wanted to join his Scrabble society. However, over the course of the last few months he had realised Campbell was homophobic, and therefore a knobhead (a word Tim had since learnt would score him eighteen points, more so on a bonus square or two).

Tim scrunched up his eyes. Thinking about school had brought the sick feeling back. Before long he will be back covering his schoolbooks in scraps of old wallpaper, and stickers of his favourite things as he prepared to be bombarded with GCSE hints and tips. In Year 8, their

French teacher ran a competition on who had the best book covering. Tim came second, losing to Matthew, the school football captain, who only won because they were in hospital with kidney stones. He still hadn't come to terms with the injustice.

"Where are you off to now?" asked his mum as he jumped to his feet and started walking in frustrated circles in the picnic area picking at low-hanging leaves on a nearby tree.

"Stretching my legs," he lied. It felt like his brain was being swamped by a huge Swedish fog that was trying its best to consume him. What if Johann had met someone new whilst he had been away? No, that couldn't be it. Oh God, what if he knew about Barista Harry (and his arms)? No, not that either. No one aside from Marty knew about Harry, and he wouldn't have told anyone. His brother could be an idiot, but he would never do that.

Finally, his phone vibrated in his hands, Johann's name flashing out like a beacon. He took three deep breaths before nervously opening the message.

**_Hey. Meet me at the end of your road. I'll be waiting. J x_**

His heart sank further. Waiting for what? To break up with him? To tell him he was a rubbish almost-boyfriend? To tell him he would never be good enough to have a relationship with?

He felt an arm around his shoulder. "Hey, we are off now," Marty said. "Look, when we get home, I'll help unload the car and you go and see him, okay?"

Tim nodded, and buried his head into his brothers' shoulder, before letting go and walking towards the car. He scuffed his shoes across the gravel car park as the family finally made their way to the car. He was lagging a fair few metres behind.

As he caught up, Marty gave him a nod. "It will all be okay, I promise."

Tim smiled, although inside he was knotted. "Thanks, mate."

"Whatever," Marty said, smiling back, before putting his headphones back on as he opened the back door of the car.

# Two

Tim had stared out the car window, watching the water droplets running down. He had been thinking of Johann constantly, whilst imagining himself to be the main character in a music video for one of *Saint Monique's* sadder songs. In her videos however, the water wouldn't have been falling from inside a mammoth claustrophobic car wash that their dad had forced them to visit ahead getting back to Oak Tree Crescent. It hadn't been the first time his dad's desire to not appear scruffy had caused unnecessary delays.

As soon as the car pulled up outside the family home, he unclipped his seatbelt and jumped out of the backseat, cracking his knee against the doorframe. "Back soon," he shouted over his shoulder as he started to limp towards the junction at the end of his cul-de-sac. After a few steps, he turned on his heels and grabbed the deodorant out of his backpack, spraying half a can over himself, disappearing into a chemical filled cloud, like a magician leaving the stage.

"Where are you off to?" asked his mum out the rolled-down passenger side window, coughing as she breathed in the fog.

"Nowhere, explain later," he said as his walk away turned into a trot.

"Leave him to it, Mum," Marty said as he opened the boot.

"Don't be long then, darling" she replied, not bothering to try and get him back to help unpack. "I can't be arsed to cook tonight so will get fish and chips from Smarts shortly. What do you want?"

"I won't, battered sausage and chips, no vinegar, love you, bye," Tim bellowed as he left, pain pulsing in his kneecap, to find Johann.

He stalked his way around the lower end of the estate, trying to spot the Swede. In late summer, the trees standing in the west Greenwood estates were full, resembling gigantic broccoli, so it was impossible to see around any of the corners, unlike in winter when the streets were cold and bare. Tim got to a corner near the hedge-lined alley where the pair had held hands for the second time ever, but he couldn't see anyone. His footsteps echoed off the walls of each house he passed. Everywhere seemed deserted. There weren't even any of the irritating local children playing football, or equally irritating middle-aged parents walking dogs. He pulled out his phone from his shorts pocket and went to dial Johann but was interrupted by a sniffing noise coming from the alley to his left.

"Down here," came the voice, hidden by shrubs.

Tim approached cautiously, finally catching sight of him. Johann was just staring at the floor. He was sat on a low fence, elbows on his knees. An oversized deep red hoodie was covering most of his face and blonde floppy hair. Tim noticed it was one that used to be his own until the last time they had been together. He took this as a positive sign, and maybe Johann was thinking of giving the relationship another chance. Tim walked towards him and took a seat, putting a hand on his knee.

"What's going on?" Is everything okay, Johann?"

Johann took a long deep breath. "No, sorry." As he turned to face him, Tim noticed Johann's eyes were bloodshot, and he looked tired, dark circles the size of bags-for-life under each.

Tim's heart skipped. "Is it something I have done? Did you not get my postcard? I sent one, I promise!" He crouched right in front of him. "The postcard, Johann. It had a sandcastle on the front with a little flag on it saying *It's Always Sunny in Clacton* and everything. I also got you a dinosaur keyring. I left it in my bag, sorry, but I can run back and get it now. I think you will like it. I mean, you might not. But I was thinking of you," Tim couldn't stop speaking at one hundred words per second.

Tim's face was pressed against his stomach as Johann stood and pulled him into an awkward hug. He could hear Johann sniffing so dragged himself up so they were back to each other's eye level. Tim held Johann tight and kissed him gently on the ear through the hoodie.

Johann responded by hugging even firmer. "I got your postcard, thank you. Mum put it on the fridge, and every time I saw it, it twisted me up inside. I am sorry I have been so bad at messaging this week."

"Are you breaking up with me?" Tim blurted. The meticulous planning he had done for finding the correct way to ask the question ruined by panic.

Johann stopped rubbing at his eyes with his sleeves. "Of course not. Why would I break up with you?"

Tim shrugged. "You said you wanted to talk. That's boyfriend code for wanting to break-up. I feel a bit of an idiot for asking now, though. Sorry."

"Stop worrying. I need you." Johann swallowed nervously. "Look, things are a bit hard right now. My uncle. He has been unwell. My mind has not been focussed," said Johann eventually.

"Oh God, Johann, I am so sorry." Tim didn't know

much about his uncle. In fact, Tim didn't even know he had an uncle, but he hated seeing Johann upset. He left a pause in the conversation to allow Johann some time before continuing. "How ill? And did you find out today?"

Johann pulled out the hug a little and shook his head. "Last Sunday. He collapsed during a round of golf. He was excited after managing to get the ball in the hole from a bunker or something near the eighteenth green. It meant he had won the Lundsbrunn Invitational Trophy against his friends, and he just got too overexcited. His heart just gave up. We got a phone call from my aunt about an hour after you had left last week saying they were rushing him to hospital. It's quite lucky really."

Tim frowned. "Doesn't sound lucky if you ask me."

"Well, the cup is for local medical professionals, so the course was full of doctors, so they knew what to do. They brought over one of those electric shock things in a golf buggy. He has been in hospital all week. I didn't want to tell you over Snapchat or whatever as I thought it would ruin your holiday. I know you'd only spend the whole time worrying about me."

"Of course I would worry, but I would've understood and done anything to have helped, you know that. Anyway, the rain had already ruined a lot of the week for me."

Johann sighed, before hugging him again. "I know, sorry. I thought it was best not to say anything before seeing you. If it's any consolation, I thought you looked cute in that picture with your rain jacket pulled tight over your head. You looked like an animated condom."

Tim let out a chuckle. "So, what happens next? Is he doing okay?"

"He is having another operation today," Johann replied. "He had something fitted on Monday, but there were complications, so they need to do more to him."

"He will be okay, though, won't he?" Tim asked again.

Johann released the hug and shrugged his shoulders, before wiping snot from his nose with his hand. "I don't know, I'm sorry."

Tim pulled out the white serviette he had picked up from the motorway services on the way home and handed it across. The grinning face of the service station's dog mascot coupled with the "Today is Your Best Day!" catchphrase on the napkin seemed very out of place in the current situation.

"You don't have to apologise," said Tim. "I know these things are hard. I'll help as much as I can. We are having some fish and chips tonight if you want to take your mind away from it." Johann looked back blankly. "It would mean making small talk with my parents, but we can eat in front of the telly. You can share some of my sausage!"

Johann laughed in response. "As good as that sounds, and how much I wish I could, that's another thing. Mum is flying to Sweden tonight to be with the family."

"I see. Are you going with her?"

"I'm not," said Johann slowly, "but I have to go and stay with my dad's cousin, Freja."

"Oh, I see," said Tim.

"He lives in Newcastle," Johann added, scraping the floor with his right trainer.

"Like, *Newcastle* Newcastle? The one near Scotland? And forever?" panicked Tim.

"Yes, that Newcastle, and no, just until Friday night. Well, until Friday at the earliest anyway, depending on what happens, y'know? The only other option was to go on an adventure week in Tenby with the local scout group."

"Where's Tenby?"

"Precisely."

"Newcastle might be fun, though, I guess?"

"It'll be nice to see somewhere new. It means I can't do my paper round at Mark's this week, though. He already gave me most of last week off."

"I'm sure he will take you back when everything is sorted."

"Maybe," Johann replied. He sat back onto the fence and waited for Tim to join. "Tim, I'm really scared."

Tim wrapped his arms awkwardly around both of Johann's shoulders. "It will be okay, Johann, he's in the best place."

"I hope so."

Tim suddenly sat up straight, pushing Johann away.

"What is it?" Johann asked.

Tim looked down at his feet. "Um, I was going to give these to you, but I don't think they're edible anymore," he replied, as he pulled the handful of now crushed strawberries from his pocket. "I just picked these from the farm a minute ago and thought you might like them, but now I guess it's not a great present unless you like jam."

Johann chuckled and forced a big smile for the first time that evening. "I like jam, so that's good, but it's better on some toast rather than out of a muddy hand if I'm honest," he said.

"Before you have them, are you a germaphobe?"

Johann screwed up his face. "I haven't learnt that word on my Duolingo yet." He held out his hand and Tim passed them across. As he did so, Johann gripped his fingers. "I've missed you so much this week, Tim," he added quietly.

"I've missed you too, like so, so, so much," whispered Tim into his ear. "Ask Marty. He was moaning

I was talking about you too much."

"Have you told him we have been on some not-dates?"

"I didn't, but he figured it out. It's cool, though. Anyway, when do you have to go to Newcastle?"

"I am getting taken to the train station with Hanna at seven thirty. I'm sorry we have to delay seeing each other again properly for a few days."

"That's okay, I totally understand. At least your sister will be with you. I will still be here when you get back, I promise."

Johann nodded. "You better be, thank you," he said. "I promise I will text you more now you know. We can FaceTime as well if you want?"

"I'd like that. Very much definitely like that."

"Cool, it's a deal."

"Have you been up to much this week? Like, to take your mind off things."

"Not really. Hanna took me to see Beans on Ghost 2: Second Serving on Thursday. It wasn't as good as the first. It was too predictable."

Tim had wanted to see the sequel since the trailer was released in March, so was disappointed Johann didn't like it. "Did Hanna enjoy it?"

"She didn't mind it. Horror isn't her thing, though. Oh, when we were on our way there we saw Leo with a boy. I can't believe I didn't tell you."

"Our Leo? Seriously?" said Tim, eyes wide.

"Yeah. It was definitely him. They were looking awkward in Poundland by the pick 'n' mix."

"What did he look like?"

"Like a generic TikToker to be honest. In shape, the TikTok haircut, wearing a Barcelona football top."

Tim let out a snort. "That will be Callum."

"Who?" questioned Johann.

"He's just moved to town. He has like a billion followers on Instagram apparently. His mum knows Leo's mum I think."

"Interesting. Speaking of mums, is yours okay?"

"Yeah, she's fine, why?"

Johann pulled out his phone. "She just posted this on Facebook."

Tim took the phone and saw she had posted a status saying *YOUR FATE IS COMING* on a colourful background, in the way parents do. "She means the school fete is this Saturday. I always tell her to wear her reading glasses before she posts."

"I thought she might have turned into some kind of end-of-world conspiracy theorist," laughed Johann.

"You can see what I mean about her always being embarrassing now, eh?"

"All parents are the same. Speaking of parents, my mum will need us to leave soon."

Tim sighed and drew circles on Johann's palm with his index finger. "I don't want you to go."

"I don't want to go either." Johann stood up again and leant on the reverse of someone's tall back garden wall opposite. He kicked around at the floor a bit again. "Before I do leave, I need to ask you something of you if that's okay?"

"Yeah, sure thing. Lemme know what I can do," replied Tim.

"Well, it's more of a favour, actually."

"Yeah, anything, as long as it isn't you asking me to look after that bloody tortoise of yours," Tim joked. Johann shuffled a bit more and pulled at a loose bit of cotton near his zip before looking straight into Tim's eyes. "Oh, it is, isn't it," Tim continued. "Your tortoise hates me!"

"Barnaby loves you. How could anyone not? He had

an adventure last time remember?" said Johann.

"That whole incident wasn't my fault remember!" Tim said defensively. An argument earlier in the summer led to Tim's mum petnapping Barnaby. It all became so out of hand that it ended up on page one of the Greenwood Gazette. The only good thing to come of it was it led to the two boys meeting.

Johann continued to stare at Tim, putting on his best puppy-dog eyes.

"Okay, Johann, as it's you I suppose I can look after him for a few days."

"See, you are the best. Leo and Lydia can help too if they want."

"I'll ask them but won't make any promises. Want me to ask mum to drive me and you around to yours now and collect him and his stuff?"

"Yes, please. There isn't much to collect. We have his outdoor pen, his food, his indoor enclosure, which you'll need to build, sorry, then there's his heat lamp and all the other bits." said Johann, counting on his hands with each new item. "I can also give you Barnaby's timetable, so you know when to feed him, when to clean his house and that kind of thing."

"Are you sure it's easy?" asked Tim. "It sounds like a lot to learn."

"Extremely easy. If I can do it, you can too. I have made you a booklet with everything you need in it," Johann added, before showing Tim a picture on his phone of the instructions, complete with a hand drawn cover featuring a felt tip Barnaby, and Tim's name in bubble writing with a heart behind it.

"That's cute," smiled Tim.

"Is it?" Johann replied, knowingly.

"Very."

"I'm glad you think so. Oh, before I forget, if he gets

diarrhoea give me a call and I will tell you exactly what to do."

"That's gross," said Tim, screwing up his face a little and doing another sick-burp.

"It's natural!" said Johann.

Tim was not looking forward to a week of bowel explosions from the new house guest. It would be up to him to clean any mess and it'd put him off Wispa's for years if he had to do that. "Are you sure you don't have time for some quick fish and chips before you go?"

"I don't feel like eating, plus I have the strawberries," said Johann. "We should best get going, sorry."

"That's cool. C'mon then," Tim said as he turned away towards the end of the alleyway with Johann just behind.

"Tim?" said Johann. Tim stopped and turned to him. "I've missed you. Like, really, really missed you."

"I've missed you too, Johann," Tim responded, noticing Johann was looking a bit happier, as if the weight of telling Tim had been dragging him down before. Johann stood as close as he could and took hold of his hands. He looked both ways to make sure they were out of sight of everyone, before giving him a quick kiss on his forehead.

# Three



## *MONDAY*

Tim was sat at the bottom of the stairs, trying to force his feet into a pair of slightly damp blue Converse. Lydia's buffet wasn't starting for another half an hour, but he wanted a slow walk in the sunshine to clear his head. All the thoughts of Johann leaving had been overwhelming him for the past fifteen hours and staying in the house just made him feel sick. There was only so many times he could catch Johann's scent on the red hoodie he had stolen back from him the previous evening.

As he grabbed his stegosaurus-keyringed housekeys, his mum poked her head around the front room door. Her hair was tied up in a bright pink towel, with a yellow one around her body. Matched with her brown slippers, she looked like a giant tub of Neapolitan ice-cream.

"Can you take this with you for Lydia's parents, please?" she asked, as she handed over a small glittery gift bag.

Tim opened it up and saw a bottle of red wine inside. "I was told we didn't need to take anything."

"Every host says that, but they don't mean it literally."

"Adults are confusing."

"You'll get used to it. If you can hand that across and

say it's from me, that would be wonderful. Tell them I will see them all later."

"What time are you getting there?"

"In a couple of hours or so. I have some bits to do first."

"Okay, cool. I'll see you in a bit," he replied as his mum disappeared back into the front room and closed the door behind her once more.

He walked across the big field towards Lydia's five-bedroomed detached house. The heatwave was still ongoing, so he took a seat on one of the swings in the playground, rocking gently forward and back. Sitting in the playground gave him a flashback to an incident he had experienced on the old wooden seesaw that used to be here. A balance misjudgement led him to slide towards the centre, with the damage being rectified by his mum removing many splinters from his backside with a pair of tweezers and a tube of off-brand antiseptic. He still got shivers at the sight of toothpicks.

After reading through some past conversations with Johann, Tim approached the gates of the old Ivy Cottage where Lydia lived. As he walked up the crazy paving towards the large oak door, he noticed Lydia's dad, Alan, on his knees, prodding at the flower beds with a trowel.

"Hi Alan," he said, trying not to startle him.

Alan looked over his shoulder, before standing, making some odd grunting noises as he did so. Alan was a stocky man, and he rubbed his short sandy beard, leaving flecks of mud dangling in the hair.

"Alright, our kid?" he said in his slow Mancunian drawl. "Enjoying your summer?"

"Yeah, it's not been bad, thanks," Tim replied, hoping Alan would not offer him a muddy handshake. He did. Tim shook it back. "I've come over for the buffet," he added excitedly.

"Yes, Lydia said you, Leo, and some other kid were coming round. There is a lot of food, so I hope you are all hungry."

"I am, definitely," said Tim. "I skipped my Weetabix this morning to leave room."

"Good planning. How's your paper round going?"

"I've been down in Clacton this week. I am back at the newsagents tomorrow. I'm looking forward to working again if I'm honest."

"You'll learn not to always enjoy work, Tim, trust me!"

"Nah, my paper round is fine. It's probably not stressful like yours." Alan was Head of Operations at IT Home Phones, which was Britain's 'third most popular communications company', according to the slogan on the white van in the driveway.

"Just take time to enjoy the summer with your friends. You'll miss it when everything changes. Life isn't all about working."

"I guess," replied Tim. "Earning money is good, though. I'd do more work for Mr Patterson if I could, Alan. I don't want it to stop, and I think I enjoy working more than sitting at home."

Alan tapped Tim on the shoulder. "You're probably feeling the way you are because you have Stockholm Syndrome," he said, before laughing.

Tim immediately felt his cheeks flush and sweat formed on his brow. He forced a half smile and walked to the house, where Lydia was waiting with the door open. She took him through to the dining room and showed him the buffet but banning him from stealing a slice of quiche. Not only had Tim beaten Leo here, but he was also the first out of everyone. He placed the wine by the microwave as she poured him a drink of orange juice before they went to the garden. He sat next to her on the patio against the back wall of the house.

"Lydia, did you tell your parents about me and Johann?"

Lydia put her drink down. "No, of course not. Why?"

He shuffled slightly. "Your dad said I'm probably feeling sad because of Stockholm Syndrome."

"Do you know what Stockholm Syndrome is?" she asked. Tim shook his head.

"Google it. It's nothing about Johann, you idiot. Stop panicking."

"Are you sure?"

"Very."

Tim had tried to convince himself to stop worrying about Johann. Hopefully it would all be better when the others arrived. "Have you met Callum yet?" he asked.

"Not yet, but I followed his Instagram. He's quite fit." She explained how he was the son of a friend that Leo's parents, Flo and John Gardner, had met at their salsa class the previous fortnight. His family had moved to Greenwood from London, and he had been introduced to Leo to try and get him to make some more local friends. He would be joining Greenwood Secondary for their GCSE year.

"Have you been stalking him?"

"No, why?"

"How do you know all that?"

"Just from what him and Leo have posted. Anyway, wait here. I just need to check the sausage rolls in the oven."

Tim sat still until she was indoors and went straight to Callum's social media. He was properly addicted to posting everything about his life online, so his account was easy to find. There were way too many hashtags under every photo for Tim's liking. #So #Many #Hashtags.

"Told you he was fit," said Lydia as she caught Tim zooming in on one of Callum's shirtless bathroom selfies.

"He's alright, I guess," Tim replied.

They sat scrolling through his photos to learn more. He was vegan (#PlantLyf), liked doughnuts (seriously, there were about ten photos of him holding doughnuts from VeganDough from the past three months alone), and he supported Aston Villa, going to games regularly.

Callum was also quite good at filming viral video clips of himself doing keepy-uppies with a football, again topless, in his garden. His Instagram had over seventy-two thousand followers. That was probably because he was tall for his age, had a toned body, and the trendy noodle-like hair. It was so much easier to get followers if you were conventionally attractive. Even his stupid doughnut photos had five thousand likes. Tim thought Callum was way too attractive and cool to be hanging around in their group.

From speaking to Leo first thing this morning, Tim had learnt quickly Callum was one hundred percent straight. He had apparently mentioned this to Leo shortly after Leo told him he was bisexual, as if to put a barrier up immediately. He also knew he was born on the first of September, so would therefore be the oldest in the school year and the first in the group to turn sixteen.

Tim was nervous about meeting Callum. He realised he needed to let go of preconceptions, though, and give him the benefit of the doubt. They would be stuck in the same friendship group for a year after all. He decided, despite being someone who craved online validation, that Callum was probably a good egg (if you are allowed to describe a vegan as such).

"Alright?" Leo said as he burst through the back gate, allowing it to clang back heavily on its hinges. Tim closed Instagram and hid the phone back in his pocket. Leo bounded across and sat opposite, cross-legged. "Your dad's out the front and told me to come straight round."

"Cool," said Lydia. "Where's Callum?"

"On his way. Why's he looking so sad? Johann?" Leo replied, pointing at Tim. Lydia just stared at him trying to make him keep quiet. "What? What's happened?"

"Johann's gone to Newcastle for a week," Lydia whispered.

"Ah sorry, man," said Leo, putting an arm round Tim and pulling him close with too much force.

"I'm fine, honestly," said Tim. "I just need to keep my mind occupied."

"Why don't you find another job to do during the day for a bit?" asked Lydia.

"Your dad told me to enjoy the summer rather than work all the time. Anyway, where would employ me? All I know how to do is deliver newspapers."

"There's restaurants," she replied.

"Yeah, restaurants could work, Tim," Leo said. "Actually, hang on!" He scrolled on his phone before quickly turning the screen to show a post his mum had shared on Facebook.

**PART-TIME LIBRARIAN REQUIRED
GREENWOOD LIBRARY
HOURS AND DAYS TO FIT YOUR SCHEDULE
FOR MORE INFORMATION EMAIL
RECEPTION@GREENWOODLIBRARY.CO.UK**

Tim screwed his face up. "Hmmm, I dunno. I haven't read many books."

"Yeah, but you don't have to read the books," replied Leo.

"Exactly," added Lydia. "That's not your job. You just show people where the books are."

"I'll see. Maybe. They probably don't want a kid,

though."

"Why not?" asked Leo. "We could see if we could both do work for them on Saturdays if you like?"

"I guess. Lemme think about it."

Clouds had now rolled over Greenwood, and the shaded back garden meant the temperature dropped quickly. "Let's go in," said Lydia.

They walked into the house, joining the other guests who had slowly been arriving. In the large kitchen, Lydia poured juice for them all as Tim rested on the AGA for some warmth. "Why were you late, anyway?" he asked Leo.

"Just…things," he replied.

"What did you do?" questioned Tim. He knew when Leo was hiding something.

"Nothing," Leo hissed.

"Ha, tell me!"

"Okay, fine. I had a big milkshake at lunch, and it didn't agree with me."

"Were you sick?" asked Lydia.

"Sort of," he replied.

"Ew, it was the other thing, wasn't it?" said Tim. "That's gross."

"Look," responded Leo, "you don't have to say it so loud. Everyone will find out."

"Johann told me to phone him if Barnaby got diarrhoea. Want me to see if he has any tips for you?"

"Very funny. I'll be fine. I've had some tablet things. Mum thinks I'm allergic to milk now. Good thing is that I've kinda been put off milkshakes for a while anyway."

"I had that once," said Tim. "If you're ill you can't eat the same thing again for a while. I couldn't even look at lemon meringue pie for about five years."

"I'm sure it was just a bad batch of milk," Lydia added.

"Trust me to get milk from a grumpy cow," said Leo as he walked through to the main room. Lydia's house was much grander than Tim's. All their furniture matched for starters, the mantelpiece wasn't full of awful charity-shop bought trinkets, and there wasn't an inch of dust obscuring Lydia's school photo hanging on the wall.

Tim picked up a paper plate and started to build a pyramid out of beige food items. "What's all this in aid of anyway, Lyds?" he asked.

"Parents seventeenth wedding anniversary. They were meant to be going to The Trout at Turnbridge, but the cellar flooded yesterday morning, so they had to do this instead." She took a bread stick and submerged it into a vat of humous.

"This would've taken me weeks to put together. Anyway, Leo you could have mentioned it was for an anniversary on the phone yesterday. I would have picked up a card from work."

"Help yourself to everything you want," came a voice from behind. Tim turned to see Lydia's mum, Amy, stood in an apron, smiling.

"Thanks, Amy, will do," replied Tim. "Oh, by the way, Mum will be over later. She asked me to drop off some wine. It's on the side there in the silver bag." He turned to where he was pointing at, to see about twenty matching gift bags, all probably filled with the same.

As he slumped onto the sofa, he looked around the room. The house was now filled with many characters from around town. Tim didn't realise so many people were free on a Monday afternoon at short notice. Even their headteacher, Mr Barakat, was here, carefully stirring a large glass bowl full of what Tim guessed to be punch.

Leo was also staring at Mr Barakat. "I do not want to go to school again, yet."

"We still have two weeks," replied Lydia.

"Still not enough time. I don't wanna do the GCSE's." Leo pulled out his phone as it vibrated in his pocket. "Back in a minute, Callum is here."

Tim sat up, and subconsciously ran his hand through his hair and straightened the collar on his polo shirt. He was intrigued to learn even more about the new arrival. Leo was soon leading him in to join the others. As he entered, Tim noted he was taller in real life than on Instagram. He was wearing a deep green football top from a company called "SoccSquad". Tim noticed how, even from across the room, he could see how good his pecs looked in it. He also knew, based on an Instagram post from this morning, that Callum hadn't paid for his outfit. Under the photo he had shared online, Callum had claimed, "*I love my SoccSquad gear! The flexible fit and new trademarked Breathware™ Technology makes SoccSquad the number one choice for sportswear. #SoccSquad #Breathware #Sponsored #fourfourtwo #gifted #Ad*". No fifteen-year-old writes like that. It made Tim cringe. Maybe he was just jealous Callum got free clothing. Tim thought he might try the technique and get some free Wispa's. You never know, do you?

Despite only following just over one hundred people back on Instagram, Callum was following Tim, Lydia, and Leo's accounts, and also Marty's, which Tim found to be a surprise. He also had been tagged in a photo with school homophobe and scrabble-knobhead, Campbell. How the two knew each other was a mystery.

"Callum, this is Lydia and Tim. Tim, Lydia, this is Callum." Leo said as he picked up a sausage roll and shoved it into his mouth whole.

"So lovely to meet you, Callum," Lydia said, shaking his hand.

"Alright Callum, how's it going?" added Tim.

Callum remained quiet but smiled.

"Come grab some food," Leo said, and dragged him away.

Tim turned to Lydia. "Ooh, its soooo lovely to meet you, Callum," he joked.

"I was just being nice," she replied, kicking his shin in return.

"We all fancy him, but let's not make it so obvious." Tim watched as Lydia blushed beetroot.

When they were all back together, Callum still remained quiet, often staring at his phone and offering one syllable remarks. His social media personality was far removed from what he was like in real life. Despite all this, Tim decided hanging around with a popular kid would be useful. In the worst-case scenario, Tim could become popular online by association. He could do with the followers. Having less than fifty was just depressing.

As the foursome polished off their food, the lights were turned out and the curtains drawn. Before long, the darkness was broken by the light from a large sponge cake with fondant roses and many candles being brought through the double doors.

"I feel like we should be singing," said Tim.

"Singing what?" asked Callum.

"Like, at birthdays. Is there a version of Happy Birthday for anniversaries?"

"Don't think so."

"I might write one," added Leo. "It feels awkward just sat here watching."

Amy and Alan blew the candles out whilst embraced, with the adults cheering as they did so. As soon as the cake was placed on the table, Lydia went to grab some, pulling Callum along with her.

"She's going to make me vomit," Tim said to Leo.

"It's so blatant," he replied. "Anyway Tim, can I talk to you about something?" he added, watching Lydia and

Callum as he sipped his juice through a straw.

"Yeah course, what about?" Tim asked, also watching the pair as they spoke to Amy. Lydia was stood so close to Callum that he must have been feeling uncomfortable.

"Not here. I just want to talk to you alone without the crowd," Leo said, gesturing at the others in the room. Tim gave him a thumbs up. They remained in awkward silence until the other two had re-joined.

When Lydia sat back down, she became excited. "Hey, I was just talking to Mum about Funtangutan. It's just reopened. She is off work tomorrow if you want to come along for a laugh. I can ask if she can take us?"

"I'm in," confirmed Leo. Tim sat staring into the distance. "C'mon Tim, it would be good for you."

"Fine, I'll come, thanks Lydia," Tim responded eventually.

"Did you defo want to come too, Callum?" Lydia asked as she manoeuvred her way on to the edge of the sofa next to him. Callum took a bite of icing but looked puzzled.

"It's a forest assault course type thing," said Tim, helping him out a little.

"Oh, yeah, course it is. I knew that. That sounds good, cheers. Depends on what time, though."

"I'll ask Mum, but probably the morning. We can pick Leo up so can meet you at his?" said Lydia.

Callum was now taking a photo of his cake. Lydia realised the only vegan options which had been provided were cucumber batons and the crisps, so apologised to Callum.

"That's okay," he said. "I had some stuff before I came round. And cake doesn't count, does it?"

Tim looked at him. "Well, it has butter and stuff so probably not the most vegan. We won't tell anyone, though. How are you finding it here anyway?"

"Here as in the party?" asked Callum.

"No, as in Greenwood."

Callum shrugged. "Um, it's alright, yeah. I mean, it's a bit boring compared to London, sorry."

"Yeah, don't worry, we know. Some days it's too boring," replied Tim.

"I don't like getting bored. Would rather be doing anything than sitting at home. There just doesn't seem to be any drama."

"Honestly, it has always been like that. At least we have Funtangutan though," said Leo. Callum didn't reply, instead opting to scoop up some icing and stick his fingers into his mouth.

Tim was quite pleased Callum wanted to do activities with them. Hopefully he would manage to get featured on his Instagram (#Monkeybars) and look popular. Callum would also be able to help their team get closer to the course record.

After a few awkward silences, Tim realised he didn't like house parties. He would rather just spend time hanging out with his friends without all the adults being nearby. He imagined parties would just get worse as he got older. He'd seen so many in American films with teenagers all piled into large houses drinking horrible, coloured drinks from red cups. He wasn't looking forward to when everyone in his year started turning eighteen and tried to copy what they had seen on screen.

Tim took a picture of the buffet and the cake and sent it to Johann. It was four o'clock and he hadn't checked his messages since arriving an hour ago. Johann replied instantly saying he was walking to see the Tyne river before getting taken to a shopping mall for new shoes. The party had obviously worked in terms of Tim taking his mind off the situation. He wished he was walking by the river with him instead, though. He slipped his phone away, trying to go back to concentrating on the here and now. This would have worked well if there was not an immediate and frantic knock on the front door.

Tim jumped off the sofa to see what the commotion was. On the doorstep, Mrs Patterson stood in her slippers looking distraught.

"Come in, Mrs Patterson," Tim heard Amy say, but she just shook her head.

"Are you okay, Mrs Patterson?" Tim questioned, standing by her side. She shook her head again, and her eyes pricked with tears. He was worried Mr Patterson might have had an accident.

Mrs Patterson took out a tissue and wiped her nose. "It's our newsagents. Someone has attacked our shop. It has been covered in graffiti. Please help."

# Four

Tim burst back into the front room, his heart pounding. He grabbed Lydia, Leo, and Callum's plates from under them. Callum, mid-Instagram post (#buffet), gave him a confused look but Tim didn't want to waste time to explain every single thing to him.

"Get your shoes on quickly, we have to go to Patterson's," he said, panic etched across his face.

"Why?" Lydia asked, remaining seated.

"Something's happened. Mrs Patterson is not in a good way. Come on!"

Finally sensing the urgency, the trio followed Tim into the hall. Mrs Patterson was already making her way down the garden path, so they rushed out of the house to catch up. Leo, struggling to pull his shoes on without bothering to unlace them, trailed behind as they reached Mrs Patterson, attempting to reassure her.

"What exactly happened?" Leo asked with a concerned look across his face.

Mrs Patterson stopped. "It's our shop. The window has been smashed, and it's all covered in paint."

The four friends looked at each other but kept pace with Mrs Patterson as she set off again down Church Lane and towards Bridge Street. Midway, Leo filled Callum in on the significance of the Patterson family and why they felt compelled to help.

"And this is the place where Tim works, right?" Callum asked.

"How do you know that?" Tim questioned.

"I saw a picture of you wearing a delivery bag online. The shop name is quite recognisable."

"Oh, yeah."

"In that case, I'll help," Callum confirmed.

The shop was only a ten-minute walk away, but their brisk pace left Tim's shins burning. His knee was starting to hurt as well after cracking it on the car door the previous afternoon. As they turned the corner past the old mill houses, the damage came into view on the other side of the road, with a small crowd already gathered nearby.

Tim crossed the road with Mrs Patterson, navigating through onlookers capturing the scene on their phones. Pat and Pet were in the crowd, too, stood with their new Jack Russell, Archie. Up close, the damage to the shop was even more distressing.

Mrs Patterson disappeared into their house above the shop through a side door, and Tim surveyed the wreckage. The front window displayed a large spiderweb crack from an epicentre in the bottom right-hand side of the pane. A yellow smiley face was drawn in spray paint across the centre, with X's instead of eyes. Below the face, the letters TJ had been sprayed on. This is what scared Tim the most. Mr Patterson was sat on a fold-out stool by the kerbside, his gaze fixed into space. Tim approached him gently.

"Are you okay, Mr Patterson?" he asked. Mr Patterson shrugged his shoulders but did not move his head. Tim sat next to him in silence. The stillness of the day made the quietness greater. "If you want me and the others to help clean this up Mr Patterson, we will be happy to do so."

Mr Patterson turned and smiled; however, his eyes did not reflect any happiness. "Thank you. But we must wait for the police."

"Do you have CCTV?"

"We do. I was checking while Mrs Patterson went to get help, but there is no clear view of the person who did this. I think it was planned."

"But why?"

"Your guess is as good as mine. I haven't done anything to upset anyone. They must have waited until they knew I was out. They could have been watching me all day. When I came home, this is what I saw. I'd only gone to the post office on the corner. Mrs Patterson had popped into the stockroom so did not hear anything. I am just glad she is safe. Someone was waiting for the right moment to do this."

"It's broad daylight, though, so someone must have seen something," Tim said, trying to sound comforting. "Has this happened before?"

"Never. I have not had any problem in Greenwood since moving here. Why now? Why have they waited until now?"

Tim didn't have an answer. He felt awkward and didn't know what to say. His initials being part of the damage made him feel uneasy. His mouth was dry. "It wasn't me, just to clarify," he said eventually.

Mr Patterson stood as his wife brought out two cups of tea. "I know it wasn't you, Tim."

"But my initials are on the window, so I thought you might think it was."

Mr Patterson shook his head and took a cup from Mrs Patterson's hand. Tim saw this as an opportunity to give them some time and went to join his friends.

Scandals were rare in Greenwood. The Greenwood

Gazette was usually as exciting as watching paint dry, with its weekly updates on pothole whinging and complaints about the newly imposed twenty miles per hour speed limits in the town centre. Last week's highlight was the saga of local goose chasing a dog. A story apparently so gripping that it secured the coveted front page. Clearly, the bar for excitement in Greenwood was low. It was no wonder Barnaby's accidental petnapping became the talk of the town so quickly. The editor must have been thrilled to have had something so shocking land in his inbox.

Flo Gardener was now also present on Bridge Street, along with around a dozen others who had been at the anniversary party. She approached the group of teenage friends as soon as she spotted them.

"Make sure you four keep out of this situation, please," she warned them.

"We want to help them clean up," Leo replied.

"What I mean is, don't go snooping around. This isn't a situation for you to get yourselves involved in. This is serious, it's not one of your fun little games to be playing. That includes Johann when he's back, too."

"We won't," said Tim. Flo gave him a satisfied nod, and walked back off towards the other adults.

When she was far away, Callum had an idea. "We need to help them investigate this."

"We can't," responded Leo. "You just heard what my mum said."

"So? I know everyone thinks we are too young to be of any use, but this isn't the biggest town so we will probably hear rumours."

"And that's all they will be, rumours," spat Lydia, backing up Leo.

"Yeah, but there is always truth in them," Callum continued, getting more animated. "Do you know anything, Tim?"

"Why would I know anything? I was with you three."

"I dunno, it's just…" he tailed off.

"Just what?"

"Well, the graffiti."

"What? Just because it has my initials?"

Callum nodded. "It is a bit strange that whoever did it has written *TJ* underneath it."

"Are you seriously saying you think Tim did it?" asked Leo.

"No, I just think it can't be a coincidence that it has his initials under it."

"It wasn't me!" shouted Tim, causing a few of the nearby crowd to look over. He went back to a whisper. "Obviously it isn't me. I might be stupid sometimes but not stupid enough to put my own name on something I have destroyed. And I love working here, ask anyone. How do we know it wasn't you?"

"Don't be stupid Tim," said Leo defensively. "He got to Lydia's not too long after me and lives on the other side of town."

"Well, he blamed me first," argued Tim.

"Will you both just be quiet?" Lydia said firmly.

"Sorry," said Callum, as he put his arm around Tim. "It obviously wasn't me either, but I still think we should investigate, though."

Tim shrugged the arm away from him. The other two didn't respond to Callum's apology. Having watched multiple police documentaries on Netflix, the thought of being a detective did appeal to Tim, but when it was something so close to home he would much rather not get involved. However helpful he thought he could be, he knew it was likely to hinder any investigation.

A siren could be heard in the distance, and everyone looked along towards Mill Street waiting for the police car to swing into view. The blue lights flashed across the roundabout and the vehicle skidded to a stop just short of the shop. One officer got out swiftly, and immediately moved Mr and Mrs Patterson to one side as they had approached the car.

A second officer, who had been driving, slowly pulled himself out onto the road, and told the crowd firmly to go home, whilst simultaneously pulling blue and white tape from his jacket as he began to cordon off the front of the store using nearby lampposts and drainpipes.

"What if they question us?" asked Leo, concerned, as he watched the Patterson's disappear inside.

"Well, we will have to say we don't know anything," said Lydia, "because we don't know anything, do we?"

"Exactly," said Tim. "We were all at yours, Lydia."

"Precisely," Callum replied.

"So, you honestly don't think it is me, then?" Tim asked.

"No, of course not. I didn't mean what I said earlier."

"Thanks."

Although Tim was pleased he was no longer a suspect, he was concerned about what Callum had said. If he thought it was weird his initials were underneath, other people would, too. He couldn't recall ever upsetting anyone, especially enough to make them do this. Knowing someone with the initials TJ worked at the shop would raise suspicions further. Before sunset half the town could think he was the main suspect. Maybe it was just a coincidence, but he couldn't think of anything else it could stand for.

As the commotion on Bridge Street slowly died down, only a small group of lingering onlookers remained. Flo took charge again, and she gathered the children up, telling them to follow her back to Lydia's house. She had offered an invitation to the Patterson's, however they had declined before the police had arrived.

The walk back down Church Lane remained subdued. Leo seemed most affected and lagged behind the group by about ten metres. Callum manoeuvred his way between Tim and Lydia at the front. "Is there a cinema in Greenwood?" he asked.

"Kinda," replied Lydia. "It's in the Town Hall, but only shows about three films a week."

"We should go this weekend. Tim wanna come with us?"

Tim shook his head. "Nah, there's nothing to see."

"What are you on about? 'Course there is. The new Marvel film is out remember, it looks sick," protested Callum.

"Yeah, in a normal cinema," said Tim. "Our cinema will show it in about six months' time. They tend to show older films. You don't realise how out of touch this town can be."

"What, like films from last year?"

"Try fifty years ago," said Lydia. "Sometimes even older. I think *The Wizard of Oz* is on tonight."

"What's that?" asked Callum.

"Have you seriously never heard of it?" asked Tim, bemused.

"I don't think so. I hate all films with wizards in though, so sounds crap."

"Yeah, I do too, but it's more of a family film thing. I dunno why people would pay to see it as it's on telly every week. It's about a girl who visits a land over the rainbow and that. Have you seriously never heard of it?"

"Nah, sounds gay. What about horror films? Do you like them? I love 'em," added Callum.

Of course he liked horror films, Tim thought, trying to ignore the subtle homophobia. Normal films wouldn't fit in with his tough boy London image.

"Have you seen *The Danger Underneath*?" Callum continued. "It is about these divers who get stuck in this big cave network because the entrance got flooded and their guide ropes broke. Anyway, after a while they lose their torches, and these alien things are swimming around them, being summoned by some secret signal. Every now and then one of the divers gets eaten and all his brains and guts go everywhere. On the surface a group of scientists are trying to rescue them but can see what's going on because they have this fancy radar system and that. They decide to blow up part of the cave to get in and save them, but when they get there, they're all dead. There's blood everywhere and it turns out the big twist is that one of the divers was already infected with this weird alien disease and it killed everyone. It's so good."

"It sounds horrific," frowned Lydia.

"At least we know the twist now so we never have to watch it," said Tim, before adding "Have you seen *Beans on Ghost 2*?"

"That's not a horror," Callum argued.

"Yeah, it is."

"It's a kid's film."

"Well, I liked the first one," he replied.

"Course someone like you did," said Callum sarcastically.

Tim wasn't sure what he meant by this but was too tired to pull him up on it. Noticing Leo was still lagging, Tim saw the opportunity to get away from Callum. He slowed down and allowed him to catch up.

"Alright, Leo?" he asked.

"I'm okay, yeah. I think."

"What's up?"

"I'm struggling," Leo said as he came to a standstill.

Tim stopped too. "Struggling how?" he asked.

"I was looking online and talking to people. Have you

ever done that? Like, to find out if you're the same as gay people?"

"A couple of times, yeah. It can get a bit much though, and everyone online is faking how good things are. I mean, look at Callum. Maybe take a break from that."

Leo frowned. "I thought that once I came out to someone it would all be fine. Like, hi, I'm bi, goodbye. I thought it would be simple, but it's not. Even when Callum found out I was bi, and you were gay, I was nervous. I told him as it seemed the best thing to do. It's messing with my head."

Tim put his hand on Leo's shoulder, which was met with a fake smile. Tim had been so caught up in his own whirlwind of Johann and understanding his own sexuality that he hadn't noticed Leo wasn't coping well. Leo had done everything he could to support Tim, and he didn't even mind he had been outed to Callum, yet Tim realised he hadn't offered the same support back. "Leo, you've always just seemed so, I dunno, confident, I guess?" he said.

"Yeah, that's not always the case," said Leo. "I probably seem that way to you, but I think just hanging around with you and Lydia makes me that way. I can be genuine around you all the time. Sometimes I even forget I'm bi because it doesn't matter to you both. Like, it matters, but you don't care about it, if you get me, and I love that. At home I'm not the same. There are times when I sit on my bed to think about it all and before I know it, an hour has passed, and I can't remember how I have spent that time. It's like its consuming me so much that I'm literally losing hours of my life without realising. Do you ever get that?"

"I guess I do, yeah. But for me, if I feel that way I talk to Marty, even if it's not about the whole gay thing. I just hang with him. I guess you can't do that with Kelis?"

"Yeah, when your sister is only seven it doesn't work. I doubt she would understand even the basics. Probably why I ended up chatting to people online," said Leo. "Like, finding out about being bi is hard. Every page talks about sexuality has all the bi stuff as a footnote. It's like I am not gay enough for gay people and I'm not straight enough for straight people. Where do I fit in, Tim?"

"I don't know, sorry. I hadn't thought about it. I just thought it would be the same as it was for me."

"Yeah, it really isn't. You're fine though, well, not fine obviously, but like, being gay is so much easier than being bi, I think."

"Being gay isn't exactly easy," said Tim. "Like just now Callum said something was gay."

"I know, I get you. I didn't mean it was easy as such, just for me it's been just as hard, but I tried coping and I realise now I'm not managing well at all. I don't know what to do. And what happens if I get a girlfriend. Everyone will just think this is all a phase. Or a boyfriend, if that happens then I'll be called gay when I'm not. I hate it. I don't fit into anywhere."

"How can I help?" asked Tim. "Tell me what you need, and I'll be there. You've been amazing with me and Johann, and I should've been there for you, sorry."

"You have been there, but I need you more. I don't want to lose what we have. I might just call you at random times more often."

"That's cool. And you don't even need to try and work it out when you call. Literally, phone me up and ask me a stupid question. Ask me anything you want just so you can get through those difficult minutes. Like ask me what superpower I would have, or I can ask you to name the last ten Olympic British divers."

"I guess that could work. Just expect a lot of phone

calls."

"More than normal?" Tim joked.

"Even more than normal. C'mon, we best get back."

∗∗∗

Back at the party, Tim sat on the sofa with a fresh plate of sausage rolls, some rubbery ham, and cheese quiche, but he did not feel like eating. The stress of seeing the damage had given him a slight headache, and he felt guilty about not realising Leo had been struggling. He pushed his food around in the ketchup a bit before saying he wanted to leave.

"Do you still want to go to Funtangutan tomorrow?" Lydia asked.

He nodded.

"If you come round for about quarter to ten then we will pick Leo and Callum up. Mum has managed to book the first slot, so all is good. We have a better chance of beating the course record that way. It won't be as slippery if we are the first ones on it."

"Good plan," replied Leo.

"Callum, give us your phone number, I'll add you to the group chat," said Tim, as he passed his phone across. He wanted to make sure Callum was not going to do any investigating on their behalf. Despite being accused of damaging the shop by him earlier, he wanted to give him the benefit of the doubt for now. He believed his mouth probably just spoke before his brain thought. He was fitting in, albeit slowly. He just hoped he wouldn't share anything about the afternoon with his Instagram followers.

When he got his phone back, he checked Callum's Instagram stories. The only updates from that day had been:

- A photo of a plate of toast.
- A photo of a seagull sat on a fence.
- A reshare of an old reel of him playing football in the garden.
- A clip of him from when he was on a fancy holiday. He was pouring water on elephants in some kind of watering hole.
- A photo of a cup of coffee.
- The photo of his cake from the party.

Flicking through, Tim realised this was quite a few updates for one person in one day. He didn't even add much to his story over a whole week himself.

Tim's mum had arrived at the party shortly after they had got back. She had seen a picture of the shop damage on Facebook. She must have been in a hurry to come round because she was wearing a witch's hat for some reason. Rather than head straight home with Tim, she stayed to have a glass of juice and tried to help the Flanagan's celebrate a bit more. Tim couldn't hear the conversation, but he watched as she started doing some dance moves in the kitchen. He prayed she hadn't got TikTok herself, now. The longer he watched, the more he realised how embarrassing it was. Everyone else present gazed on with expressionless faces.

Performance complete and glass empty, she passed Tim a tin full of cake and told him to come home. Walking would have been quicker, but he thought it safer to stick with her for the journey.

"Do you know anything at all about the shop?" she asked as they drove down Oak Tree Crescent.

"No, honestly. We were all together at Lydia's."

"If you hear anything, let me know. Mr Patterson was round ours when it happened."

"Really?" asked Tim. "He said he had been down the

post office."

"Maybe he had been there, too."

Tim felt as if something was being kept from him. He just hoped he would be able to do his paper round in the morning.

It was shortly after six when he jumped in the bath. He laid back in the warm water and tried calling Johann, but it went straight to voicemail. He hated talking to voicemails, even if it was someone he knew well. He always sounded weird. After three failed attempts, he sent a voice note on WhatsApp instead, which was slightly less embarrassing.

"Hi Johann. It's Me. It's Tim. Um, I hope you've had a fun day. We went to Lydia's for a party, um, but there was something at the shop. Um, someone threw a brick through Mr Patterson's window and drew a graffiti face on it. I took a picture which I'll send to you when I know you're alone. Um, I hope you have had a fun day, hang on I've said that already. Um, anyway, I am in the bath so lemme know when you're about for a chat. I'm sounding awkward so I'm going now. Miss you, bye."

Johann would know what Tim should do next. He always did.

As he was drying himself, his dad shouted from downstairs. Lydia and Leo had arrived unexpectedly.

# Five

"What is it going to do?" asked Leo.

"What do you mean, 'what's it going to do?', it's a tortoise. This is what a tortoise does," replied Tim.

Leo, Lydia, and Tim were sat on deckchairs in the Johnson's back garden around Barnaby's outdoor pen. The tortoise was sat in the middle of his enclosure eating leaves. It was just after seven o'clock and the creature was still getting used to his new surroundings.

"What I mean is," continued Leo as he chewed on some gum, "all it has done is sit there and eat. It's not very exciting."

Tim looked at him. "As I said, Leo, this is what tortoises do. I mean, I can try and teach him to do a backflip or something, but don't get your hopes up."

Barnaby did move about four inches at one point, which was a highlight, but then stopped to restart munching lettuce. He had the ideal life. No school, no homophobic classmates, and no teenage worries. The only decision it had was whether to eat or sleep. Idyllic really.

The clouds had moved on and the sun was again beating down onto them. Tim's mum had agreed to collect Barnaby the previous evening with no fuss, not that he had given her an option. It had taken two trips to bring everything they needed over, and Tim had held onto the pet on his lap the whole journey home. He had been placed in a shoebox with airholes and Tim had held him carefully so he didn't get carsick.

The three best friends hadn't spent a great deal of time together during summer. Lydia had been in France for two weeks with her family, and Leo had been away visiting family in the Midlands. Add in the Johnson's week in Clacton and they had only had about nine days in total where they were all in the same county at the same time. The only thing of note they had done was to go out together for Lydia's birthday in late July. It was getting towards the end of August and before long the new academic year would be here. He was unsure how he was already entering Year Eleven. It didn't seem five minutes since they first stepped foot into Greenwood Secondary.

"How's Johann?" asked Lydia.

"Fine, I think, thanks," responded Tim. "He sent me a picture a minute ago, look!" Tim held out his phone in excitement and showed the others a picture of Johann, his sister, and an older lady who he assumed to be Freja, stood on a path with the Tyne Bridge in the background. "He looks happy, though, I think, all things considered?" Tim added. "Urgh, this is going to be such a long week without him again. I hope he does manage to get back on Friday."

"Yeah, I'm sure he will," said Leo. "Did he say how his uncle's operation went?"

"Yeah, he said it was successful, however he is still heavily sedated so it's still all a bit worrying."

"What was it he had to have done?"

"I dunno exactly, but Johann used some long medical term which I didn't understand. I'm not sure if it was a Swedish term or British but either way it was confusing, and I couldn't even spell it close enough to Google it properly. All I know is it's something to do with his heart. Apparently, he had a heart attack a few years ago as well, so I'm hoping that him recovering from one is a good sign for this one as well. I don't think he wanted to talk much about it on the phone, so we spoke about Newcastle instead. He said it is colder up there, which is something when you have been living in Sweden all your life. I wish I had asked him so much more about his family this summer instead of just talking rubbish."

"That's no different to us three, though, is it? And anyway, it's not always cold in Sweden. You should do more research if you like him this much," replied Lydia, leaning back in her chair and readjusting her oversized heart-shaped sunglasses. "When was the last time we had a meaningful conversation anyway? We just talk about general things happening in town."

"I guess," responded Tim. He pulled out his phone again. His lock screen was a picture of the four friends sat in the park. The moment captured was about five minutes after Johann had silently taken his hand as they were cloud watching. The happiness on Tim's face was clear. As if by magic, a message from Johann flashed up on the screen.

***Miss you x***

Tim opened the app.

***Miss you too. Hope all is ok? X***

***It is what it is x***

Tim turned back to the others. "Friday. Urgh. It's so far away." He slumped back on his seat and punched his knees.

"It will soon be here," exclaimed Lydia. "It's only, what, three days? We will keep your mind off it a little if you want?"

"Thanks, Lyds," smiled Tim. "It's just I didn't see him last week either, so it has felt like ages. I mean, I thought going back to work would help but after what happened at the shop today, I don't think that will happen either."

"Have you heard any more about the shop?"

"Nothing. Have either of you?" They both shook their heads.

"Look," said Lydia positively, "we can work out things to do in the afternoons for the next couple of days with you."

"Also," interjected Leo, "at least Johann will be back for the school fete on Saturday!"

"That's true. Well, hopefully anyway." Tim had become a bit more animated. "Johann will be allowed, won't he? Like, even if he doesn't go to our school?"

"Yeah, course he will," replied Leo. "It's not an exclusive event like the Oscars or something. It's just a load of stalls in the school field. I might bring Callum, if that's okay?"

"I guess," mumbled Tim. "Where is he by the way?"

"Said he had to help his dad with something out of town."

"I still can't believe he accused me of the graffiti."

"He apologised at least," said Leo.

"Even so. Least he can't cause me any trouble when he's with his dad."

"Have you seen a picture of Callum's dad?" questioned Leo. "He looks just like Ed Sheeran. Y'know, ginger hair, tattooed arms, plays a guitar."

Tim and Lydia laughed.

"He is gonna be at the fete too, by the way,"

continued Leo.

"What, Ed Sheeran is? That's quite a good booking," replied Lydia.

"Obviously I mean Callum's dad. He is running the bouncy castle. Part of his business is to run an inflatables-for-hire service."

Barnaby was now clambering over one of the rocks in his enclosure, and the trio watched as he lost balance and fell onto his back. Lydia stood, turned him up the right way, and sat back down. He immediately went back to his food.

"Anyway, is there any good entertainment on Saturday?" asked Lydia.

"The usual," said Leo. "Meat raffle, classic. Also, there is a dog display, general stalls, face painting, ice cream van, welly wanging. That kind of thing."

"Welly wanging? Wow, all the big sports then," joked Tim.

"It's Greenwood Secondary, Tim, not the Olympics. Anyway, yeah, there's welly wanging, the annoying Greenwood Secondary Cheer Squad, who we will obviously avoid like the plague, a jazzercize dance off competition, a baking demonstration from someone who nearly got on The Great British Bake Off, and also Thames Valley's Strongest Man."

"Just Thames Valley's?" asked Tim.

"Yeah, he lost in the regional heats of the nationals."

"And what will he do?" enquired Lydia. "Just stand there and look all big?"

"Probs. Might pick up some bricks or move barrels. He's a mussel man."

"Of course he is," said Lydia. "Wouldn't be strong if he wasn't muscley, would he?"

"No, mussel man. As in M-U-S-S-E-L. He works on the seafood counter at the market. He's the one who has the manbun and only wears vests, even in winter."

Tim laughed at how so-bad-it-will-be-good this fete would turn out.

"The vicar is also running a tombola, if you like games?" added Leo.

"Are you allowed to gamble if you're Christian?" questioned Lydia.

"Um, I think so, and it's not gambling, is it?"

"Yeah," agreed Tim, "I don't think winning a bottle of old wine or a tin of corned beef counts. It's hardly playing high-stakes poker in Las Vegas, is it?"

"I guess."

"Should be a good laugh, if nothing else," said Tim, looking at his phone in case anymore messages had come through. "I'll need it this week, with Johann being away and that."

"Try not to think of him, Tim," said Lydia, trying to be helpful.

"I can't. I have not stopped thinking about him since the day I first met him."

"You need to be boyfriends," said Leo. Lydia nodded.

"I know, I want to be, but I also don't want to scare him off by being too keen."

"Stop being so pessimistic all the time, Tim," Lydia said sternly.

Tim slumped back in his chair and started to pick grass off his socks quietly. None of them had ever dated before, another thing which Callum had an advantage over them with. Tim was excited about having a boyfriend, but equally as nervous. Having an official boyfriend would mean he might have to come out to more people, and he was not ready for those at school to find out yet. The bullying would become targeted at him directly.

"I wish Honey Latté would bring her drag act here for it," said Tim.

"Her show last month was so good," replied Leo.

"Yeah, it was the best. She was kind as well."

"It's weird to think it was at her show you first hung with Johann properly," added Lydia.

"Yeah, it seems so long ago now," Tim replied.

"We will have to invite her down here again someday."

"I'd love that. I wanna see her again."

"I think we all do," said Lydia, as the others nodded. "Oh, I was meant say, I hear Marty is in a band now."

This was something else making Tim nervous. Marty was now such a cooler older brother that he had helped form a rock band. They were made up of Marty (bass), Gary (drums), Michelle (aka 'Shell', guitar) and Danny (vocals. Well, vocals-ish. He struggles to find the key). They had met in the college canteen during Spring Term and had a shared love of rock bands like Devil's Advocate and The Thunderdomes. Their band name was not as epic or legendary, though. No, Marty was about to introduce the world (well, Greenwood) to *Haberdashery Menagerie*.

Tim didn't know which of the four had come up with the name. He had told Marty it was a rubbish name and wondered what worse ones they had rejected. *Haberdashery Menagerie*, come on. Marty argued it was memorable, which Tim guessed was true, but he doubted he would see it written across a poster for Glastonbury in the future. They only had one original song as well, and it was called *Checkout Check Out*. It had been written by Shell about her ex-boyfriend who had cheated on her with a girl who worked on the tills down at the big Asda.

Before Tim could tell them about the band, the conversation was interrupted by Lydia's phone. She walked across the garden and answered. Leo turned to Tim.

"If you could have a superpower, what would you choose?" he asked.

"Would people know I had this power?" Tim replied.

"Maybe. I don't know, it doesn't matter."

"It does. If people knew then that would make a load of difference."

"Just answer the question, Tim. Stop adding in unnecessary stipulations."

"Um, I guess time travel," responded Tim, before adding, "Well, not time travel, but that thing where you can sort of travel anywhere immediately."

"Like doing the beep-beep-bop noise and coming out somewhere completely different?"

"Yeah, that one."

"Why?"

"I think it would be cool. Also, I could get my paper round done in, like, ten minutes!" said Tim excitedly.

"Right, you would have a superpower, literally picking from any superpower that there is, only so you can do a paper round a bit quicker?"

"Yeah, what's wrong with that?"

"Well, it's a bit boring. I thought you'd pick to be Spider-Man."

"I wouldn't look as hot in the suit. Anyway, what would you choose?"

"To be able to fly. It would be amazing."

"But what if you crashed into a building or something?"

"I wouldn't. It's a superpower so it would all be good. You're being pessimistic again."

"Fine," said Tim, and crossed his arms.

"Callum said invisibility."

"Why?"

"He said it would help him get away with things."

"Sounds dodgy to me," Tim replied.

"Nah, I think it's a good choice. Like, you could rob a bank, and no one would know!"

"Exactly. Dodgy."

Leo didn't respond, instead sitting with his hands linked across the top of his head. They waited until Lydia came back to join them.

As they sat finishing their drinks, Tim's mum came through the back door. For some reason she was now dressed in a bright pink leotard, with lime green wristbands. The witch hat was back on her head. She looked ridiculous.

"Tim are you free for a minute?" she asked.

"Is it important?" he replied, looking at her with a worried expression. He knew she was up to something, and he would do his best to find out what.

"Mr Patterson is in the front room. He said he needed to speak to you, so you best come in."

"Is it about the shop?"

"Just come inside, please," she responded.

Tim was desperate to hear if he still had his paper round. His mouth was dry again, and thinking of the damage earlier in the day was starting to get him down. He swallowed, before standing up and heading inside.

# Six

Tim walked through the kitchen, followed by Lydia and Leo. "Did you want to stay and speak to Mr Patterson?" he asked.

"I have to get home," Lydia replied. "I need to help unload the dishwasher after earlier."

"Yeah, and I am babysitting Kelis tonight, so I best go as well. Sorry."

"It's alright. I'll let you know if I find anything out."

"Stick it in the group chat," said Leo.

"Righty-o."

Tim saw Lydia looking around the kitchen. "Why is there so much pastry in here?" she asked.

The kitchen table was stacked with ready-rolled pastry packets and at least five bags of sugar. Tim rolled his eyes. "Mum's doing Bake Off at the fete this weekend. That's why she made us pick all the berries yesterday…"

"Nice. I love pie," said Leo.

"Well, I'll bring you some. There will probably be enough to feed half of the town."

Tim opened the front door and fist-bumped them both as they left. As he turned, his mum was leant casually on the banister. She smiled and gestured for him to enter the front room.

"Dare I ask why you are dressed like that?" he asked.

"I have aerobics later. This outfit arrived in the post today so I was just seeing if it would fit when Mr Patterson arrived," she answered, removing the witch's hat and placing it on a coat hook nearby.

"You're not wearing that outside, are you?" he said nervously, fearing he already knew the answer. He didn't want to be embarrassed by her being seen walking around town like she had stumbled out of some 1980's horror-fitness crossover video.

"Well, we have a dress rehearsal tonight down at the youth centre, so I will have to. I'll put a jumper on though, I promise."

"And the stupid hat?"

"No, I won't wear that, don't worry."

"I'll still worry," he replied. "And a dress rehearsal for what?"

"Our competition, of course."

"What competition?" he quizzed.

"On Saturday. I must have told you about it?"

Tim raised his eyebrows. "Oh, you definitely didn't. Is it in public?"

She approached her son and ruffled his hair. "You need a haircut."

"Stop changing the subject."

"Look, I will tell you about it later, okay? Just come and talk to Mr Patterson."

"You can tell me as soon as possible," Tim replied reluctantly, as he was led into the front room.

As he entered, Mr Patterson was stood, leaning on the windowsill. He was watching Lydia and Leo walk along Oak Tree Crescent. "You have nice friends, Tim," he said, turning around and giving his trademark smile.

Tim joined him by the window, crouching as he rested his head on his arms. "Yeah, they're alright those two." He meant it, too. He would be totally lost without them. Across the road he could see Pat crouched over Archie the Dog.

"That dog is a bloody nuisance," said Tim's mum as she came to join them. "Anyway, I'll get the kettle on for some tea. Make yourself at home please, Mr Patterson."

Tim watched her head back towards the kitchen. It was cooler in this room than it had been in the garden, and the breeze was wafting the net curtain gently. Mr Patterson moved to walk to one of the floral armchairs, using a cane to steady himself. Tim waited until his boss had slowly sat, and then took a place at the end of the sofa nearest to him, curling his feet under himself.

"Are you okay, Mr Patterson?"

"Yes, not bad thank you, all things considered."

"Okay, that's good. I've only seen you with a cane once before so was worried you weren't well."

"Oh, yes sorry. No, I am okay thank you, just my old hip injury flaring up again. These things happen when you get older like me."

"Ah okay," smiled Tim back. "Is there any news from the police? And is Mrs Patterson okay after today?"

"She is getting there, thank you. She has gone to our neighbours for a bit. She is still shaken, as you can imagine."

"Send her my best, won't you. And the police?"

"Nothing yet, no. They have taken the CCTV and have said they will start some enquiries. I hope it is sorted soon. My wife had told me to stay at home and watch the cricket on the television to help me relax, but I needed to get some fresh air." Mr Patterson cleared his throat. "Actually, Tim, if I am being honest, that is what I want to talk to you about. I wanted to come and see you here in person about it."

"The cricket?" asked Tim. He had played a few times

in PE at school but was not in the best position to talk about techniques and tactics.

"No, I meant the newsagents," Mr Patterson replied, tapping on his cane with his wedding ring.

Before he could start explaining, Tim's mum entered the room with three mugs on a tray made from an old, framed picture of a seagull. None of the mugs in the Johnson household matched, they never had. There were two on the tray which had come free with Easter Eggs earlier in the year. Tim and Mr Patterson remained silent as they watched her place the mugs on the coffee table in the centre of the room, pushing old magazines aside as she did so. The milk was placed next to the cups in an old measuring jug, slightly stained orange from it being used to microwave baked beans in over the years.

"Milk and sugar?" she asked Mr Patterson.

"Just milk please, thank you," he replied, and waited to be handed his Kit Kat cup.

Tim was handed a royal blue mug with "Greenwood Pony Club Gymkhana 2005" emblazoned in yellow down the side. He didn't even know there was a pony club in the town, let alone how this mug had then ended up in his house. When he was older, he would own a house where all the crockery matched, like Lydia's. None of the mugs would have a stained ring of tea just under the lip either.

His mum took a seat opposite the other two, her leggings making a weird squeaking sound as she did so. "How is the hip?" she asked.

"Sore but getting better, thank you," Mr Patterson replied.

Tim sat there through the small talk, taking sips of his tea to pass the moment.

Mr Patterson leant forward steadily before placing his cup carefully on a coaster. "I was about to tell Tim why I have come round," he said.

Tim sat up and put his cup down, too.

"Is it about my initials on the window?" Tim asked.

"No, no. As I say, there is no more news."

"But what is it?"

"Well, and this isn't easy Tim, but as I have been saying, time is beginning to catch up with me. This hip injury is becoming more frequent. We have been thinking about making some changes for a few months now, but never acted. After today, though, we feel now is the best time for us to move on."

"Move on to where?" questioned Tim.

"Well, not move geographically as such. I mean in terms of our life. We have taken a lot of time to think over our decision, but sadly we are going to leave the newsagents."

"What, no, please don't!" begged Tim.

"I am sorry, Tim. It has been a hard decision. I am seventy-four now—"

"No way are you seventy-four," interjected Tim. "You only look about sixty."

Mr Patterson laughed. "Well, thank you, but sadly sixty seems a long time ago for me. Look, I wanted to tell you first as you are simply the best paper boy I have ever had working for me. You are always on time, you don't moan about the places you deliver to, you are kind-hearted, you care about the customers, and you always seem willing to go that extra mile. It breaks my heart that I am going to have to let you down."

Tim slumped into the cushions. "Is there anything which could change your mind?" He loved the paper round, and not only because of the money he got from it. It had been part of his routine since Year Eight and he wanted to keep doing it. He hated change and wanted to take on the new school year in a comfortable place.

"I am sorry, but I have made the decision. We both have, Mrs Patterson and me. We should be enjoying our free time whilst we are still blessed to be able to do so. You know, traveling around England, visiting Yorkshire more, spending more time with friends and family. The shop takes up about fifty hours of my time each week, and it is always an early start, even on Sundays."

"So, what happens now? Will someone be taking it over?"

"We did some small enquiries earlier in the summer, but no one has come forward so far with an offer. Now it is definite we are leaving, we will work to try and find a suitable person to replace us. It is a lovely opportunity for someone."

"Mum, can you buy it?" said Tim, turning towards her.

"Where would I get the money from, darling? I wish I could but that's not possible." She moved to sit next to him.

"When will you close?" Tim asked, turning his attention back to Mr Patterson.

Mr Patterson took a long drink from his mug. "This is the hardest part, I'm afraid. Because of what happened today, we have decided to close on Saturday. It was going to be closer to Christmas, but the damage today has made us uneasy. Mrs Patterson currently does not feel comfortable about being there alone."

"Saturday is only five days away. That's not long. I hope someone does want to take it from you. I love it in there!"

"We've been taking you there years haven't we," said his mum. "I remember taking you there when you were little to get you stickers and Lucozade when you were off sick from work."

"I must be your longest serving customer, Mr

Patterson," Tim replied.

"I know, I know. I remember you as a little boy as well. Those days seem so far away now."

"If you want me to do a poster or something to advertise the shop, I will."

"Thank you, however It will not just be the shop. You know we live in the house above it, so it all comes as part of a package. We will move home too. We will want to stay in Greenwood, but it is too big for just for my wife and me. We currently have three bedrooms and a small study, and we simply do not have enough to fill all that space. We need to find a buyer who wishes to take on a retail opportunity as well, of course."

"And if you don't?" asked Tim.

"I have a meeting today with an advisor. It is most likely that if the shop is not taken up as an option, it will be converted into part of the house. Of course, these days it is more likely an investor will come in and split the property into flats. There is a lot more money in it for them, I believe."

"That's sad," said Tim quietly. "I can't believe I only have five more days of delivering papers for you, Mr Patterson."

"I know, I am sorry."

Tim sat back on the sofa and remained quiet.

"We won't be opening tomorrow but are will still be doing the deliveries as normal. If you wish, have a bit of a lie in and come a little later to see us. We can have a coffee together before you go out delivering."

"Everything just seems so unfair," Tim grumbled.

"I know. Life is like that. Just remember this is not because I don't want you, Tim, more I don't need you. If you would like to help me out this week, though, that would be nice. You can come over on Sunday and help us clear stock and tidy. Your two friends can come along also if they want?"

"It won't be the same, but I will." said Tim, deflated.

"There comes a time when good things have to end."

Tim's mum moved closer and placed an arm around him, giving a smile to Mr Patterson as she did so. Tim leant his head into her chest and became silent.

"If there is anything you'd like me to do, Mr Patterson, let me know. I have a quiet week. I am only working at the doctors on Wednesday and Thursday."

"That is kind of you, Katherine, thank you. I will give you a call. Please don't be sad, Tim."

Tim let out a soft muffled sound and then sat up slowly. Earning less would mean missing out on summer plans. He didn't want to have to go back to asking for money from his dad every time he wanted to do anything fun. He was just thankful he had enough money for Funtangutan already.

Mr Patterson continued, "I know a couple of people who may be looking for someone of your age to help them out Tim, if you would like that?"

"I can't deliver from Mark's," replied Tim. There was no way Tim would take a job at the same place that employed Johann. Life was stressful enough as it was without having to try and look presentable to his (hopefully future) boyfriend early every morning.

"No, no," said Mr Patterson. "It won't be delivering. Leave it with me and I will be in touch."

"Will you still be at the fete, Mr Patterson?" Katherine asked.

"Of course. Will you be there, young man?"

"Yeah, gonna head down with Johann and the others," Tim replied.

"And how is Johann?"

"He's fine. Why?"

Every mention of Johann's name from someone

other than Lydia and Leo made him feel as if everyone knew his secret.

"I was just asking sorry," said Mr Patterson, holding his palms up.

"Sorry, Mr Patterson, I just didn't know you knew him." He hadn't meant to reply snappily.

"Well, I don't, it's just you always talk about him."

Tim felt himself blush so buried his head in his hands to hide this from the others.

"He mentions him a lot here now as well," his mum added. "It's good they all have a couple of new friends. Are you on a stall at the weekend, Mr Patterson?"

"I am on announcement duty. Wherever you are in the field, you'll hear my voice telling you what is going on. Hopefully I won't be busy when you do your display though."

Tim saw his mum shake her head quickly at Mr Patterson, but it was not swift enough for it to go unnoticed.

"Display?" Tim asked cautiously.

"I'll tell you later."

"Today is already bad enough, so you may as well tell me now."

"Fine. There is a dance competition and…"

"Leo mentioned this," Tim interjected. "You can't dance!"

"It's not just me."

Tim raised an eyebrow. "That somehow makes it worse. Who are you doing it with?"

"It's me and my Dolly Mixtures," she said while faking lifting weights with her left arm.

"You're called the Dolly Mixtures? Mum you are such an embarrassment. I legit want to vomit." Tim wasn't sure if the name was better than *Haberdashery Menagerie* or not. Both were terrible.

"It's not that bad. We have been practicing hard."

"No, it is bad. I mean, look at you! Is that why you are wearing that hat?"

"Well, yes. Each group had to pick a theme, a bit like *Strictly*. We have chosen Halloween."

"But Mum, it's August." Tim wondered why she couldn't be normal like other mums.

"I know, but we thought dressing up as scary things would be quite groovy."

"No one has said *groovy* since the nineties. And you won't be groovy or cool or whatever. You'll be a joke. Are you all being witches?"

She shook her head. "Only me. Elaine is dressing as a mummy, Pat as Frankenstein, and Wendy as a headless woman."

"It's Frankenstein's Monster. Anyway, I need to make sure me and my friends aren't around at that point to see this."

"Why not? Everyone else's children will be there. Elaine's sons are both dressing as skeletons. They will come on at the end of the display and spray us all with fake blood."

"Yeah, but her sons are young."

"They're only two years younger than you!"

"Even so, I wouldn't be seen dead with you."

"Shame, cos if you were dead you would fit into the theme quite well and we would get extra points."

"This is ridiculous," argued Tim.

"Listen, let's not discuss this in front of Mr Patterson."

"I'm going to my room," he said sternly, before downing his tea, taking a couple of digestives out the packet on the table and heading towards the door.

"Before you go," said Mr Patterson. "I have something for you."

Tim stopped and sat on the arm of his chair, allowing him to continue. "Now, I know it won't make up for your job going, or, or this," he said, gesturing with a loose hand in his mum's direction, "but hopefully you enjoy them."

Mr Patterson leant down to the side of his chair and pulled up a floral bag for life, taking some effort in doing so. "I want you to have these."

Tim took the bag and looked inside. It was about a foot deep and full of purple wrappers. "Every Wispa I could find in the shop," laughed Mr Patterson. "I think there are about two hundred and fifty."

Tim laughed back, finally smiling a little again. "Thank you, how did you know I liked these?"

"How couldn't I know? You have had one every morning for the last two years."

"True. How much do you want for them?"

"Don't be silly. They're all yours. I don't want any payment. Think of them as your bonus."

"Thank you," said Tim, and then immediately opened a bar and downed it in three bites before moving onto a second.

"Don't scoff them so quick," his mum said, taking the bag and putting it out of his reach. "You'll spoil your dinner."

"I'm not that hungry."

"You look it with the rate you're eating those."

"Wispa's don't count."

"If you say so. Maybe you could pop to the newsagents after your delivery and help Mr Patterson to say thank you for bringing them to you."

"Sure. Oh, actually, I can't. We are going to Funtangutan tomorrow."

"I didn't think you liked it there?"

"Nah, it was alright. We want to go and beat the

course record."

"Fine, so long as you clean that tortoise enclosure out this evening."

Despite it only being built the previous evening, there was already a musty smell lingering around the front room and the open window was doing little to solve the issue.

"Will do, thanks," Tim said. "And thank you, Mr Patterson, for telling me. I appreciate it. I'll see you in the morning."

"Cheerio, Tim. I am going to stay and have a quick chat with your mum, but I shall see you in the morning for that coffee."

Tim smiled, before taking out another Wispa as he left the room.

# Seven

## *Tuesday*

After the upheaval in his world over the last forty-eight hours, Tim was happy Tuesday would finally bring back some of his normal routine. He had taken Mr Patterson's offer of a lie in, but still woke with Johann on his mind every time his alarm broke the snooze cycle.

He took to Instagram and sent a "Are you up?" message to Johann, before checking Callum's feed. Thankfully there was no mention of the shop. The only post since Lydia's party showed Callum stood in a wood somewhere with mud on his face like fake war paint.

He pulled open his curtains. The air outside was already hazy from the heat. The fields on the farmland in the distance were becoming scorched, and the football pitch on the big field was already changing from a rich green to a hay-like yellow. His phone vibrated on his bedside table, and he rushed to answer it.

"Johann!" he called out.

"Morning," came a weary voice on the other end.

"You sound knackered. Are you still in bed?"

There was some clattering of plates and cutlery in the background before the reply. "I am in a café in the centre. Freja has taken me to get new school shoes before she has to head to the office. How's everything down there?"

Tim explained the shop situation again over

loudspeaker as he pulled on some old jogging bottoms and an oversized t-shirt.

"Has anyone ever said anything about wanting to get back at you for anything?"

He thought for a moment. "Nothing at all. I don't think I have ever done anything to annoy anyone."

"Hopefully it is all a coincidence that your initials were there. Keep a notebook on you this week, and if anything occurs, write it down so you don't forget."

"Will do," replied Tim, as he pulled out a Jurassic Park notepad from his desk draw and put it into his paper bag. "What's for breakfast?"

"Bacon and pancakes."

"With maple syrup?"

"With all the maple syrup," replied Johann laughing.

"D'you still fancy coming to the fete on Saturday?" asked Tim.

"If I'm back, yeah." The phone went muffled, and Tim could hear Johann talking to Freja. "Sorry, have to go in a minute. Are you doing a stall at the fete?"

"Nah, just going there to hang out. Leo wants to have a go at the wellywanging."

"What's wellywanging?"

Tim sighed. "One of those games you probably only get in towns like Greenwood. Basically, you have to stand behind a line and see how far you can throw a boot."

"And then what?" asked Johann.

"That's it. That is the whole game."

"I bet I can beat you."

"You probably could," replied Tim. "I have the upper body strength of a five-year-old."

Johann laughed down the phone. "Either way, it'll be nice to spend time with you again. Look, my pancakes are arriving, so I have to go. Message me later, okay?"

"Will do. Enjoy!"

Moments after hanging up, a picture of eight sad and flat looking pancakes came through to Tim's phone. When Johann returned to Greenwood, Tim would need to take him somewhere better. He deserved better than a cheap breakfast bar, and they couldn't keep continuing to go on not-dates to the same place every time. The last thing Tim wanted was for Johann to think this was all he could afford, even if it was the truth.

He dived onto the floor and pulled himself into the darkness under his bed, flashing the torch on his phone around to try and find his secret money-saving pot, hidden in the clutter amongst the jigsaws and discarded old toys. It was in the shape of a TARDIS, given to him when younger by some family member who didn't know he couldn't care less for *Doctor Who*. He has used this pot recently when saving up to pay for his diving lessons. He sat by his desk and sellotaped a note saying 'First Date Fund' to the front, before throwing it back under the bed.

As he moved downstairs, he stopped to look in the oval mirror that hung halfway down. His eyes look tired and his skin dry. He wasn't sure if it was the stress causing this, or that he was bad at keeping up with any form of skincare regime. Tim had a record of two days in a row at remembering to moisturise. His forehead looked a bit oily around the level of where his cap usually sat.

He poked at his face and stretched his skin as he examined himself closely, wondering why anyone was willing to actually date him. As he stood looking at himself, he heard a clatter from the kitchen. There was a sickly-sweet smell drifting down the hallway. His mum's pie making conveyor belt must already have been in full swing. It was unlike her to be this active at such an early hour. He jumped down the remaining four stairs and stuck his head around the kitchen door. Once his eyes had adjusted to the thin layer of dusty air, he saw what looked like the aftermath of an explosion at a bakery. Every surface was covered in a thin white layer of flour, and the floor resembled newly fallen snow.

"Morning, Mum," he said as he moved into the room, avoiding touching anything by climbing across two dining chairs towards the back door, as if playing a game of the Floor is Lava. His mum was also covered in flour. "Did you get any ingredients in the bowl?" he asked.

"Morning, darling. Do you want to try some of my cooking?" she responded, pointing at a large fruit pie sat on top of the microwave.

It was perfectly baked in the middle; however, the circumference was dark, making it resemble a reverse solar eclipse. Tim didn't respond.

"Yes, I know it isn't perfect, but that one was my first go," she added defensively.

"I'm sure it's fine, but it's a bit early for pie. Why are you making them now?"

"I need to practice for the fete!"

"But that's still four days away. Won't they go off?"

"These are test runs. I am making the proper version on Friday. There are prizes for the best three bakes."

Tim knew he would be eating a lot of pie this week, not that this was a bad thing. "What's in this one?" he asked, pointing to the one nearest to him on the kitchen table.

"Apple and Gooseberry."

"Is that a normal combination?"

"No, and that's what makes it great. Everyone else will be making boring apple ones, won't they."

"I guess. I'll try some when I'm home."

"We will get bonus points for picking all the fruit ourselves, too. Don't forget you have Funtangutan today."

"I haven't. I'll be home with plenty of time to get ready. Have you heard anything more from Mr Patterson?"

"No, no news today."

"Cool, he hasn't text me either so I'm gonna head down there now."

"Give him my best wishes, won't you?" she said. "Ask him if he'd like a pie as well."

"Will do," he replied, as he moved across his chair walkway and out into the garden. He was leaving when he was interrupted.

"Oh, I was speaking to Flo yesterday. She tells me there is some work going at the library."

"Yeah, Leo showed me that. I'm not sure if it's for me if I'm honest."

"Why not?"

"It means speaking to the public. You know how awkward I am. Also, I'm used to doing work at this time, not in the middle of the day."

"You'll be fine. You can't be a paper boy all your life."

"Why not?" he asked.

"You'll look a right numbnut if you were still doing this paper round in fifty years' time."

"Hmm. Okay, I'll think about it."

"Please give it a try."

Tim thought for a bit longer. Maybe having a new focus would do him some good. People always say a change is as good as a rest, but he would prefer a rest. "I'll definitely consider it."

"Good. They have a shift that runs between ten and two. It's available so there is cover for lunchbreaks. It pays well also. They said it would be five pound twenty an hour for someone your age. That's a lot more than your paper round. You won't get soaking wet during winter, and you won't have to get up at silly o'clock each morning. And, at the end of summer, if you're any good, you can then do Saturdays as well, maybe doing a full day."

"That's true," said Tim, before adding, "How do you know all this?"

"I enquired on your behalf. I text Jill last night who works there."

"Thanks, I think. Maybe I will give it a go sometime."

"You start tomorrow," she said as she turned back round to decant more fruit pulp into a pastry tin.

"What? You've already signed me up?". Tim re-entered the kitchen, leaving footprints on the lino.

"If we didn't get in there quick then someone else would have taken it. You need to keep yourself busy once your paper round is done. We know what you get like when you get bored."

"But what if I have plans tomorrow?"

"Do you?"

"Well, no, but what if I did?"

"But you don't, so that's irrelevant."

"Urgh. Fine. If I must. I was gonna do it with Leo, though."

"You can't do everything together. Anyway, it's only for four hours. If you don't like it, at least you say you have tried."

Tim rolled his eyes and headed out to get his bike from the shed. As he placed his phone on the workbench, Leo started calling. He didn't answer. Instead, he sent a message to Johann to let him know about his new job. A reply simply saying **'nerd x'** came back within seconds. Tim would have been angry if he didn't like him so much.

***

The cycle to the shop was uneventful, however the temperature was already too warm to be wearing trousers. His legs were itching with the heat. He knew he'd be boiling on the assault course later. There were rumours on the radio during the morning it could reach close to forty degrees by the start of the following week.

At Patterson's Papers, the police tape had been removed and the broken part of the window was boarded up. As he approached the front door, a handwritten note had been stuck to the glass at an angle asking paper boys to knock on the side entrance.

Despite having been here many times, this would be the first time Tim had gone into any part of the building other than the shop. He pressed the doorbell, which rang to the tune of *God Save the King*, and then tapped with his knuckles at the end of the chorus when it still hadn't been opened. Eventually, Mr Patterson appeared to let him in. He seemed to have more colour in his face than the previous evening.

"Morning Mr Patterson, all okay?" Tim asked.

Mr Patterson half-smiled. "Come in, Tim." He began leading Tim up the steep staircase and into the kitchen, which was cluttered with stacks of newspapers on every surface. "Have a seat, son" he said, as he flicked the kettle on. "I have got your pile of papers ready to go. Coffee?"

Tim put his bag on the floor. "Yes, please. One sugar, please. How are things here?"

"Not so bad, thank you. My wife is still a little shaken, but things are moving forward. The police have the CCTV, and I have spent two hours on the phone to the insurance company already. The police did say the culprit is likely to strike again, though. Other than that, nothing much to report." Mr Patterson dropped sugar cubes onto the floor as he spoke. Even if the insurance company would cover the physical cost of the damage, it was clear Mr Patterson was still slightly troubled internally by the attack.

As Mr Patterson headed to get some milk from downstairs, Tim took in his surroundings. He was surprised at how spacious the house was. He could see a generously sized front room painted maroon off to the left, and a corridor on the right, with another set of stairs towards the end.

"I'll have to give you the tour tomorrow. This place is much larger than you'd expect," Mr Patterson said, catching Tim staring. "Would you like any breakfast before you head out?"

"I would, thank you, but I have to get ready to go to Funtangutan after my round. I have an Oatie Bar with me, so I'll be fine," Tim replied.

"No problem." Mr Patterson moved across to take a seat opposite, placing a mug of coffee on the table.

"You said this had three bedrooms yesterday, didn't you?" Tim remembered.

"That's right. If you were to go by those stairs," he said, pointing down the corridor, "there's a door on the left. That is our bedroom in there, and the study is attached. Up the stairs are two loft-converted rooms. We use them for storage these days. Everything me and my wife require tends to be kept on this floor.

"I'd love to live in a loft," said Tim. "It'd be much nicer than my tiny cell I have at home."

Mr Patterson laughed, but it had a thread of sadness running through it. "Tim, promise me when we no longer have this time together that you will still come and visit me and my wife, won't you."

"Of course, Mr Patterson. I'll be around quite a lot, wherever it is in town you end up."

"That's good. I hope you don't miss this round too much. I hear you have a job at the library now, also?"

"I think you knew before I did," Tim laughed. "Mum only told me about twenty minutes ago."

"We were discussing it yesterday when you were in the garden with your friends. I think you'll be good there," he said as he put a splash of milk into the two (matching) mugs.

"Do you think?"

"Of course. You're likeable, good with people and have your head screwed on."

"I try."

During the coffee, Tim tried to help Mr Patterson decide where they might want to move to. He said Mrs Patterson's dream home would be one like Lydia's.

"She'd love a large kitchen with the room to cook properly," Mr Patterson had said.

Before long, Tim set off around the six estates he delivered to. Normally, Tim rushed his round, trying to complete it as fast as possible, however today was different. With his time as a paper boy coming to an end, he wanted to take in every moment.

Rather than put the papers through the letterboxes, he planned to knock on doors and speak to the customers. It would help him feel more comfortable when facing the public for real tomorrow. He had met many before and wanted to say goodbye to them all while he still the chance. Even taking the time to do this, he would still have an hour to shower and grab a snack, probably pie, before leaving for Lydia's.

Everything started off fine, and he spoke to a few in Ash Street and Birch Avenue, and many of the residents gave Tim a goodbye tip. He'd earnt around thirty pounds before getting to the upmarket Elm Meadow. His first date TARDIS fund would be off to a good start by lunchtime.

The larger houses on the second half of his round would take longer, mainly as he had to leave his bike at the end of their long gravel driveways. It was when delivering to number 64 Elm Meadow that his plan to speak to everyone changed.

The front of this house had two Greek-style pillars outside the front door. Off each, a large green bauble of fake flowers were hung. After knocking twice and receiving no answer, he pushed the financial paper through the door and turned to move on. Unfortunately, and although not being the tallest kid in Greenwood, his head collided with one of the flower balls, causing it to spin quite dramatically.

He rushed to put his hand up to stop it, but this caused it to come loose and fall to the ground with a thud. He picked it up, noticing it was now more egg-shaped than it had been thirty seconds prior. Not wanting to cause a scene and run away, he knocked on the door again. No answer.

He tried the doorbell, but still no response. Not wanting to give up, he took hold of the bronze lion door knocker and banged it much louder than before. He waited and heard a noise in the distance, which started increasing in volume quite quickly. The sound was coming from the left-hand side of the property, and he watched in horror as a large black dog bounded onto the driveway, doing quick laps around the Mercedes and BMW parked a few metres away. It barked violently halfway between Tim and his bike.

"Hi there," he said in his best talking-to-a-dog voice.

It did nothing. He tried various other commands such as 'heel' and 'sit', and even tried throwing some of his Oatie Bar near it from the depths of his jogging bottoms pocket. The dog would not move and kept barking angrily at him. He needed the owners to help but this didn't seem to be happening.

Not wanting to be caught, he moved steadily off the porch, hearing his own pulse inside his head. The dog came closer and growled. He moved. The dog moved. He held his hands up like a hostage being freed, but the dog didn't understand this gesture. He thought his best bet was to run. He waited until the dog was silent, and then sprinted across the gravel, feet slipping like in cartoons, running faster than he was actually moving. It was as if he was running across sand in bare feet. He could hear the dog barking behind, each yap seemingly louder than the last. He didn't dare look back.

He flung the gate open and noticed the 'Beware of the Dog' sticker on its outer side. He wished he had seen this earlier. He grabbed his biked and sprang into the seat, pedalling quicker than he ever had before. As his breathing became heavy, he took the opportunity to glance over his shoulder. The dog was following him up the road at pace. People out on walks stopped and watched as he passed, followed by the canine a few paces behind.

His bag was weighing him down on one side, but he couldn't give up. He put his head down and cycled as fast as he could until he had reached Beech Close, making use of all the small alleyways he knew of.

If he had the beep-beep-bop superpower, it would come in handy, he thought.

His thighs were burning, the lactic acid racing through his bloodstream, until his legs couldn't go on. He leant against a wall, panting for oxygen. When he turned, he was glad to see he was now alone. His shins on fire, and sweat was pouring down his neck and running the whole length of his spine. His whole body trembled from the adrenaline. Knowing he still had twenty papers to deliver in Elm Meadow did not make the situation any easier.

He locked his bike to a lamppost and went to deliver the next few papers by foot. He had given up on the idea of knocking on doors now. The first date fund would need to wait to be filled even further. He wanted this round to be over. If this was to be one of the last times he'd deliver, at least it would be memorable.

***

"Hi, Mum," Tim said as he came through the back door. The house was quiet, with the only addition since he left being four more pies sitting on the kitchen side. Each one was slightly less burnt than the previous effort, so by the end of the week there should be a decent pie available for judging at the fete. *One out of fifteen would be a job well done*, he thought.

He flicked on the television in the kitchen, cut himself a slice from the warmest dessert and sat watching the morning news. He took a first fork-full of the pudding and put it in his mouth, his face screwing in on itself immediately after being hit by the sharpest tasting fruit he had ever tasted. He stood and pulled the sugar out of the cupboard above the microwave, throwing five heaped tablespoons on to it to make it edible. Within a minute his bowl was empty.

However challenging Funtangutan would be, it was sure to be easier than the panic of his paper round. The clock in the hall chimed, signalling thirty minutes to go until he had to leave. He threw his tips into the TARDIS, and stripped so he could have a long shower before having to meet the others.

# Eight

Before heading to Lydia's, Tim spent ten minutes laying on his bed scrolling through Johann's old Instagram posts. It was the best way to feel connected to him during the absence. His account went back two years, and it provided a glimpse into his life before they had met, each handily timestamped.

There were family gatherings for Midsummer celebrations from June the previous year, Johann stood in snow on New year's Day, and a collection of other random pictures of him taken whilst doing the everyday things all kids do. Tim had been able to see what his Christmases and birthdays looked like, who his friends were at his old school and where he had travelled to. He skipped over the post of Johann and his ex-boyfriend quickly, the jealousy prickling at his skin even though it was all resigned to the past.

Tim's favourite photo was of Johann stood slightly away from the camera, looking out to sea from a rocky coastline. The boy in that photo had no idea his life would change so much, or he would captivate a different boy in a different country, each unaware of the others existence when the camera lens had captured him. The scrolling made Tim desperate for their evening FaceTime to come around quickly. He needed to hear his voice, see his face.

Although the weather was good, Tim had decided to wear his bright orange waterproof trousers, just in case the ropes and slides at Funtangutan were as wet as their previous visit. He knew he was likely to get soaked on the assault course and didn't want to ruin any of his nicer clothes.

He realised halfway through the walk to Lydia's that wearing waterproofs for the journey may have been a mistake. If jogging bottoms were a mistake earlier, waterproofs in the sun were a gigantic cock-up. He felt like a chicken being roasted in tin foil.

"Morning, Lydia," he said as he walked down her driveway, the car already on its way to being completely packed with cool boxes.

"Alright Tim," she replied as he stared into the boot. "We had a lot of buffet food left over yesterday so Mum has packed it in here for us to eat after running around all morning."

"Ah nice, thank you. Any sausage rolls in there?"

"Plenty. Did you want one now?"

"Nah all good thanks, I've eaten a stupid amount of pie."

"Why are you eating pie for breakfast?" she quizzed.

"Do you need to ask?"

"Mum still baking?"

"Bingo. How did you guess?" he laughed. "If you and your family want some let me know and I'll bring a whole one round for you later. At her current rate there would be one available for everyone in Greenwood. The kitchen will be full of them. Have you messaged the others to say we are leaving?"

"Yeah, I wanted to make sure Leo hadn't overslept. He's ready but Callum isn't there yet. Should be fine though, we've got loads of time. What's with the trousers? They're blinding me."

"I couldn't find my dark ones, so you're stuck with glow-in-the-dark-Tim I'm afraid. I probably put the others in that old suitcase on top of my wardrobe at the start of spring."

The front door of the house opened, and Lydia's mum exited, hands full of trays. Tim rushed across. "Want me to take those?" he asked her.

She passed him two colourful square box-bags and he took them to the boot of the gold-coloured car. There was a lot to eat if all the bags contained food.

"I think that's everything," said Amy as she opened up the driver's door and climbing in.

"Shotgun," shouted Lydia, who then jumped in beside her. Tim closed the boot and took a seat behind her.

Just like their house, the Flanagan's car was too big for the size of their family. It had two sets of back seats which folded down if needed. Even with the four children and all the food, you could have squeezed five medium sized dogs (or fifteen rabbit-sized rabbits) in with them all. Within minutes, Amy pulled the car up outside of Leo's house and beeped the horn twice.

Callum opened the door and ran down the path. He was wearing another new outfit, probably gifted. He resembled a life-sized Action Man. He opened the door opposite and threw his backpack onto Tim's lap, before strapping himself into the middle seat. A few minutes later Leo ran out. One day he would learn to be on time.

"More bad milk?" Tim asked as Leo climbed in. Lydia chuckled in front.

"Nah, couldn't find my stopwatch," he replied.

Tim wiped his forehead in an exaggerated fashion. "Good, good. The last thing we want is for your bowels to explode halfway around. It would be like doing an assault course with a ticking timebomb."

As they passed through town, there was silence in the car, aside from Amy asking Lydia about school, which Tim knew she didn't want to think about yet.

Leo seemed to sense this too, for as soon as they had driven past the industrial estate, he turned to Callum. "Did you ever go to one of these places in London?" he asked him. This simple question somehow unlocked a side of Callum they hadn't seen at the party. He was suddenly animated and sat bolt upright between them.

"Nah, I've never been to anything like this," he said in his estuary accent. "I've always wanted to but there wasn't really a chance. I mean, there are a few around East London I think but travelling there was never the easiest. My dad can't drive, and my mum hated driving 'cos it was all so busy, so we didn't have a car. Was always having to get the Tube everywhere. I nearly went on one for a school trip, but my mum wouldn't let me."

"Why not?" asked Lydia, turning around and gazing at him.

"Dunno," he responded. "My parents used to get funny if they thought it could lead to something that might get me in trouble. A few of my friends from school had fallen in with the wrong crowd, y'know, hanging around in groups at night, robbing things from shops, smoking, criminal damage and that kind of thing. Mum thought I would end up doing the same so banned me from doing too much. Everyone I knew was allowed to do what they wanted, and I was being held back. Never got to make a name for myself in anything, y'know. She doesn't even know I'm going here today. I told her we were being driven to the shops. She'll probably check up on me. Football was one of the only things that was fine for me to do in the evening, and even then, the coach, Steve, was one of our neighbours. It's why I ended up spending so much time online posting stupid videos of me in the garden. Only so much you can do when you're stuck in a tiny ground floor flat with mould growing up the walls. It got even worse when my parents split up last year."

He stopped and looked at the others. He predicted Leo's question. "Yeah, that bloke that goes to salsa with Mum ain't my real dad. He's my stepdad, Bryan. He lets me get away with loads more than my actual Dad does. My dad is a waster most of the time. Protective though, but a waster. If Mum's working, Bryan lets me be myself. I can stay up later, watch what I want, head out later and do all sorts, that sort of thing."

"What sort of thing?" asked Tim.

"Just catch up with the things I missed out on with friends."

The three had learnt more about Callum in two minutes than from the whole day at the buffet or from anything on his Instagram. Tim guessed sharing bad news doesn't do much for self-promotion online, though.

"Is your real dad still in London?" asked Tim.

"Yeah, he lives on the Isle of Dogs, y'know, the bendy bit on the river you see on the start of *Eastenders*. I haven't gone back to see him for ages, but probably should before I start at the new school."

"What does your mum do?" asked Lydia.

"Supermarket. She works at weekends and then does a couple of shifts 'til ten at night during the week. I dunno if she likes it. The breakup with my dad wasn't great so we moved out here. Bryan used to live in the flat above so when he left, Mum decided to come as well."

"Seems like they were quite close, then," said Leo.

Callum swivelled quickly and stared at him. "They weren't having an affair, if that's what you mean?" he snapped.

Tim got the feeling this was a rumour that had surfaced before. "So, what does Bryan do?" he asked, trying to change the subject.

"This and that," Callum replied vaguely. "He doesn't work, though. Well, not really anyway. He says he's sort of a mechanic. Helps repair or do up old cars and stuff like that, and does the odd job for some people he met down the pub. He hasn't had much work since being here, but it's something."

"I thought he ran an inflatables business?" asked Lydia.

"Well, yeah, he does that too. Someone he knows, knows someone nearby who actually owns it. He helps every now and then. He's got a bouncy castle at the fete this week."

"Yeah, Leo told us about that the other day," said Tim. The trip being a secret from Callum's mum had blown any hope Tim had of being featured on his Instagram. Before he could say anything more, Callum was already continuing.

"Like, no offence to you lot, but Greenwood isn't my thing still. It's so boring and quiet. I hate how my mum moved me from my school before my last year. I'd rather go back and live with my dad for a bit to be honest, even if he isn't the best parent in the world. People are different there y'see. My school was quite rough, I guess. Well, not to me, but you'd all hate it so much. Lots of fighting and stuff. Everyone is trying to be the most popular person, and you keep close to your small friend group and that's it. Being told to stay home so much meant all my mates were doing so much without me, and I was kinda becoming an outcast. Everyone was doing what they knew. No one had any ambitions unless they thought they could be a footballer or earn money on TikTok. Most would want to do the same manual jobs their dad did. I'd probably be doing a building apprenticeship or something next year if I had stayed. Bryan wants me to go to college but I dunno. Here is much different. Like, this is bad, but I'd never met anyone who was gay before and now I've met you two already."

Tim felt blood rush to his head and clenched his fists tightly. He wasn't sure if Lydia's mum had heard this new information, but the quick glance she gave in the mirror to the back seats suggested she had. Leo must also have noticed too as he shrunk down into his seat. Leo wasn't even gay which made it worse.

In one throwaway sentence, Callum had not only outed Tim to a parent, which was a huge deal, but also erased a key part of Leo's identity. Tim's fear of his mum finding out before he was ready seemed a step closer. After their conversation the evening before, Tim knew Leo was feeling as vulnerable as he was. They needed to stop Callum from saying more as soon as possible. Luckily Lydia had sensed this and changed the subject.

"Do you have any plans for your birthday, Callum?" she asked. Tim didn't listen as he started talking at length again, instead taking his mobile out of his pocket and messaging the front seat.

*Lyds, If he continues being like this and saying stuff like that then I'm not being his mate.*

*Hopefully mum didn't notice*

*If you heard, she heard.*

*She might not have. Don't panic!*

*He's a #knobhead*

*#agreed*

### I need to speak to your mum

Lydia didn't respond, instead putting her phone in to the glovebox and turning to look out of the window. Somehow Callum was still going. "Of course, I'd have a proper party if I was still at my old place. I told Mum and Bryan I'd rather be in London, and they told me to get used to it. Hopefully one day I'll go back but I could be doing so much more if I was there. Dad was the one who took me to Villa Park after all, and now I can't even do that this season. It proper sucks."

The others waited, but this time he had finished ranting. Tim wondered if London had made Callum grow up faster than Greenwood had allowed himself to do so. The things that angered Callum were the things Tim had grown up knowing. His palms still felt sticky, and he wanted to be anywhere else than in the car. The atmosphere had changed, and silence took over again for the final five minutes of the journey.

Amy Flanagan swung into the venue through the large wooden Funtangutan arch, complete with wooden carvings on each side. They were the first ones there so had the choice of spaces. The four children got out, before putting their phones and wallets into their bags.

You weren't allowed to carry anything with you on the course. If you did, you might run the risk of something falling out of your pocket and into the bushes below, never to be seen again. Also, if you took your own phone with you, it meant you were less likely to purchase one of the Funtangutan Experience photographs sold in the Jungle Café after you have completed the challenge. They didn't buy one last time. Tim hadn't needed the evidence of him looking terrified up a tree. It was still firmly engrained in his memory.

"Have fun!" Amy called as they started to head to the entrance cabin, as she started to move to get a cup of coffee from a flask. Tim allowed the other three to walk ahead and get ready, but he hung back. He saw Lydia with her arm around Leo's shoulder as Callum went into the wooden building. Tim waited until the others had disappeared from view, before turning to Amy.

"Can I speak to you please?" Tim asked.

She looked up from behind the boot. Tim knew she was aware of what he was about to say as she pulled him into a hug.

"Please don't tell my mum. Or Flo," he said.

"I won't. Are you okay?"

"I dunno. I'm freaking out a bit. I think Leo might be worse."

She released him but held onto his shoulders. "Look, you can trust me, Tim. What he said does not matter to me. I've known you for fifteen years, so I care as much as if you were mine. Tell Leo the same as well when you can. I know it must be hard, I can't imagine how hard, but try and have fun out there now, try and take your mind off what he said. Afterwards, I'll drop that idiot off at his and then you and Leo can come over to our house. That's if you want to, of course. I'll be in the café, so if either of you need me at any point you can come there."

"Thank you," Tim said, glad she also thought the same of Callum as he did right now, although he would have used a stronger word to describe him.

Amy stroked Tim's arm. "Go and make sure Leo is okay. Things will be alright."

"Thank you," he replied quietly. He dragged his feet as he went to join the others.

# Nine

Tim entered the cabin and took a seat on one of the wooden benches near to Leo, who was looking angry and upset. Callum was messing about on the opposite side and was still muttering but Tim wasn't in the mood to listen.

"Why did you have to say that?" Tim snapped.

"What?" asked Callum.

Tim assumed he must have been as stupid as he was annoying. "You told Lydia's mum that me and Leo are gay. Do you not think before you speak ever?"

"I didn't know she didn't know."

"Well in future, assume no one knows anything, okay? And anyway, Leo is bi not gay so if you're going to announce it to the world you could at least get your facts right."

"It's the same thing."

"It really isn't," Leo replied.

"Alright, sorry," he said and then continued getting himself ready. Tim wanted to rant more at him but was stopped as a lady in a green Funtangutan hoodie came in with a clipboard. Lydia moved and sat close to Leo, giving his knee a shake with her hand to comfort him.

"Good morning kids, you must be the Flanagan party, I assume?" the staff member said, her bobbed haircut bouncing as much as her voice.

"Yep, that's us," replied Lydia.

"Marvellous. I should have a Leo, a Lydia, a Timothy, and a Callum. Is that correct?" Lydia confirmed it was. "Faaaaaantastic. If you'd all like to get your safety gear on, Mike will be with you shortly to get you started. Have fun guys!" She left as quickly as she had entered.

"So, what's our gameplan then?" asked Callum.

"Go as quick as possible," responded Leo, flatly.

"Well, yeah, but you need a plan."

"We didn't last year," Tim said. He sensed this was going to be a disaster.

"And did you get the course record last time?"

"No."

"Well, there we go. We need a plan. As I am the strongest, I should go on each obstacle first, and then I can help pull you lot up when you struggle."

"You've never been before Callum," Tim responded. "How do you know you'll be any good?"

"I'm a good climber."

"Any proof?" asked Lydia. Tim could even sense anger in her voice.

"Look at me, I'm clearly stronger than these two," he said, pointing between Tim and Leo.

Leo pounced to his feet. "Look, you're not in London anymore, mate. You can drop your hardman act. Anyway, we both dive. We have done a lot of strength stuff in the gym recently."

"Even so."

"Go first if you have to, just don't start crying when we have to rescue you," jibed Tim.

The previous year they had completed the course in thirty-four minutes. They were hindered by having to have Campbell and Michaela from school in their group, though, who had been there on a date. Campbell had blamed Tim and had spat that Funtangutan was 'gay' and 'for kids'.

The four didn't speak until they were greeted by Mike, a burly, stocky instructor with huge biceps. He had been here the last time also, but now came with a shaved head and veins that seemed like they were about to burst from his forearms. Tim found him intimidating. Now he was here, he started to feel nervous again. His fear of heights was becoming more prominent than his current anger.

He should never have agreed to have come here. Yesterday he had thought he would have been okay dealing with heights this time around, however now he was about to be sent up trees he started sweating again. His trousers were uncomfortable, and he felt as if his legs were slowly boiling. Mike threw safety harnesses at them, and they clambered in as best they could. Leo helped Tim tighten his, making it pinch in all the worst places. Once he had adjusted it to be comfortable, he noticed Callum had somehow put his on back to front. Maybe he wouldn't make the best leader, unless he planned to do everything backwards.

"Now before the final briefing," started Mike, "you need to get your helmets on. We don't want you cracking your skulls like eggs if you fall to the forest floor."

Tim tried to move but was trapped to the spot by fear. He pictured himself freefalling through branches and crunching onto a leafed floor below. "Can one of you pass me a helmet, please?"

Callum took a purple one off the wall and threw it in Tim's direction. "Your head looks small so you can have the smallest. I don't know if that's a number one on the front, or an I for idiot," he said laughing.

"I'm gonna kill him," Tim whispered to Lydia. He put the helmet on, and in the mirror he caught a glimpse of himself looking like a blackcurrant. He was determined not to let Callum get to him today. He had given him a chance, which he had already blown. He was always acting as if he had a point to prove. Tim preferred it when he sat there quietly at the buffet, not causing any problems for the other three. They were stuck with him for now, though, so he would have to give him the benefit of the doubt for the time being. If he was going to act like this for the whole of year Eleven, he needed to create some distance. He needed to convince Leo and Lydia to do the same. Hopefully Callum would be more happy hanging around the popular kids on the football team once school restarted, you know the ones who are all abs and confidence rather than having social skills.

Finally, fully suited, Instructor Mike made the quartet stand in a circle and do one of those 'go team!' type hand things where you all stack your hands on top of each other and pretend to be like an enthusiastic American teenager in some high school basketball film. It all felt cringy.

A red digital clock flashed on the wall, starting the countdown to their start time. Three minutes to go.

"Team name?" said Mike bluntly.

"Um, we were Team Greenwood last year," replied Leo.

"Bit boring ain't it?" said Callum. "We need something more epic."

"Like what?" asked Tim.

"I dunno, Team Dragon or something."

"Callum, that makes us sound like we are about five years old," Tim complained.

"Two minutes to go," said Mike, forcefully.

"Okay, Team Dragon," said Leo.

Tim wasn't happy with this, but it was too late now.

"Sit!" demanded Mike. They all sat close on a bench

as he pulled out a flipchart. "We have five small obstacles for you today, all of varying difficulty. Each team member must complete each section, and once done, hit the big red button. You can't miss it. Once you hit that, the gate opens to allow you entry to the next challenge. Understand?"

They nodded. Tim wanted Mike to go. Didn't he have a protein shake to down or something?

"TEN!" shouted Mike. "NINE! EIGHT!"

Tim wanted more time to compose himself, but it was too late.

"THREE! TWO! ONE! FUNTANGUTAN!"

The cabin door swung open, and the forest stretched out in front of them and into the distance. The forest floor could be seen far below from their high starting point. Tim wished he remembered the car park and entrance were at the top of the hill. The taste of sick hit the top of his throat, but he had no choice but to move forward and get on with it. Five obstacles, nineteen minutes. That's all it was, after all.

Callum was the first to leave the hut. Tim followed the rest and hunched small when he found himself on a small rectangular platform. By the time he had the confidence to open his eyes, Callum was already being strapped onto a zipwire. A zipwire isn't too taxing if you're comfortable with that kind of thing. Sadly, Tim wasn't. Callum crashed onto the landing area in no time, with Lydia behind. They both seemed to glide down effortlessly. Tim was shaking at the edge. He tried his best to not look down, however this was difficult when the only thing you could see was the ground far below. All he needed to do was jump off, slide down the wire, land in the pile of leaves and wait to be unclipped. It took two false starts before Tim got the confidence to go.

As gravity took over, he realised he was sliding down

fine and needn't have been worried. He felt like a red kite soaring above a farmland. Halfway down, a sudden breeze of wind caught him from the right-hand side. Before he knew it, he started spinning in fast circles. He looked around but couldn't tell left from right, or up from down. The dizziness this brought meant he crashed into the leaves at the bottom at speed, rather than land gracefully. He was jerked to a halt and was immediately unclipped by a teen.

Leo and Lydia grabbed his arms and pulled him through the gate towards The River.

"This isn't much of a river," said Leo.

Lydia shook her head. "It's more of a muddy trench."

Team Dragon had to build a bridge out of five large blocks to get across. Arguments broke out within the team by the time they were only a quarter of a way through. Tim could feel the course record slipping away already. He was hoping Callum would end up falling, but sadly was left disappointed.

After conquering the next stage, consisting of five damp rope bridges which allowed Tim's waterproof trousers to come in useful at last, they were on their way back up into the trees on the Treetop Climb. The metal walkways had been greased to make it more challenging, and Tim's triceps burnt as he desperately tried to drag himself upwards. Callum was finding it easy.

"C'mon Tim, use your strength training," he mocked.

Tim slumped onto his backside. His heart was beating as he feared he would lose his grip and tumble to his death. Although only around ten metres long, it felt much longer but he relied on the others to get it out the way. As Tim held onto a coarse, frayed rope, he slipped onto his front. He held on tight as he was dragged upwards without any dignity, dirt collecting on his face with each yank by the others.

As he sat at the top, he desperately took deep breaths to try and get some energy, before realising the worst was yet to come. The Death Drop. The final bit. The final horrible, vomit-inducing, last bit.

"You're first," said Leo to Tim.

"Why me?"

"Well, if we left you alone up here then you'd never jump, and it'd be dark before we got home."

"You'll be fine, Tim," said Lydia encouragingly.

Tim shuffled to the edge after being given the thumbs up to do so from the staff. He looked over the edge to the ground below. For the Death Drop you had to jump from the treetops onto an inflatable. It was large and black and had the word Spitfire written across it in large letters. Seeing about eight staff members around the landing area (including at least two who had FIRST AID emblazoned across their back) did not help Tim's confidence much at all.

By now, all in his team sensed how bad his fear of heights was currently. Having the three others stood behind him made the nerves worse, yet they started to give more encouragement (and a gentle push every few seconds).

Tim took a step back before re-approaching the edge. It looked so far down.

"Just jump!" shouted Callum.

"Piss off," he replied. "I am courageous," he repeated to himself quietly. He was certain he would be projectile vomiting within seconds. He closed his eyes to gain some composure.

"Eyes open!" shouted Mike from down below. "Remember the terms and conditions you agreed to when signing up!"

Tim counted himself down from three and jumped. As soon as he was plummeting through the air, he let out an horrendous scream all the way down. He hit the inflatable with a giant thud, which threw him back up in the air when it regained its shape. After bouncing a bit, he tried to get to his feet, but the staff had other plans. They grabbed hold of each limb and carried him towards a wooden bench.

"Well done," said the teen who had somehow got here quicker than the team. He couldn't have been much older than they were.

"Cheers," Tim replied, out of breath and out of enthusiasm.

"You've got two options now," he continued. "You can either sit on the bench here and wait for the others to jump, or you can go and sit in the finishers hut."

He chose the latter. He wanted somewhere to get warm and was promised a towel if he went on ahead. As he approached the wooden door, he heard the screams as Callum fell to the inflatable. He watched as he slid onto the floor, his head landing in a puddle, ruining his Instagram haircut. At least that would stop him mocking for a bit.

Tim took one final look up to Lydia and Leo, gave them a quick wave and opened the door, taking a seat on a bench inside, leaving the door open to speed up the last part for the others. He draped a blue towel around his shoulders and sat back with his eyes closed, glad it was all over.

Two minutes later, Lydia, the last of the group, entered. Leo punched the final big red button. It was over. They looked up the large digital display waiting for their time to show. The clock started flashing, before the time of twenty-seven minutes and eight seconds was displayed. They had taken nearly eight minutes off their previous time. Callum pulled them all reluctantly into a group hug, and Tim knew the other three were all as relieved as he was.

Tim needed a coffee and a Wispa. "If I ever agree to come here again, tell me its's a bad idea."

"Tim?" Lydia asked.

"Yeah?"

Rather than say anything more, she looked straight over his shoulder. Tim turned around to follow her gaze. On the inside section of the door was another graffiti face. Again, the eyes were represented with crosses. Again, the initials TJ had been scratched underneath. This time it had been hastily drawn in chalk, with the writing implement discarded in two pieces in the corner of the cabin.

# Ten

"What the hell, Tim?" said Callum as he walked over to the chalk face and rubbed at one of its eyes with his index finger.

"It wasn't me!" Tim argued back. "And stop wiping it off."

"Who else could it have been?" Callum continued. "It wasn't here when we arrived and yet, when you're left alone for a minute, it appears." He continued to rub out some of the lines.

Tim didn't respond this time, instead he unclipped his harness, picked up his jumper off the hook and went to storm out of the hut.

"Wait," said Lydia.

"I'm going," Tim said, firmly.

"No listen, we can't leave it here. We need to tell someone because it's obviously linked to the attack on Mr Patterson's shop."

"Tell who? The police?" asked Tim.

"Well, yeah. Wait here, Tim. Going anywhere may make people suspicious of you. Callum we've said to stop rubbing it," she said, pulling Callum's arm away from the back of the door.

"Callum thinks it's me anyway," said Tim.

"Tim, stay," begged Leo, tugging on his t-shirt.

Reluctantly he sat back on the bench, not in a mood to talk to the others.

It was only two minutes before Amy Flanagan entered the hut. "Gather up your things and come to the café. Now!" As they grabbed their clothing, Funtangutan staff entered, and Tim could overhear them talking about closing this part of the venue until "this stupid stuff is over". Tim walked with Lydia and Amy back across the car park, with Leo hanging back, but walking silently, with Callum.

On arrival, they were told to sit around the large table towards the back of the room, which had views of the forest from a large window that filled one wall. The bags of food from the previous days buffet were brought through and the four children started to silently pick at it.

"I have phoned your parents, and they are all on their way," Amy said as she joined them, carrying over a wooden tray with a hot chocolate for each.

"Including mine?" asked Callum.

"I left a voicemail. Your mum didn't answer."

"I'll be in trouble now," Callum replied.

"What did my mum say?" asked Tim, not caring about Callum's problems at all.

"She said she will be here soon. Same with your mum, Leo. I have told them both not to worry unnecessarily, though."

Tim pulled out some slices of quiche from one of the bags, which were now even more rubbery than they were yesterday. He wasn't feeling in the mood to speak to the others, especially Callum. He hated the way he had come into the group and accused him twice, on top of the fact he had been outed by him on the journey. Amy was doing her best to keep Tim occupied but backed away slightly when he didn't engage with any conversation she tried to start.

Out of the window, Tim saw the family Volvo pull into the car park and park up outside of a designated bay. His mum and Flo got out and walked at pace towards the café. As they entered, a police car pulled in behind them. The seriousness of the situation hit Tim like a tonne of bricks.

"Where was it today?" Tim's mum asked as she took him to a separate table.

"In the hut over there," he replied pointing out the window. "It appeared after we had finished. I didn't do it, Mum, I promise."

She took hold of his hand. "I believe you, it's okay. Was it the same as the one at the shop?"

"Basically yeah, although it was in chalk this time."

"Did it have your initials?" she asked.

"Yeah. It was the same, Mum. I don't know why it's happening. Callum already thinks it's me."

"Look, we will work this all out okay, don't worry."

"It's easy to say it'll be fine if you're not the one being accused."

"I know, darling, but please don't work yourself up about this. The police will help sort this for you. Promise me you will tell them everything you know. And I mean everything. Even if you have heard rumours and anything like that. Will you promise me that?"

"I promise. But I genuinely don't know anything."

"Then tell them that." Tim didn't respond. "When you get home, have some of my pie and maybe give Johann a call. It would be good for you to speak to someone close and who wasn't here today."

Speaking to Johann was already his number one priority, but this was the first time his mum had hinted she knew the two were close. Did she know everything? Tim nodded and went back to nibbling at the quiche as his mum grabbed a coffee from the counter. He looked around and noticed Flo had also taken Leo off to be on his own, while Amy was speaking to Lydia and Callum on a third table. He wished this wasn't happening.

The police had taken up a table near to the front of the café, and Amy moved across with Lydia to sit with a lone officer. He was making notes in a small pad as they answered his questions. The music over the speakers was so loud that Tim couldn't hear what was being said. Lydia was sat back in the chair, arms folded across her stomach. Her face was not giving anything away. Once complete, the officer shook both their hands, and Amy came over to the Johnson's.

"I am going to take Lydia and Callum back now," she said as she took Tim's empty plate away.

"Leave those, Amy, I'll help sort that. I can drop your bags around to yours this evening," his mum replied. Amy smiled and led Lydia and Callum out of the room.

"How come Callum didn't have to speak the police?" asked Tim. "He's the one accusing me."

"He probably isn't allowed to because his parents aren't here, that's all."

"It feels unfair," argued Tim.

"I know, but don't beat yourself up about this. The police are only asking questions to try and find out the information they need, they aren't accusing you of anything, remember."

Tim didn't respond, instead sitting back drinking hot chocolate. He watched Leo and Flo as they sat with the police, which only took a few minutes. Tim was nervous as his time approached. The top of his chocolate vibrated in his shaking hands. Once completed, Leo gave Tim a wave and a 'text me' hand signal before he too left. As soon as they had exited the door, the police officer gestured to Tim's mum.

"Come on, Tim, let's get this done. Remember, be

honest, okay?" she said.

"I will," he replied, dragging his feet on the floor as he was led to take a chair opposite the officer.

As they sat, the policeman gave a wide smile, and swept his sweat filled ginger hair off from his forehead. "Good morning, Tim, Katherine. My name is PC Hughes. I am part of a small team looking into the incidents which have occurred around Greenwood this week. Before I start, I need to state no one is being accused of causing the damage, just we need to ask a couple of questions so we have a full version of events that happened here today. If you need some time at any point, please let me know and we can take a short break. Does that all make sense?"

Tim nodded.

"Okay," continued PC Hughes. "Just to confirm firstly, your name is Timothy Louis Johnson of 247 Oak Tree Crescent."

"Yes," replied Tim. He felt his mum retake hold of his hand under the table, before giving it a squeeze.

"Thank you. Now, as you know there have been two instances of criminal damage we are now looking into. The first occurred on Monday at Patterson's Papers Newsagents, Bridge Street, Greenwood. The second incident occurred this morning here, at Funtangutan Leisure Ltd, Northlee, Greenwood. Do you understand?"

"Yes," Tim replied again.

"We will start with yesterday. When did you first hear of the criminal damage of the newsagents?"

Tim shifted in his seat, sitting on his right hand. "I was at a party and Mrs Patterson came round to tell us about it."

"And where was this party?"

"It was at Lydia's house on Church Lane."

"And this is Lydia Flanagan, correct?"

"Yes," said Tim. "She is the one you spoke to a minute ago."

"Were any of your friends here today also at this party?" the officer asked.

"Yes, all of them."

"And did you arrive together?"

"No, we didn't. I was the first one there, and then Leo came about quarter of an hour after me because he had bad guts because of drinking milk, and then Callum came around just after."

"And how long did it take you to get to the Flanagan's house?"

"Not long. About ten minutes. I was at home with Mum. I wouldn't do anything to that shop. Mr Patterson is my boss. I deliver papers for him."

"That answers my next question, thank you. And it is true Mr Patterson had spoken to you to confirm your role at the shop would be coming to an end, is that correct?"

"Yes," said Tim, "but that was later in the evening. I didn't know when we went to the shop to see the graffiti. I'd never damage his shop. I like Mr Patterson. I was there today to do my job."

"Tim," interjected his mum, "they are not accusing you, remember. He is just making sure they know the situation."

Tim leant forward and put his arms on the table, cupping his head in his hands.

"Your mum is correct, Tim. These are just some questions I am obliged to ask," added the officer. "Now, of course, on the graffiti, your initials have been present. Do you know of any reason why this might be?"

"No," said Tim into his hands.

"Is there anyone you know of who share those initials, or anything related to those initials?"

"No."

"Okay. Please do keep thinking, though, and if there is something which comes to mind, please let me know, is that clear?"

"Yes."

Tim watched the officer made a few scribbles in his notebook, before looking blankly at his mum, who responded by stroking her son's shoulder.

"Now, onto today," said PC Hughes. "The people who were here with you were the same as those with you at the party. Is that correct?"

"Yes. It was us four again, and Lydia's mum."

"When did you first discover the graffiti today?"

"It was when we got to the finishers hut over there," he said pointing again at the wooden building through the window. "Lydia noticed it, though, not me."

"Yes, again, this is not about accusing anyone of anything, or who saw what first," said PC Hughes.

"I wasn't accusing Lydia, sorry, I was just saying I didn't know about it," added Tim, exasperated.

"Tim, please keep calm, we are nearly done. We just need to understand the facts. With the visit here today, were you, at any point, alone in that room?"

Tim nodded slowly, he could feel the colour drain from his face.

"Okay, and for how long?"

"'bout a minute, if that. I had just done the Death Drop."

"Death Drop?" asked PC Hughes.

"Yeah, like you have to jump down onto this big inflatable thing. I was knackered so went into the hut rather than sit on the bench as I wanted to get a towel and try to stop myself panicking 'cos I hate heights."

"And you didn't notice the graffiti when you sat in there?"

"No, honestly. I left the door open cos I wanted it to be easy for the others to get in."

"And this was the door with the face on?"

"Yeah."

"Great, thank you." PC Hughes wrote some more notes in his book, and then looked down the answers given by the others on previous pages. He nodded to himself and then looked at Tim. "I think that is all we require today, Tim, thank you. And thank you, Katherine, for being here."

"Have you got the CCTV from here?" asked Tim.

"Tim, we will be doing all we can to work this out, okay? Please just let us do our jobs," PC Hughes replied, standing up and picking up his items. His radio beeped, and then a fuzzy voice said something which made no sense. "I will be in touch should I need to ask either of you anything further, but at this stage I think we have everything we need. Here is a card with my details. If you think of anything, give me a call."

"Thank you," said Tim as he took the card and passed it to his mum for safe keeping. They waited until the officer had bought a takeaway coffee and left towards his car.

"Well done, Tim, that wasn't too bad, see?"

"I guess. Can we go home now please?"

"Yes. You absolutely stink."

Tim put on a sarcastic smile. "Cheers."

***

At home Tim was ushered straight into the kitchen. He removed his dirty trousers and top, having refused to do so on the doorstep in full view of the neighbours. He sat at the table in his boxer shorts. His dad came to join him, passing him a bowl of warm blackberry pie from the microwave, and custard from a tin. He preferred cold custard on hot desserts, which others found odd. His dad took a seat opposite and moved a folder of paperwork onto the dresser.

"Where's Marty?" Tim asked with his mouth full, realising he hadn't seen his brother since their fish and chips on Sunday.

"He was at band rehearsals last night," said his dad. "I think they have driven somewhere today. He'll be back later I expect. Why?"

"I just want to talk to him."

"About what?"

"Everything," Tim replied.

"You can talk to us, darling," replied his mum, bringing a cup of tea across.

The truth was, he couldn't. They would only be able to hear half of his problems. "I'll wait for Marty."

"Well, he isn't here. We do need to discuss what is going on, though."

"Can I call Johann first and do this later? I haven't done anything remember, Mum, I promise."

"Call him when we are back. As for the graffiti, I believe you," she replied. "I think you did well with the police this morning. If you think of anything else, let me know and we can give PC Hughes a call."

"I believe you, also," added his dad, before gesturing for his wife to carry on.

"It is just strange this is happening, though, I'll be honest," she said.

"I don't know anything, and if I did, I would tell you," repeated Tim.

"I know, but you need to take care. We all do. Just make sure you let us know where you are at all times."

"But that feels like I'm being punished," argued Tim, dropping his spoon into his bowl with a clang.

"It's for your own benefit," his dad responded.

His mum nodded. "I have to go to town soon, so you can come with me, Tim."

Tim wanted to bury himself in his room. He didn't want to go out but could tell by the tone of his mum's voice he had no choice. He ate his pie slowly and headed up to his bedroom. He opened Instagram.

**Hey Johann. Are you free to talk? X**

After messaging, he laid back on his bed, delaying a much-needed shower. Funtangutan was meant to be one of the highlights of the week, but now the memory had been tarnished. He pulled out an old music magazine to read to take his mind off all that was happening. It took twenty minutes for a reply to come from Johann.

**Heya. Sure! I am just out for a walk at the moment. I'm so bored. I want to be back with you. X**

**I really wish you were here too x**

**How was Funtangutan?**

**I'll explain later**

**What's happened?**

Tim sent the photo of the chalk face to Johann.

**Another one??**

**Yeah. I'm getting a bit worried now. People think it's me**

*But it isn't you*

*I know. Callum has already accused me though
He's a dick then*

*He did something worse too. He told Lydia's
mum I'm gay*

*Seriously? Why?*

*Because he's a dick. And Leo*

*What's Leo done?*

*No, Callum told Lydia's mum Leo was gay too*

*Oh god. Did she say anything?*

*Yeah, she was nice about it. I'll explain all later*

*I hate Callum*

*Agreed. We're stuck with him though*

*Not if he's being like this. I'll be home in a
couple of days hopefully*

*Can't wait!*

*Me neither :). I best get on with this walk. I'll let
you know when I'm home*

*Cool. I'm off up town with mum anyway. Speak
in a bit x*

**Speak soon! xx**

Tim put his phone on charge and went to shower. Once clean, he pulled £20 from his First Date Fund jar. He needed to treat himself today. Anything to save this day from being the worst one ever.

***

Tim walked across the car park towards the express supermarket, fighting with a mini trolley that had wheels that wanted to go in every direction except the one he needed it to. His mum had given him the shopping list to manage. It only had about ten items on it and Tim knew this was all a badly disguised plot for his mum to keep an eye on him.

He couldn't go through every day like this for the rest of the summer holidays. Although he had been strictly told to keep out of the investigation by Flo yesterday, it was playing on his mind too much. He would secretly start working on solving this during the afternoon but could not do this on his own. He needed Johann's help.

As they entered the small shop, a woman with a severe blonde bob haircut and red wine lipstick bounded across. They hadn't even picked up their first item. She was called Miriam according to her name badge. "Oh Katherine, so good to see you!" she said as she fake kissed her on both cheeks.

"Have you got the goods?"

Miriam smiled. "I do."

Tim waited as they started discussing the upcoming fete. Tim did not have any idea who this lady was and can't recall ever seeing her before.

"Back in a minute, darling" his mum said, before she followed Miriam through a staff only door.

Tim started browsing the shelves, but the selection

was poor. He did sneak a couple of packs of chocolate desserts into the trolley, however (they would make a change from all the pie). He wandered briefly, but after five minutes, his mum still hadn't returned. He put the trolley to one side and took a seat on a pair of steps by a large pillar. He pulled out his phone.

"Hey Leo, are you free later?"

"Can be. You okay?"

"Yeah, a bit better now thanks. Still angry."

"I wouldn't worry."

"You would if they put your initials everywhere."

"Yeah, but I'm innocent."

"Me too!"

"What did you wanna do?"

"Can you come to mine?"

"Time?"

"4?"

"See you there. I'll message Lydia and Callum."

"Nah don't do that."

"Why not?"

"I want it to just be us two."

"OK. Can I talk with you about something later?"

"Yeah course."

He put his phone back in his pocket and continued waiting. After a further ten minutes, he became restless. He stood up to stop his legs becoming dead and took a walk to the newspaper section, flicking through various magazines, stopping only when he saw the face of Olympic diver Marco Rodriguez staring back at him from the latest *Sports Monthly*. Staring at Marco would be a much better use of his time waiting.

With his money still in his pocket, he took it to a man who was staring into the distance from behind an overstocked till. He had a plain face and lank hair that was trying its best to hide the fact he was balding, but not doing a convincing job. He looked like the human equivalent of the colour beige. His grey uniform wasn't helping him. Tim put the magazine on the short conveyor belt.

"Did you find everything you were looking for today?" he asked monotonously.

"Yes, thank you."

"Would you like to pay for the items in your trolley as well?"

"No thanks, my mum will pay for those shortly. Just the magazine."

"Do you have a rewards card?"

"No."

"Would you like to buy one of these chocolate gifts for just one pound?" he added, waving lightly at a stack of large Fruit 'n' Nut bars.

"No, I'm fine thanks."

"Would you like to round up your purchase to the nearest pound for charity?"

"I am fine, sorry."

"Would you like one of our new savings cards?"

Tim sighed. "No, just the magazine."

"With the savings cards you can purchase stamps to help pay for Christmas items when Christmas arrives."

"Honestly, just the magazine is fine, please."

"There are now only one hundred and thirty days until Christmas," he continued, pointing at a Santa shaped countdown on the wall behind him.

"Only? One hundred and thirty is quite a lot."

"It will soon arrive. Our Christmas range will be on sale from next week. Would you like a bag?"

"No, that's okay, thanks."

"Would you need a receipt?"

"Yes, please."

"Is there anything else I could help you with today?"

"No. I just want to take the magazine."

"Three pounds and fifty pence, please."

Tim had no idea why people who worked in shops were taught to interrogate every customer that came in. Why did he have to answer fifty questions just to buy a magazine? He handed a ten-pound note across, and when asked, confirmed the change in any form would be fine. He'd have said anything to get away from the world's most boring man. Once the transaction was complete, he forced a fake smile at Mr Beige and went back to the steps by the pillar.

He opened his magazine and went straight to the Marco interview. Tim wasn't one to lie and would happily admit he fancied him. The feature was an in-depth interview about his home life and career to date, alongside his top diving tips. He would ask his instructor Mrs Brute at tomorrow's diving lesson if they could incorporate some of these. He was looking forward to going diving on Wednesday evening. It would take his mind off everything else happening around Greenwood.

Marco lived in North London and trained at the old Olympic pool five times a week, doing a mixture of dives and gym work. He spoke about working on his fitness to be in shape for the upcoming World Championships. He had missed the British Championships due to a frozen shoulder. Any injury made Tim feel a bit squeamish. The only disappointing moment in the article was when he had spoken about his girlfriend, not that Tim was in any position to date such a megastar.

Having read the article and having stared at the pictures for slightly longer than normal, Tim's mum still hadn't emerged from the depths of the warehouse. It had now been nearly twenty-five minutes and other customers kept looking at him oddly. He decided to give her mobile a call. There was no answer. He rang the house phone. After three rings, it was answered.

"Hello?"

"Hi, Dad, it's Tim."

"Hiya, you okay?"

"Yeah fine, just wondering if you had heard from Mum at all?"

"She's in the garden, did you want a word with her?"

"Are you sure?"

There was a slight pause. "Yeah, I can see her out the kitchen window from here. She's putting something into the shed. Why?"

"Well, I was with her in the shop, and she told me to wait a minute."

Tim heard a long, loud laugh. This didn't make him feel any better. If his parents were planning on keeping him within their sight, then they should be doing a better job of it. Once the laughing finished, Tim heard his dad put the phone on the side and go to shout out of the kitchen window. A distant conversation could be heard.

"Katherine, did you forget something from the shops?"

"I don't think so?"

"What about a son?"

Tim couldn't hear her response as his dad was laughing again. After a few moments, Tim heard him approaching the phone. "Hello, you still there?"

"Yep."

"Mum says can you pick up the rest of the shopping and bring it home. She'll pay you back of course."

"If I must," he replied.

"She's sorry, honestly."

"She owes me big time," Tim replied, before jabbing the screen to hang up.

Despite being forgotten, Tim quickly collected the other bits from the shopping list (except for stuffing, which he couldn't be bothered to track down), throwing two extra packs of chocolate desserts in for good measure. He took the trolley back to the till and picked its contents out onto the conveyor belt. Mr Beige looked up at him.

"Did you find everything you were looking for today?"

Tim sighed again, defeated.

# Eleven

Tim kicked off his shoes and took the shopping to the kitchen. He opened the fridge and was faced by six and a half different pies, all of various quality. He hoped the people at the fete would be hungry as this was a lot of food to eat and there were still three days of baking to go. He started to squeeze the shopping into the small remaining gaps, trying his best not to squash the cheese.

As he sat at the table with a tea, his mum came into the kitchen, hugging him from behind around the neck.

"I'm sorry, darling," she said.

"I'm not speaking to you," he replied, not taking his eyes away from a stretching article in *Sports Monthly*.

"I just got caught up in all the excitement."

He threw the magazine down. "Excitement? You were in a supermarket."

"Come with me and I'll show you what I picked up."

"You owe me twenty pounds."

"Twenty?"

"Are you in a position to argue?" he asked, making sure his magazine cost was covered as compensation.

"You're a cheeky one, but fine. I guess I owe you."

"Didn't you think anything was odd when you got in the car?"

"I was just in the moment. I had some boxes on the

front seat with me so didn't notice. Let me show you."

She opened the back door and led him outside. Barnaby was in his pen on the lawn perched with his front legs on a rock, taking in the heat. Opening the wooden door of the shed, she stood to one side and gestured inside. Tim walked around her and saw a stack of boxes taller than he was in the middle of the floor. He approached them and pulled open a flap of a box halfway up and peered inside. All he could see were pumpkins. There must have been ten in this box alone. He didn't say anything but turned his head to stare at her with a blank expression.

"Well, you don't have to look so impressed," she said.

"I assume this is for Saturday?"

"Yes. They aren't as easy to get at this time of year, but Miriam managed to pull some favours down at Quicksave and get them in for me. The Dolly Mixtures have a better chance of winning the top prize now. What do you think?"

"I don't think much to be honest. I, just, well, I dunno." He perched on his dads work stool. "I'm not sure exactly what you want me to say?"

"I just thought you would like them," she said, before approaching and closing the box back up.

"Right, fair enough. The pumpkins look good. Happy?"

"That's better. You can help me carve them."

Tim sighed. "I assume there isn't an option for me to say no here?"

"Correct. Pat and Pet are coming over this evening to help as well."

"Are they bringing the dog?"

"Probably."

"Can I ask Leo and Lydia over?"

"If you want. I can pick them up."

"Mum, you don't have to keep us under surveillance. Let them walk round together."

"I am just trying to protect you all, sorry."

"Well, you don't have to. Anyway, who was that woman who gave you these pumpkins? I've never seen her before."

"Yes, you have. Miriam used to babysit you and Marty when you were young."

"Are you sure?"

"Yes. Very. She used to have dark hair and a lot of make-up. You must remember?"

"That's her now? She looks so, well, so dull and mum-like."

"Her emo phase went when she had kids of her own. And don't say mum-like as if it's an insult."

"She used to scare me a bit," Tim said truthfully.

"That's why she was so good. You never caused any trouble for her."

Tim took a final look at the pile of boxes and went back into the house, throwing some more lettuce to Barnaby. The tortoise was seemingly the only sane creature left. It was coming up to four, so he headed to his room to prepare for the investigations to start. He took two chocolate mousses from the fridge on his way. He had an hour before dinner to make a start forming a plan.

His room was cluttered, not having had chance to put away his washing or replace all the books onto his shelf. He took a seat on the floor and pulled his phone out, ringing Johann on FaceTime.

"Hey hey!" Johann shouted happily. Tim couldn't see his face and the camera work was shaky.

"Heya, Johann. What are you up to?"

"Sorry, was sat in the front room so just heading

upstairs to my room. Gimme a sec."

Tim waited until he was settled, listening to thumping footsteps. It took some time. "How many floors does that house have?" he asked when the video settled.

"It's three storeys. And there's the loft, which is where I am." Johann came into view, sat back on a beanbag with his phone propped up in front of him. "Hanna has the room in the basement so I've kinda got a good deal!"

"I wish I had a huge house. I didn't realise your family were so rich."

Johann laughed. "Oh, they're not, it's just they've lived here for like twenty-five years. Freja's husband Nils was a bank manager for ages so they could afford to buy it back then. What are you eating?"

Tim held up a dessert to the camera. "A cheap chocolate pot. Have you got windows in there, Johann?" The room looked dark to Tim. He saw Johann give a thumbs up and then pick up the phone. Johann span the camera around and the screen was flooded with sunlight. Tim wasn't quite sure what he was being shown.

"This is the view," said Johann eventually.

"Ah, okay. I can't see much."

"It's like a view of some of the city. You can see the football ground. It's massive. I'll send a picture later."

"Cool." Tim waited for Johann to sit back down.

"How's Barnaby?"

"Yeah, all good! I'm enjoying him being around. He's in the garden again now."

"You haven't lost him then?"

"Nope. All is good. I'm gonna clean out his pen again after dinner."

"Do you have enough bedding still?"

"Yeah, a little bit. Dad knows someone who can lend us more, though. I can collect it later."

"Cool. If you need more, though, go round to mine. There should be some in a plastic box thing down the side of the house. Just help yourself. I'm kinda missing him. Send me a picture, won't you?"

"I will," replied Tim, before adding "Do you miss him more than me?"

"About equal."

"Thanks!" Tim laughed. "Oh, quick question. Can tortoises eat pumpkin?"

"Um, I think so. Google it. Why?"

"No reason."

"Sure, sure. Anyway, are you okay after Lydia's mum found out about you?" he asked.

Tim took a moment to think. "Yeah, I guess so. She's promised me she won't tell anyone, but I'm still gonna go and speak to her at some point."

"Does she know we are, y'know, me and you are sort of hanging out together?" Johann asked.

"No, I don't think so." *Hanging out.* Is that how Johann was going to describe it? Tim was desperate for it to be more but was still too afraid to ask right now. He just needed to find the best way of asking. Over FaceTime didn't seem right. What if Johann got weirded out and ended the call? "Do you think I should mention us to Amy?"

"I don't know. I guess it's up to you. We can wait until I'm back, though. Like, there isn't any rush is there to sort of tell the world?"

"True. I want to, though. I want to tell everyone."

"Maybe take things one step at a time."

"I will. I might not be able to see Amy again until you're back anyway, so feel free to come with me."

"So, what happened at Funtangutan?"

Tim filled Johann in on the questioning that had occurred at the Funtangutan café but said they needed to wait for Leo to arrive. "Did you want to help me investigate? Secretly, of course."

"Absolutely."

"Thanks. Leo should be here in a minute or so." As they were waiting, Johann gave Tim a tour of the house, which included a games room, complete with snooker table. The back garden was also incredible; landscaped with small walls and a beautiful patio.

"Tim, Leo's here," shouted his dad up the stairs as Johann was showing Tim a small waterfall.

"Send him up," he bellowed back as he put his phone on the bookcase and sat back onto the floor. Leo entered the room a few seconds later and sat next to Tim with his legs stretched out across the floor.

"I'm knackered." he said.

"Why?"

"I was gonna be late, so I ran round, and my legs are stiff from the climbing. I hope you don't wanna walk anywhere far."

"Well, no, nowhere at all. I need your help here," Tim confirmed.

"Cool. What's up?"

"We need to investigate the graffiti," Tim said, wanting to get it out in the open immediately.

"You heard my mum, though, and with the police already speaking to us I don't think it's a good idea. What did they ask you this morning anyway?"

"Just where I saw it, if I knew about my initials being on there, that kinda thing. How about you?"

"Same. I don't think I should get involved, though, sorry." He stood back up.

"You are here now, and I know you want to investigate this just as much as we do."

"We?" questioned Leo.

"Me and Johann."

"Is he back?"

"Not yet, no."

"Urgh, you best not be miserable all evening, then. Just tell him you want to be his boyfriend and give yourself something to be happy about."

Tim jumped to put his hand over Leo's mouth and told him to shut up forcefully as he wrestled him to the ground. Leo pushed him off.

"Hey Leo," Johann said from the phone.

"Oh, heya!" he responded, before the penny dropped. "Ohhh," he said dramatically to Tim who just held his hands out. "Didn't know you would be here, Johann, sorry. Did you hear all that?"

"Hear what?" laughed Johann.

"How's Sunderland?" said Leo, changing the subject.

"Newcastle. Yeah, it's okay but I am a bit bored."

"And your uncle?"

"Still in the hospital but he's awake and eating and stuff so it's looking good."

As the two were chatting, Tim opened a drawer and pulled out a new A4 pad and two marker pens. He moved his phone again so Johann could see them both as they sat sharing the chair at Tim's desk. Tim took the lid off of a red marker and to draw a copy of the graffiti face on the front cover.

"That's weirdly accurate," Leo told him, taking hold of the pad.

"Well, it's hardly the Mona Lisa, is it?" snapped Tim.

"So then, what do you know so far?" asked Johann, stepping in before any arguments started.

"Well, there was one on Mr Patterson's yesterday. And one at Funtangutan this morning," said Leo, giving the pad back to Tim.

"Right," responded Johann.

"Um, that's literally all we know," added Tim.

"You two would be rubbish detectives," joked Johann.

"Why?" they both replied defensively before Tim carried on. "That's literally all there is."

"You need to think outside the box." said Johann.

"How?"

"Okay, listen. Let's take the first one. Where was it?"

"On Mr Patterson's window," said Leo.

"Correct. Now, what was it drawn with?"

"Yellow paint. Spray paint, I guess," said Tim.

"There you go. Write that down." Tim did as he was told. He was glad to let Johann take the lead.

"Now, what time, Tim?"

"I got to Lydia's at three-ish."

"And you Leo?"

"About half hour later. Then Callum came round not long after that."

"And what time did Mr Patterson say it happened?"

Tim thought for a moment. "Um, Mrs Patterson came round at about four, maybe four fifteen. I can't remember exactly."

"So, it happened just before then?" asked Johann.

"Maybe, yeah. Mr Patterson had been to mine just after I left at three so some time in that hour?" guessed Tim.

"Seems a reasonable timeframe," added Leo.

Tim wrote this down. Johann was much better at this than he expected. They had no suspects yet, mainly because the only people they knew of who were linked to Tim were either with Tim at the party, preparing to go to dance rehearsals dressed as a witch, or in Newcastle. The only person he hadn't seen was Marty, but Tim couldn't bring himself to think he would be responsible for it. It wasn't in his brothers' nature.

Despite his initial protests, Leo was getting into the

investigating. The three followed the same process for the face they had found at Funtangutan. Initially they narrowed it down to the time they had been on the course, until a thought dawned on Leo.

"Tim, obviously I believe you," he said.

"This feels like there will be a 'but'," Tim responded.

"No, not at all. What I was going to say was I believe you, but Callum accused you because we found it after you had been left in the hut alone."

"Told you there was a 'but'. But, yeah. I can't explain that," said Tim, dabbing at the page with the pen.

"But think. When we got to Funtangutan, what did we do?"

"Lydia's mum went to the café, and we went and got changed."

"Precisely," said Leo.

"I'm not following," said Johann, who was now eating a Wispa. Tim noted his influence on him.

"But think, Tim. We got into the hut to change. What mood were you in?"

"Why does that matter?" asked Tim.

"Just answer."

"Well, angry, obviously. You?"

"Yeah, same."

"Because of what Callum said in the car?" asked Johann.

"Yeah," they both replied.

"We were both angry, right?" continued Leo. "Then, when we were inside, we were forced to talk about the course record and our game plan."

"Yeah, and Callum was still being an idiot saying he was stronger than us."

"Right. What do you remember about the inside of the hut at the start?"

"There was Mike and his biceps," said Tim.

"Biceps?" questioned Johann.

"Honestly, they could crush you, Johann," said Tim.

"I see."

Leo continued. "Aside from Mike and his biceps, what else was in there. What was on the walls?"

Tim pulled out two Wispa's from his stash, chucking one at Leo. "Um, there was the clock, and then the map of the course."

"Yep," said Leo. "What else?"

"I don't know. I genuinely can't think of anything else I saw."

"Do you remember anything else, Leo?" Johann added.

"No. And that's my point. We were busy getting ready and arguing, and you were also crapping yourself about heights," he said, whilst pointing at Tim.

"I did alright!" Tim argued back.

"I know, but that's not the point. None of us were concentrating, so we didn't take in our surroundings."

"Hang on," Johann said with a mouthful. They waited for him to swallow. "So, what you're getting at is, if you weren't concentrating, then the face may have already been on the wall before you started?"

"Exactly!" said Leo, triumphantly.

"Maybe, but we can't be sure," said Tim.

"How were you feeling in the hut at the end Tim?" asked Johann.

"Awful. I had just done the death drop."

"What's that?" asked Johann.

"Basically, you jump off a platform onto a big inflatable. I feel sick thinking back to it now."

"Stop being so dramatic, Tim," said Leo.

"I'm not. Seriously, even if I see the word Spitfire now it would make me nervous."

"What's spitfire?" asked Johann.

"Oh, it was just written across the landing place when you jump."

"Fair enough. Anyway, write down everything we have just said, Tim," said Johann. "Leo is probably right, and it was done before you two entered the hut."

Tim made a note of everything in a new column on the page. If Leo was right, and it was there before they arrived, then this narrowed down the timeframe to approximately one year as that's how long it had been since the last time they had visited.

The staff at the centre would surely have noticed it quickly after it was done, though. They couldn't go and ask them, so their investigation had led to more questions than answers. They promised each other not to tell anyone else just yet. Johann had suggested they tell Lydia, but for now to keep Callum out of it. He was still new and, having already accused Tim, Johann agreed they should wait until they could fully trust him.

"We have to tell him soon," said Leo.

"No, we don't," replied Tim. "I don't want him involved."

"Tim, mate, you can't keep on being so angry all the time. It's not all about you, y'know."

"I can be as angry as I want for as long as I want, Leo. He outed us both. I don't know why you aren't still angry."

"I am, but it won't help. Just leave off him a bit."

Johann tried to ease the tension by asking about their diving, but neither answered more than one word.

As Leo left to go to the toilet, Marty entered. Tim threw his pad under the bed. Marty had his bass on his back and was dressed in the trademark black. He had now added a tartan bandana to the outfit.

"Alright?" he said to him. "What are you up to?"

"We're just chatting to Johann."

"Fair."

"Where have you been, anyway?" asked Tim. "I've not seen you for ages."

"Just places. Went on a road trip in Shell's car today. Just got back. Also, yesterday we had a rehearsal."

"With the band?"

"Yep. I have something for you to listen to," Marty said, as he pulled out a CD from his pocket. "Welcome to the first ever Haberdashery Menagerie demo."

Tim took the CD out of his hand and went to put it in the player immediately.

"Wait until I've gone," Marty said. "I don't want to be here if you hate it."

"Did you do this today?"

"Yeah," said Marty, looking proud. "Shell knows someone who has some equipment, so we recorded it in their garage. It took ages."

"But you only have one song?"

"We have two now. And we've changed the name of *Checkout Check Out* also as that was rubbish."

"It was," confirmed Tim.

"Are you free on Thursday?" Marty asked.

"I am, but only after two because I might be working at the library that day."

"The library? Since when?"

"I start tomorrow. I'll fill you in on the details later."

"Sounds like I've missed a lot these last two days. Someone told me down the pub last night Mr Patterson is closing his shop."

"Yeah, it's rubbish," said Tim.

"Yeah. Anyway, we have a gig at The Bell on Thursday, and I wondered if you wanted to come?"

"I'll come," said Leo as he came back into the room.

"Are we allowed in?" questioned Tim.

"Yeah, it's in the garden as a part of some music

festival thing. We are on at about three for twenty minutes. Johann, will you be here?" he asked, with his face now close to the phone.

"Um, I can't sorry. I won't be home until Friday."

"Ah that's a shame. You'll have to come to the next one."

"Will do."

"Leo, I've given Tim our CD. Let me know what you think. I'm gonna go and write some new basslines." He left the room and closed the door behind him.

"I have to go out for food again shortly," said Johann. "Let me know what the music is like. I'm kinda excited."

"You sure you don't wanna listen with us?" asked Leo.

"Nah, I genuinely don't have time. Anyway, it'll sound all tinny through this phone. Try and send it to me somehow, though."

"I will," said Tim. "I'll message you in a bit, okay?"

"Sounds good. See ya later Leo."

"See ya, Johann."

"Tim?"

"Hello."

"Miss your face," he said smiling.

"Miss yours, too," Tim replied, a warm sensation filling his chest. "Speak shortly."

Leo mimicked being sick.

Once Johann had hung up, Leo turned to Tim. "Can I speak to you about something else?"

Tim pulled his old CD player from out the bottom of his wardrobe. "Nah, that can wait, we can talk later. I wanna hear this music first," The CD was put in the player and Tim hit play. This would be an experience.

# Twelve



"This is pretty bad," Tim said, as they listened to the *Haberdashery Menagerie* CD for the second time. Although *Checkout Check Out* was now called *Goodbye*, the supermarket themed lyrics still were still awful.

"We've got to go along on Thursday to the gig and pretend to like this," joked Leo. "Also, how are they going to fill a twenty-minute set? These two songs are about six minutes in total."

Tim shrugged. "I guess they'll do some covers. Hopefully of good songs."

"Anything will be better than this."

After the second run-through had finished, Tim took the CD out and messaged Marty to say he liked it. He didn't want to appear unkind. He heard Marty shout 'thanks!' through the bedroom wall. He would listen to it again later when on his own. He was looking forward to seeing them live on Thursday. Marty had always been quite shy about playing bass in front of anyone in the family so the gig would be a big step for him.

"What you up to tonight, Leo?" Tim asked.

"Nothing, why? More planning?"

"Nah, my mum is hosting a pumpkin carving session later if you want to get involved. Pat and Pet will be here as well."

Leo thought for a bit. "I don't have much on so can't think of a valid excuse unfortunately, so may as well."

Tim noted Leo didn't question the appearance of pumpkins in August. "Cool, thanks. I'll message Lydia."

"And Callum?" asked Leo. Tim didn't want him around the house so didn't answer. "Come on, Tim," Leo continued. "I'll bring him round and then you can settle this together rather than fall out anymore."

"Fine. But if he starts—"

"I'll make sure he won't, Tim," said Leo, stopping Tim's response.

After Leo had left, Tim went back over the notes they had written during the afternoon. Despite them writing a few points for each face that had been found, Tim couldn't find any connections between them, and could not work out who would use his initials when doing so. He could trust no one.

***

Tim had cleaned out Barnaby, using the last of his hay bedding, and had a soak in the bath before Pat and Pet had arrived just after seven. So far Barnaby's bowels were behaving, but he was nervous every time he held the animal on his lap. He was becoming quite attached to the tortoise, despite thinking at the start of the week he would be the complete opposite. Tim headed down into the kitchen. His mum was already setting up, putting newspapers across the top of all counters.

"You should have done the same when doing your baking," he said, realising they were likely to cause less mess than the pastry party she had held previously.

"Give me a hand shifting this table, will you?"

They dragged the table into the centre of the kitchen, and by the time Tim had brought through all the emergency chairs, Pat and Pet were sat with knives in their hands. Archie the dog laid under Pat's chair, seemingly asleep, his sequined rainbow colour projecting sunlight across the room like a canine glitterball.

"So, Katherine, what do we need to do?" asked Pet, who was sat opposite from her wife.

"Anything you like. They're just to go around the edge of the stage so they don't have to be perfect."

Tim had spent a few minutes downloading carving templates. If he was to be forced to do this out of season task, he was going to do it properly. "Is Marty helping?" he asked.

"He is meant to be but no idea where he is," said his dad as he now joined the group. "Too obsessed with his blooming music, that one is."

"Oh, leave him alone," said his mum. "He needs to practice for the gig. We don't want him to be an embarrassment."

"Not with you on Saturday as well," said Tim. She didn't answer, instead just putting a pumpkin in front of her son and telling him to get carving. "Have you heard his CD by the way?" he asked.

"He won't let us," said their dad. "Have you?"

"Yeah. It's good," Tim half-lied.

"I'll just have to wait until The Bell to hear them, I guess. I'll let you know what they're like, Katherine."

Tim stopped cutting the lid off his pumpkin. "Are you not coming, Mum?"

"I've got work so I won't be able to, I'm afraid. Make sure you film some of it for me. I'd love to see it."

"If he will let me," said Tim. As his mum started the

usual catch-up of gossip regarding all the neighbours with Pat and Pet, Tim moved it to the kitchen counter. He thought it would be easier to carve it whilst standing up. He went through his templates and decided to start with an easier one, pulling out an outline of a cat. All the fruit from the middle was to be put in various mixing bowls on the countertops so they could be added to more pies. He had explained to his mum this wasn't how you made a proper pumpkin pie, but she said she wanted to experiment.

After five minutes, his cat looked more like a chubby owl. Deciding an owl was still suitable for Halloween, he continued prodding until eventually the last part of the side fell onto the counter. "How many more are there to do?" he asked as he placed his first effort on the floor in the hall.

"Just two boxes, so about twenty in total. Not many," replied his mum. "The rest of them are just going to be placed around the front of our performance area. Oh, that reminds me, I was meant to bring the candles in. Can you run and grab them for me please?"

"Why do you need candles? It won't be dark at the fete."

"There's no point carving them if you don't have candles," she replied.

"Fair enough. Where are they? In the shed?"

"No, they're in the boot of the car. Keys are in my coat pocket on the banisters."

Tim headed towards the door and pulled out the keys from his mum's long white coat. As he did so, a small envelope fell out of the pocket. As he picked it up, he noticed it had been sent from The NHS Waterside Surgery. At first, he thought it may have been a letter about her job, but she didn't work at that practice. He wondered if she was ill. Maybe she was changing jobs again. As curious as he was, he knew it would be wrong to read it so folded it back up and put it back into the coat.

"Alright, Tim?" came a voice from behind him as he limped across to the car in flip flops. Tim turned around and saw Leo, Lydia, and Callum walking towards him. Callum was dressed in more sponsored sports clothing, with shorts so high up his thighs they were bordering on the offensive.

"Alright?" Tim replied.

"What are you doing out here? Thought we were carving pumpkins," asked Leo.

Tim opened the car boot. "Yeah, there's some candles in here somewhere that Mum forgot."

"Cool, I'll take them in," Leo offered as he helped find them. The boot was filled with a collection of random items. There were picnic blankets, wellington boots, a carrier bag with a spade and first aid kit, and a roadmap which was dated 2005. He had no idea why this was still there considering the Satnav made it obsolete. Many of the roads in Greenwood wouldn't even be on the map, either, considering the town had nearly doubled in size in recent years.

"Here they are," said Leo, pulling a bargain pack of one hundred tealights from underneath a mini-carjack and a multipack of hardboiled sweets. "Callum wants a word," he added as he pulled Lydia away with him towards the Johnson house. Tim closed the boot and locked the car but decided not to start a conversation. Callum stood opposite, not making eye contact.

"You alright?" asked Callum.

"Fine," responded Tim, as he started off across the carpark.

"Wait a minute. I wanna say sorry."

"About what? Telling Lydia's mum I'm gay, or being

a dick at Funtangutan?"

Callum looked to the floor. "Um, both, I guess. But I am sorry."

"Okay, fine," Tim said, not feeling fine at all. "Oh, my parents don't know, and nor do Pat and Pet so I'd appreciate you keeping your mouth shut. If you're unsure if you should say something, you probably shouldn't."

"Who are Pat and Pet?" asked Callum.

"They're our neighbours. They're married just in case you fancy offending them as well."

"I'll keep quiet," Callum promised.

"Good. We best go in. Come on."

Tim led Callum into the house and told him to take his shoes off. When they had got into the kitchen, there was still a spare seat between Pat and his dad, so Tim made Callum sit there to make sure he kept himself out of trouble. Tim went back to the counter, picking up another pumpkin on his way. He handed templates to Lydia and Leo, who had started but were also struggling.

"Can't we just do the generic face thing?" asked Lydia.

"As long as you don't mean like the one on the shop?" Leo replied.

Lydia's face flushed. "Oh, yeah, I didn't mean that, sorry. I just meant the usual pumpkin face thing."

"Would be quicker I guess," said Tim.

The three all put their templates into the bin and went back to hacking out two circular eyes. Everyone was concentrating so much that there wasn't any conversation for a few minutes. This silence was interrupted by Pat.

"I hear you have a job at the library, Tim?" she said.

"Um yeah, sort of," he replied, without turning around. "I'm working there tomorrow, but it's only a trial thing."

"You didn't tell me this," said Leo.

"Or me," added Lydia.

"Yeah, sorry. I was meant to, but with everything that happened earlier I didn't get round to it."

"I didn't think you were interested when I showed you the advert yesterday," Leo said.

"Well, I wasn't, but *someone* gave me no choice," he said.

His mum pointed at him with a wooden spoon, but spoke to Pat. "If I had left him to make his own decisions then he'd never have gone for it. You know what he's like."

"Hey, what does that mean? I'd have done it. Eventually," Tim responded.

"Exactly," his mum replied. "Your eventually would have been too late."

"Ask if they have any shifts for me, would you?" said Leo.

Tim turned his attentions back to his friends. "Yeah, will do. Lydia, wanna join as well?"

"Nah, you're alright ta."

Callum moved away from the table and took his first finished pumpkin into the hallway. He had annoyingly done quite a good job and took a photo to upload to Instagram, before coming back to the room. He had taken this as an opportunity to come and stand with the others rather than sit at the table.

"Do you think Funtangutan has reopened yet?" he asked.

"Probably," said Leo. "Did the police leave when you did, Tim?"

"Yeah, just before us."

Callum nodded. "I imagine they opened just after that, then. If they lost more money, they'd probably close."

"When did they lose money before?" asked Lydia.

"I was speaking to someone in the café when we were all waiting there. They had some issues last week with faulty equipment so had been closed for a couple of weeks. My stepdad dragged me there last night as he had to drop off some elastic cords or something. We were the first ones to go back on the course," Callum said.

"I'm glad we found this out now and not before we went," said Tim. "I'd have never gone on those zip wires if I knew we were the guinea pigs for it."

"Pretty sure they would've tested them, mate," added Leo.

"Yeah, but even so. I ain't going back there for a while anyway, for obvious reasons."

"Me neither," said Leo.

"Have the police spoken to you yet, Callum?" asked Lydia.

"Yeah. They came round mine this afternoon. Mum was angry because I had lied about where I had been."

"What did they ask you?" questioned Tim.

"Asked what I knew about each of the graffiti faces. Asked where I was, who I was with, that kinda thing."

"Did they ask about the initials?" asked Leo.

"Um, yeah, course they did," he replied.

"What did you say?"

Before he could answer, Tim's mum moved across towards them to empty some pumpkin innards into a bowl. "You four know you should not be discussing this here," she said firmly. "The less you all speak, the less that can come back to you. Do you all understand?" The children nodded. "Now, get on with these pumpkins and once you're done, I'll get you some food and you can all stay and watch some telly in the front room."

Lydia had now finished her first pumpkin and went to collect another. "Only six left to do," she said, as she carried two back with her.

"Thank god for that," said Callum. "Are you working all day tomorrow, Tim?"

Tim could tell he was overcompensating now. He'd rather Callum just kept quiet. He tried not to let these feelings show. "Nah, just ten 'til two. I get to cover lunchbreaks."

"Cool. Much planned afterwards?" he asked.

"Nothing."

"I'm not about," said Lydia. "I have to go with Dad to look at a new car.."

"I can't do anything either, not until diving anyway," added Leo.

"We can all meet up Friday or something if you want?" said Tim, not wanting to have to hang around with Callum alone. "We can do crazy golf?"

"Yeah, sounds like a plan," said Leo. The others confirmed they were both in.

"Also, if Johann is back by the afternoon we can get him to come along, too," said Tim excitedly. "I'll let him know."

"We can't do pairs if we have an odd number though," said Callum.

"Well, you can stay at home then," replied Tim, before Leo gave him an elbow to his ribs. "Sorry," he added.

The hallway of 247 Oak Tree Crescent was now full of carved pumpkins. Their quality varied, but Tim was pleased the work had been completed quickly.

"Did you four want food?" his mum asked. Only Lydia declined, saying she had to get home. Callum made his way through to the front room and started to scan through Netflix to find something to watch. As long as he didn't pick a horror it would be okay.

"He's being alright, see," said Leo as he topped up three glasses with lemonade.

Tim grabbed a new pack of Wagon Wheels out the cupboard. "You know what they say. Keeps your friends close. Keep Callum closer."

# Thirteen

## *Wednesday*

Tim had got home from his Wednesday morning paper round just after eight. When he had arrived, and after turning down a coffee, Mr Patterson had explained plans were in progress to reopen during the afternoon. As Mr Patterson had spoken, it was clear he was still slightly shaken by the events on Monday. His voice trembled occasionally, and he was more forgetful than Tim had ever noticed previously.

"Mr Patterson, I'm not sure if I should say anything to you, but they found more criminal damage yesterday," Tim had said.

"Was this the one at Funtangutan? If so, yes, I was given an update by the police last night, thank you," he had replied.

On any other day during the holidays, Tim would have a lazy morning once home and showered, before heading out to the park by the lake on the edge of town with Leo and Lydia. Today was different though as he started to mentally prepare himself for his first shift at the library. The thought of a 'proper' job, as his dad called it, was a stepping stone that he wasn't expecting to come so soon. As for Greenwood Library itself, Tim had not been there for a number of years.

There was a time where he would be taken by his mum each Saturday morning to choose a book for the week. This was back in the late days of primary school however, where they would be set reading challenges each term to help improve their literacy. Even earlier than this, he had attended the Library Little Learners sessions, where young children would be read chapters from a book twice a week and then do potato printing during the school holidays to help parents with childcare.

He had since found out Leo had attended these sessions at the same time, and they both remembered a book about a man going around his big house setting clocks to the correct time. It was strange finding out things they had in common from before they had met. Since moving up to Greenwood Secondary, visits to the library had ceased, as any books he now needed were available at school, or could be borrowed from Pat and Pet. The amount of fiction Tim was reading these days was much lower than those old times. Even during half-terms and holidays he had fallen out of the habit of taking time to sit and read (unless it was a magazine). All the books he read these days were for homework.

At home, Tim threw his paper bag under the stairs, wondering if it would be the last time he would wear it. The speed at which life was changing meant nothing was certain. He negotiated the pumpkins and made breakfast. He was halfway up the stairs when his mum caught him as she came out of the bathroom at speed, wearing another new kaftan and almost knocking the bowl out of his hands.

"No eating breakfast in your room," she said to him before he could move too far, as she stuffed a large ball of toilet roll into her pocket.

"I was just going to watch some TV before work," he protested.

She waved her hands in his direction, forcing him to retreat. "Nope, go and sit down in the kitchen."

Tim trudged downstairs and back to the table. "Aren't you meant to be at work today, anyway?"

"I am, but I don't start until midday today now. I'm covering Holly as she couldn't get childcare. I'm only in until four as well. After, I am going to go round to Mr Patterson's to give him a hand with some paperwork. I'll be back by six so I will take you and Leo to diving if you like. When you have finished your shift, come and see me to let me know how you got on, won't you?"

"Thanks, I'll message Leo. And, yeah, will do. Where are you both going anyway?" he asked as she pulled on some trainers.

"Me and your dad need to pop up town quickly. I'll see you later. Don't forget to wash your bowl." She kissed him on the head, wished him good luck, and power-walked out of the house.

***

Tim changed into one of his white school shirts and pulled on his smartest trousers before heading to the library on his bike. He was oddly nervous as he approached. He locked his bike up in the racks on the edge of the lawn and walked to the front doors. His phone vibrated and Leo's name was on the screen. He hit cancel and put it back in his pocket.

The library was a single-story building with bad symmetry. It had large double doors at its centre with a tall, red-framed glass roof over the entrance hall. The doctor's surgery his mum worked at was sat directly opposite on the other side of the road, and the old orthodontist Marty had once gone to when having his braces fitted was next door. This was an odd road, and the police and fire stations were just further up. There used to be a football ground and large carpark too, but that was now gone, replaced with a small shopping arcade and flats.

He was a few minutes early, and as he pushed the front doors, they wouldn't budge. He pressed his hands and face to the glass and had a look inside. The whole building seemed deserted. All he could see were noticeboards filled with bright and colourful posters advertising all kinds of clubs and new release books.

"Hello?" he called through the letterbox, yet still no movement from inside. He stalked around the perimeter of the building, passing through a small but well-maintained garden before looking through the rear windows. There was a light on, but his tapping went unanswered. As he used his sleeve to wipe off the grease mark he had left, he suddenly saw the briefest glimpse of movement. He moved down to the next window, and on the other side he could see a pair of plimsole-covered feet stood at the top of a stepladder. He banged on the glass, with more force than before.

Inside, he heard a scream, before a pile of books clattered to the carpet. The feet moved down the ladder and revealed the top half of a woman with a sensible chocolate brown cardigan, and glasses that had a golden chain linked to each arm. After looking nervously from left to right, she eventually spotted Tim's waving head-height silhouette at the window. She smiled and motioned him to go towards the front doors again.

"You must be Timothy," she said in a cheerful primary-school-teacher voice as she relocked the door behind him.

"Yes, hello."

"Are you a Timothy? Or a Tim or a Timmy?"

"Um, Tim is fine please, thank you."

"Tim it is. Follow me."

Tim walked behind her through the main library, the

only noise being the gentle hum of an air conditioning unit that was plugged into the wall by the welcome desk. The library appeared much more modern than it had been when he had last visited. The old wooden chairs had been replaced by neon plastic ones, and there were beanbags and benches scattered in every free space.

"Here we are," the woman said as they entered a back room which held the smell of instant coffee. This, coupled with the low sitting foam chairs, reminded him of the school staff room.

"Would you like a drink?" she asked.

"A tea please," he responded. "Are you Jill?"

"Oh, sorry, I completely forgot to introduce myself. I'm Charlotte, I'm sort-of the manager. Jill will be here in a minute. She usually arrives one minute before we open."

"Nice to meet you. Sorry to make you drop your books a minute ago," Tim apologised.

Charlotte chuckled. "That's okay. I always think it's the ghost when I hear a noise and I'm on my own."

Tim frowned. "The ghost?"

She smiled. "There is a rumour the library is haunted by a Victorian girl. She sits in the rocking chair in the Children's section sometimes."

"Have you seen her?" Tim asked, slightly pessimistically.

"Well, no, but others have, apparently. I'd just ignore those people, though. Ask Mrs Whataday about it when you see her."

"Who's that?" he questioned.

"She is our regular. She will come in at ten fifteen this morning."

"How do you know?"

"She comes in a ten fifteen every day. I would say it is because she is lonely if I didn't know she still had her husband. I think it's more likely she comes in just to get away from him."

"And she has seen this ghost?"

"Claims to. Ask her."

"I will. I wouldn't have thought this building is old enough to be haunted?"

"It isn't. It was built in the early seventies. Anyway, take a seat."

Tim sank into one of the chairs, and picked at some loose foam bursting out of the side of its green covering. Charlotte came across and passed him his coffee. "Thank you."

"No problem. Feel free to use this room whenever you need to. If it's quiet, you can drop in and get a drink or a biscuit or whatever. They're stored in the tin over there," she said, pointing to a deep metal Quality Street tin which was much larger than the plastic ones you could get nowadays. "There is a new box of Family Circle in there so get the chocolate ones before they go. Just make sure you don't put ginger nuts in the tin. Jill hates ginger nuts and can tell if the other biscuits have been contaminated." Charlotte tapped a spoon on the side of her mug, and then came to take a seat opposite him. "Now, Tim, how familiar are you with Dewey Decimal?"

"Um, I've not heard of him. What books has he written?"

"No, it's not an author. Dewey Decimal is the numerical system that determines how the books are arranged. I'm surprised they don't teach that at school these days."

"Oh, sorry."

"It isn't your fault. Anyway, each book out there has its own code, so you know what section to find things in when people ask you for books on a certain subject. Every library uses this system so it's easy for you to find something for someone quickly. I can give you an example. Name something you are interested in."

Tim thought for a couple of seconds before stating dinosaurs. Charlotte closed her eyes for a moment before saying five hundred and sixty.

"Is five hundred and sixty all the dinosaur books?"

"Factual ones are around there, yes. Five hundred is the sciences. After that, each number above is a division of science. I know five hundred and sixty is palaeontology so that would be the best section to take someone to."

Tim was impressed. "That's quite cool. Do you know all the numbers?"

"Most, however, I have been doing this for twenty years, for my sins. Your example was easy though as we are always asked about dinosaurs. Don't worry too much, though, there is a cheat sheet by the till, and the computer lists the number for every book we have. I'll ask Jill to test you later."

During their coffee, it was agreed Tim would be working for a two-week trial period, taking him up to the end of the summer holidays. Then, if he was doing well, he would be able to work on Saturdays and an evening or two after school. Despite being there for less than quarter of an hour, and without having met a member of the public, Tim was quite glad to be at the library. It would be a suitable replacement for his paper round for sure.

Just before opening time, Jill arrived. She was flustered from striding across from the car park a few hundred metres away. She was wearing a fluffy yellow jacket, a furry hat that was coloured like a fried egg, and a black skirt over bright rainbow leggings, which must have been warm in the current weather. She put her bag behind the welcome desk and went into the back room, quickly grabbing a cup of coffee and a Party Ring. Tim had been allowed to wander around so he could get used to where each section was.

In the children's section, he sent a picture of himself to Johann. He had placed himself to make it look like he was being eaten by a large cardboard cut-out of the Very Hungry Caterpillar. Johann didn't reply but did give the message a thumbs up emoji. For some reason Tim was expecting a rush of people to flood through the doors as soon as the library had opened, but instead only one person came in during the first ten minutes, and that was only to ask for directions to Poundland.

He took a seat on a stool behind the desk and watched as Jill went through the procedures for how to scan a book that was being checked out, and then how to check it back in again. It all seemed simple.

"Hopefully everything makes sense, but if you get stuck give me a shout," Jill said to him.

"Will do, thank you. How long have you worked here?"

"About five years or so now. I started when my youngest went to nursery," she replied, as she readjusted her brown hair back into its ponytail, holding an elastic hairband between her teeth. "I like working here as I still get my free time in the evenings and at weekends."

"What do you like to do when not here?" he asked.

"This and that," she said unhelpfully. "How about you?"

"Hang out with friends, um, go out on my bike, the usual things."

"As long as it keeps you out of trouble, that's all good. Are you coming to the fete at the weekend?"

"I am," said Tim. "Are you?"

"Of course, I'm dancing with your mum."

"You're in the Dolly Mixtures as well?"

"Sure am. Are you looking forward to watching us?"

Tim shook his head. "Um, I wouldn't say that exactly, no. Mum always embarrasses me. What are you dressing as?"

"I'll be a vampire. I think your mum is a witch, isn't she?"

"Yep," Tim confirmed. "She has a stupid hat for it and everything."

He turned to the window and noticed it had started to drizzle slightly. One good thing about this job was that if it was raining, he wouldn't get soaking wet whilst doing what he was meant to. The paper round had served its purpose and, despite thinking differently two days ago, moving on was probably for the best. He could start earning real money now.

The library computer system was outdated compared to his computer at home, and the internet took a while to load up. He was just starting to read a story on the Greenwood Gazette website about a car that had crashed into someone's garden wall when the front door of the library flung open, knocking some leaflets off the noticeboard as the handle cracked into the wall. A lady, around sixty years of age, came in. She was wearing a long, padded, lilac coat and a see-through rain hood. She looked like a cling-filmed aubergine.

He watched as she shuffled her way across to him at the counter, dragging a tartan shopping trolley behind her. She put one hand on her hip and slapped the other on the counter in front of Tim, making him lean back as far as he could. She shook herself to get the water off, a bit like a dog would.

"WHAT A DAY!" she shouted.

"Good morning," replied Tim, unsure how else to respond.

"What a day, I say," she repeated.

This time Tim didn't respond. She looked up slowly,

before a confused look crossed her face.

"Who are you? I don't know you."

"I'm Tim."

"You look young," she said.

"Um, yeah, I'm fifteen."

"What are you doing here?"

Tim wasn't sure about her already. "I work here."

"Since when?"

"Today is my first day. How can I help?"

"I need a book," she said, which Tim found to be not too helpful considering where they were.

"On what subject?" he asked, trying to narrow it down.

"That programme last night. With the old man. Did you see it?"

"I didn't, sorry. I was carving pumpkins all night."

"In August? Are you mad?"

"Yes," he agreed, just to save any hassle. "What was the programme on?"

"An old man."

"Right, okay, and what was he doing?"

"Talking," she said.

He hoped other customers would be more concise. "And what was he talking about?"

"Dead animals. Old ones."

"Old dead animals? Are you sure?"

"Of course I am sure. You must know him. He's always on. Very famous. His name escapes me. Wears the blue shirt and beige trousers. Talks slowly about animals?"

"Do you mean David Attenborough?" Tim asked, finally solving the puzzle.

"Yes, him. He was talking about the dead animals in the rocks down by Lyme Regis."

Tim wasn't sure how someone could watch an hour

documentary on fossils, narrated by David Attenborough, less than day ago, and then not remember who he was or what he was actually talking about. Luckily, he knew where the dinosaur books were after testing Charlotte on arrival so assumed the fossil books would be in the same place.

"Follow me," he said. "Is this Mrs Whataday?" he whispered to Jill, who nodded. He started leading her across the library, passing the children's section on the way. "Oh, I've heard you have seen the ghost here?" he stated.

"Poor old Mary. Bless her soul. I can't sense her here today, though."

"Maybe she's busy," Tim replied.

"Perhaps. She may be looking after her sick brother. The poor children."

Despite not being a believer in the paranormal, Tim felt a little freaked out and he made a mental note to keep his distance from the rocking chair. As they reached the science section, Tim scanned the shelf for the relevant topic and pointed it to Mrs Whataday. She thanked him, and he set off back to the desk at the first opportunity.

"Did you ask her about the ghost?" Jill asked.

"I wish I hadn't," he replied.

"Wait 'til you get her started on the healing power of crystals, and how the paranormal dictates your future."

Tim would not raise this. Ever. The next forty-five minutes were even less eventful. A group of children came in just before eleven and Tim was happy to see the Little Learners programme was still running. Even better was his first ever teacher, Miss Bailey, was running the group today. Even though he had left her class around eight years prior, Miss Bailey still recognised Tim immediately, and even remembered his name. Miss Bailey told Tim the children were currently being read a story about a goldfish that grew to be a giant because of something in the sewer system.

Once the session started, Tim listened in. It took him back to when he was that age, a time where life was much simpler. Joining the book midway through made the story impossible to follow, though.

As the clock above the reception chimed for midday, Charlotte came back across. "You can grab your ten-minute break now if you'd like to?" she said.

Tim jumped off the chair, put the kettle on and took two chocolate digestives from the tin. He ate these as he walked out into the back garden to call Johann. He was on another walk.

"I'm so bored up here," he said to Tim. "I need to come home."

"It's only two more days. It'll fly by."

Johann took a moment. "Hopefully it will be Friday. No one has said anything yet. I want to come home and hang out with you again. We can do some more investigating together then as well."

Tim definitely needed Johann back. The library could only do so much to keep his mind from the police enquiries. He started on a second lap of the garden and started talking about the *Haberdashery Menagerie* CD.

"How bad actually is it?" Johann asked.

"It's not the worst. But I wouldn't say it's good, either."

"Sing me one of the songs."

"Absolutely not," Tim replied. "I can't sing, you know that."

"Go on!"

"No," he said firmly. "Anyway, you've agreed to come to their next gig now and I'm not letting you get out of that!"

"Maybe I'll stay up North forever," he joked. "Oh,

did you get more bedding from my house for Barnaby by the way?" Johann asked, changing the subject. Tim didn't reply. "Tim, you still there?"

Tim stood frozen in the centre of the garden, a sick feeling brewing in his stomach. "Johann, it's happened again."

"What has?"

"I'll call you back," he said, slowly dropping his phone onto the grass. Tim stared across the garden at the back of the library. In the centre of the brickwork was another face. Again, it was in yellow spray paint. Again, underneath, were the initials *T.J.*

# Fourteen

Back at the library welcome desk, Tim couldn't concentrate. He no longer wanted to be at work. He knew the police would soon hear of the latest criminal damage, and he was fully expecting to be made into Suspect Number One. Jill even had to show him twice more how to scan a book, despite it being the easiest task ever. She realised something was not right so sent him to get a drink and have five minutes to compose himself.

As he was sat in the staff area, he sent a picture of the graffiti and a text to Leo, Lydia, and Callum in the group chat.

"Meet me at Freddie's Diner at 1pm."

It was time to involve everyone to help solve the problem. He sat back at the desk, watching the clock as it slowly ticked over, minute by agonising minute. Maybe this job wasn't what he needed right now, the change not bringing anything positive to his life as he had hoped.

Charlotte came across and put a fresh cup of coffee in front of him, with two Jammie Dodgers. He did not have the appetite.

"Sorry, Charlotte, would it be possible if I left early, please?" he asked as she moved away.

She stopped and rubbed his shoulder. "Oh, are you not enjoying it?" she asked, slightly surprised.

"I am, sorry, it's just I have a bad toothache and can't

concentrate," he lied.

She pulled out a chair and sat next to him. "You go and grab your bag and get some rest. I can text your mum to book you into the dentist, if you'd like me to?"

"No," he said, firmly. "Sorry, I mean, I can pop by on my way home. My dentist is only up on Church Green."

Tim knew his mum would see through his lies straight away. He picked up his bag from the back room and headed straight to the diner. Feeling like he should eat, he ordered some chips, but only managed to eat two in the ten minutes it took for Callum to arrive.

Callum threw his backpack under the table and sat opposite. "Hi," he said. "Are you okay?"

"Not really," he replied, stirring a straw around his half-drunk glass of flat cola.

"The police will probably speak to us again," said Callum.

"I know. That's what scares me. It was me that found it so they probably will only speak to me again. We just need a plan to help me sort this. Me and Leo have met before but we didn't want to tell anyone we were trying to work out what was happening."

"So why have you told us now?" Callum asked as he looked down the laminated menu.

"I dunno. I'm panicking a bit, I guess, and you lot might be able to help."

"If the police ask me then I wouldn't be able to tell them anything, anyway," said Callum.

"Where were you today?"

"Why? Are you accusing me?"

Tim shook his head. "No, just asking."

"I was out with Bryan. He wanted me to go with him when picking up some old car. My mum thinks all this is strange."

"Have you told her?" asked Tim.

"Yeah, I showed her the picture you sent."

Tim growled. "You shouldn't have shown her, Callum. She will tell Leo's mum and she will have probably already let my mum know…"

"You didn't say not to tell anyone."

"And I didn't say you should've, either." Tim sat back, crossing his arms tightly. "Do you actually have any brain cells at all? You have gotta stop doing this."

"Doing what?"

"Everything. You're always talking too much, and it keeps ending up with me being in trouble."

"It's not my initials on it, is it?"

Tim didn't answer this, the anger in him was too much. He got up and went to the toilets, taking five minutes sat in the cubicle to update Johann. Sitting surrounded by the smell of bleach was much more preferable than having to talk to Callum any longer.

When he came back out, Leo was sat with Callum and Lydia was ordering some ice cream from the counter. He helped her carry her drinks across and took his seat. As soon as he had sat, his theory was confirmed.

"Mum knows now," said Leo. Tim stared at Callum, who just shrugged his shoulders.

"Can you tell her not to tell my mum, please?" he asked.

"It may be too late. Did you tell the people at the library?"

"I was too scared."

"Lame," said Callum.

Leo turned to him quickly. "Not now, Callum."

"Lydia, Leo, where were you this morning?" asked Tim.

"Why?" Leo asked.

"We all just need to know where everyone else was.

Like, I was at the library, and Callum was with Bryan."

"I was at home," Leo said. "My sister has just got a new swingball set so I was playing in the garden with her."

"And I was just at home with Mum," added Lydia. "Did you see anything odd when you were at the library?"

Tim pushed out his bottom lip. "Nope. I just saw the face when I went for my lunch break. You can't see the back of the library from the desk I was at, and no one weird came in apart from this random woman who thinks she can see ghosts, but it wouldn't have been her."

"So, we ain't no further than when we started," said Leo. "This is pointless," he added, standing up.

"Leo, don't go. There will be something, we just need to figure out what it is," replied Tim.

"Well, I'm out of ideas already," said Callum. "You got anything Lydia?"

Lydia shook her head, Tim wished he had his notebook so he could try and see if he could work out any link at all. The only common factor so far was Tim.

The server brought across Lydia's chips. "Look, let's talk about something else," she said as she scooped three into her mouth. "I hear Marty has a gig, Tim."

Tim sensed she knew how mixed up he was feeling. "It's at The Bell tomorrow afternoon if you wanna come." He knew it would be a long afternoon watching a bunch of amateur bands so needed his friends there. Leo started explaining to the others how bad the music was.

"I used to go to gigs a lot in London," Callum said.

"Who did you see?" asked Leo.

"I've seen loads," he replied, but not naming anyone specifically.

"Just to warn you, The Bell is hardly the O2," added Lydia. "It should be fun, though."

Tim listened as Callum explained how to put on the perfect gig, ignoring any attempts to get him to join the conversation. "I wanna go," he said, picking up his backpack.

As Lydia and Callum went to the toilets, Leo turned to Tim. "Is your mum okay?" he asked.

"I think so yeah, why?"

"She was round ours this morning. Your dad was there also."

"What were they saying?" Tim asked, confused about why they had told him they were going to town.

"I don't know, I was told to leave the room."

"Do you think it was about all this?" Tim asked.

"Maybe."

"I hope not."

"I don't know what else it would be. Like, Mum knows, your mum will know before long 'cos Greenwood is too small for the gossip not to spread, and then the police will get involved and you'll have to answer all those questions again."

"Don't say that," whined Tim.

"It's true, though. It had your initials again and was in the building where you were working. They're gonna think it's you."

Tim kept quiet. He knew Leo was right. Lydia came back to the table with a wooden spoon with the number six on it. "I've ordered some nachos," she said, sitting back down.

"I thought we were all leaving," replied Tim.

"I know but we aren't letting you go yet. Just please eat something."

He felt as if he was being held captive by the other three now. The nachos arrived and he had realised he had been zoned out for around five minutes, not taking in anything the others had said. He poked around at some food but wasn't in the mood for guacamole. It reminded him of the horrible mushy peas the school used to serve, all lumpy and bitter.

It was as if there was a large weight on him and that he was starting to suffocate. He waited until the others were fully engrossed in another farfetched Callum story and slipped out of the diner unnoticed.

***

As he arrived home he was glad to see everyone else was out. The car wasn't parked up, and Marty's room was dark when he poked his head through the door.

"Marty?" he said, making sure the lumps under the blanket were just his pillows. There was no answer. Worried his dad might return soon, he quickly changed into comfortable clothes and headed back out on his bike towards Johann's house. Being at his home was the next best thing to being able to speak to him. He cycled across with a bag for life on his handlebars. Collecting new hay for Barnaby was a perfect excuse to use in case he bumped into anyone he knew on the way.

The lock on Johann's gate was rusty and stiff. He put his weight on his heels as he leant back to try and get it to shift. After a few moments, a large groan came from the metalwork and the gate swung open. Tim tumbled onto his back, the lock mechanism still in his hand. He got to his feet, brushed himself down, and hid the evidence in a large plant pot by the front door.

As Tim entered the side path, he noticed stacks of plastic-wrapped hay in a low shelter backing onto the side wall of the house. He crept along the path and sat cross-legged in front of it. As he began to gather hay into his bag, a voice came from the other side of the fence.

"Do not move!"

Tim ignored this and turned around to spot an elderly man with round glass staring over the fence. "Hello. I'm just getting some straw for Barnaby?"

The man creased his face. "Oh. The odd blonde boy?"

"Um, no," said Tim. "Barnaby is a tortoise. You're thinking of Johann, but he isn't odd."

"Do you have any identification on you?"

Tim shook his head.

"How do I know you are not a thief?"

Tim stood up. "I'm just collecting hay as I am pet sitting Barnaby whilst the family are in Newcastle."

"Newcastle you say. The woman told me they were going to Sweden."

"Well, Johann's mum is in Sweden. Johann and his sister are in Newcastle. Look!" Tim pulled out his phone, gulping when he saw four missed calls from home. He opened the photo app and found the picture of the Tyne Bridge Johann had sent earlier in the week. "See. That's Newcastle, and there's Johann and Hanna," he said, pointing at the screen.

The man took the phone and put it an inch away from his face. He studied it as if it was some ancient artefact. "Hmmm. I will give you the benefit of the doubt."

Tim put his hand out to take his phone back, but the old man suddenly jumped and sent it spinning in the air, landing with a clunk in the rockery. Tim hoped it wasn't broken, but when he picked it up it was even worse. Somehow the neighbour had hit accept on another phone call from home. He put his ear closer and could hear his mum calling out his name. He panicked and quickly ended the call without responding. He tied up the hay bag and turned around. "I've got to go. Nice to meet you."

"Cheery-bye," the man said as his head sank behind the fence.

Tim's heart was beating like a drum solo, which was quite apt considering he now had to go and face the music. He pulled the gate shut, wedging a garden gnome underneath it to stop it from opening.

In his head, he planned out what he could say. *'Mum, I was ill so came home.'* He decided she would see through that straight away. He would need to tell her the truth. He saw the face. He freaked out. Maybe he would leave out the part about meeting the other three in Freddie's Diner.

Thoughts swimming around his head, he hit the button on the pedestrian crossing. As it turned green, he scooted into the road. He was snapped back to reality when the bag of hay was grabbed. He turned to his right and almost fell off his bike. Two large white horses towered over him. One of them tearing the bag from his handlebars and spreading hay across the road. If he thought the situation couldn't be worse, he was wrong. As he kneeled on the floor trying to recover Barnaby's supper, he caught glimpse of the waiting traffic. The horses were attached to a carriage. In the back, a coffin could be seen through long glass windows. He slowly got to his feet. Three black limousines queued behind.

"S-s-s-sorry," he mumbled to the well dressed, grey-haired gentleman in the carriage, who held a long whip high as if he was about to strike. A younger man next to him gestured at Tim to get out of the way. He was only too keen to oblige. He picked up his bike and dragged it to the side of the road. Stony faces stared at him from the dark windows of the cars in the funeral procession as they moved on at a slow pace. It felt like an hour had passed before they finally disappeared from his view.

Now with only a quarter of the hay left, all being held

together by what remained of the plastic bag, he jumped into the saddle and made his way back to Oak Tree Crescent.

Before going into the house, he took a seat on the same fence he had met Johann on Monday. The dozen missed calls proved word had got out about the new graffiti. There was no way anyone would believe it wasn't him.

His breath became short, and his eyes prickled with tears. He wanted to go home, and not go home at the same time. He couldn't face seeing his family and the fallout that would come, but he needed the sanctuary of his bedroom. He needed to just hide away and not get up until everything was right in Greenwood again.

"Oi," came a voice from the shadows. Tim straightened up. "You good?" it continued.

Tim wiped his face and turned towards the end of the alley. Marty was looking awkward, hands buried deep inside of his skinny jean pockets.

"Go away," Tim demanded.

"No. Are you good?"

"No," replied Tim, tightening his arms across his stomach.

Marty approached slowly and sat next to him, taking a hand into his. "Wanna talk?"

"No."

"Well, that's tough, cos I am gonna sit with you until you do."

Tim remained quiet. The silence hung in the air, heavy as it could be. After what felt like five minutes, Marty spoke again. "Mum will want to know where you have been. You're like two hours late home and you didn't see her at work when you finished your shift."

"I don't want to speak tonight. I just want to go to diving and then go to bed."

"Good luck with that."

"Does she know about the graffiti?" he asked.

Marty nodded. "Look, Tim, I'm worried about you."

"I'm fine, honestly."

"You've been gone all day, and now you're sat crying in an alleyway, so that's not true, what's wrong?"

"I am going to get blamed for everything," he said.

Marty put an arm around him. "Was it you?"

Tim wiped his nose. "No. Was it you?"

"Why would it be me?"

"No one has seen you for three days, Marty. What's *your* alibi?"

Marty let go of his brother. "Tim, mate, c'mon, I am on your side, okay. Don't throw that away."

Tim stood and walked past Marty and out the alley, dragging his Converse along the floor as he wheeled his bike towards home. Marty jogged to catch him up and grabbed his shoulder. Tim shook him off and started pedalling. As he reached the house, he threw his bike on to the lawn and entered the already opened front door, before heading upstairs. As he moved his mum came out of the kitchen. She was covered in flour again.

"Where the hell have you been?" she shouted as he started taking two stairs at a time.

"With Leo," he responded before continuing.

His mum followed close behind, but not near enough to stop him slamming his bedroom door shut.

"Leave him, Mum. He will be alright," he heard Marty say on the other side of the door.

"Absolutely not. This is not acceptable," she replied.

Tim sat hugging his knees, back against the bedroom door, tears flowing down his cheeks.

"Open it up. NOW!" shouted his mum.

He stayed silent.

"Look, I'll have a chat with him," Marty said.

"Timothy, open this door now or I will force it open," she said, ignoring his brother.

"Go away!" Tim shouted.

"Mum, please, just leave him for a minute," begged Marty.

"Keep out of this. He has a lot of explaining to do."

"Mum, please!" continued Marty.

"Go to your room and leave this to me," she demanded as she started pushing the door with force against Tim's back.

He used all his strength to try and keep it shut but it was a losing battle. He jumped up and ran to his bed, burying himself deep under the covers. He heard the door fly open and crash into his wardrobe. She pounded across the floor and tried to rip the covers from him.

"Leave me alone!" he screamed. "Just… just leave me alone."

"Not until you tell me what's going on."

"Nothing. I'm fine, please, just go."

The sheets stung Tim's hands as they were torn away from him. He was crying harder than he had all day. He tried hiding his head in his t-shirt, but he knew it was no good.

"What's going on?" she asked again.

Tim let out a loud moan and began punching his pillows.

"You were meant to be home much earlier, and it's gone six now. What is going on?"

"I was out with Leo," he mumbled into his arms.

"I know that's not true. Flo was around here earlier, and she was telling me how he was with Lydia at the cinema. She also told me about your latest stunt at the library."

"I was at the cinema with them," he said, confused as to why Lydia and Leo had also lied about their whereabouts.

"No, you weren't. Please stop lying and just tell me where you were."

"I just need some space," Tim said.

"You need something, that's for sure. And Tim, when I asked you to tell me how your first shift went, you ignored that. Don't worry, though, I've heard all about if from Jill. Said you got bored after a couple of hours and walked out. Then, I came home to find you not here. Also, I went to pack your diving gear in your bag, and do you know what I found?"

She left the room briefly before coming back in, slamming a can of Bristow's yellow spray paint onto his bedside table next to Marty. "All along you've denied this was you, and I don't know what's got into you, but this isn't acceptable. Things do not work like that in this family. First, you destroy Mr Patterson's shop, and then Funtangutan and now, after I've got you a new job, you deface the library as well."

Tim sat up, genuinely confused. "I've never seen that before," he said, pointing at the spray can.

"Oh, of course not. It just fell into your bag after being sprayed around town. You could have at least not added your initials to it each time."

"Honestly, Mum, it isn't me," he begged.

"Stop lying. The police will be coming over again later to ask you some questions and you better have answers for them. You can go to diving tonight, but after that you will be staying with me or your dad until we have got you back on the right track."

"Marty, tell Mum it wasn't me."

Marty tried to jump to his defence but was told to keep quiet again. "All the work I put in to help you have something instead of your paper round, Tim, and you throw that back in my face. What has got into you?"

"Mum, please!" said Marty again. "Don't shout at him."

"Marty, go away. Now!" she replied.

Tim shuffled in the bed until he was curled in a ball facing the wall. He could barely breathe and felt like the walls of the room were collapsing onto him. His ribcage was moving in and out rapidly. Marty approached the bed and sat on the pillow. He put his arms around his younger brother.

"Do you know something I don't?" their mum asked.

"No," Marty replied softly. "I just want to make sure he is okay."

"One of you knows something so you better tell me. You do not treat me like this in my house. The police will get it out of you if I can't."

"Johann," said Tim.

"What?" she replied.

"Mum, it's okay, honestly," Marty said reassuringly.

"What has Johann done?"

"Nothing," the elder brother said.

"Well, he must have done something to make him like this," she said as she made another attempt to pull Tim up.

"Honestly, Mum, leave him alone a minute, this isn't helping."

"I should have trusted my instincts from the start with that family," she spat. "I didn't like his mother when I first met her. I can't believe I forgave her. I can't believe I was made to think the whole family were fine. They are nothing but trouble."

"No, they're not," argued Tim, through sobs.

"From the day you met him you have been nothing but trouble. He must be the reason you have changed into this. You've become rude, you go missing, you skip work, you've started to destroy our town, everything."

"It's not like that, Mum," said Marty.

"Oh, and you're an expert now, are you?" she continued.

"No, but listen, Johann is—"

"I know exactly what he is. He is a troublemaker. He is leading Tim astray. I don't want you ever seeing him again, okay?"

Tim sat up. "No, Mum, I have to."

"Absolutely not. This is the end. Me and your father will not let this continue."

"But Mum—" Tim said before being cut off.

"*But Mum* nothing," she snapped. "Why on Earth should I let you see him and that bloody family of his again?"

"Mum!" shouted Marty, but she wasn't listening.

"Give me one good reason why, Tim."

"Because I think I love him, okay!?" Tim screamed as loud as he could.

Marty let go of his brother and stared at his mum, who stood back slightly. She took a few steps back and then sat on his chair.

Tim looked at her through tears. "I love him, Mum. I'm sorry," he continued, quieter, but now sat upright. "Are you happy now?"

"What do you mean?" she replied quietly.

"Me and Johann. That's what I mean. I'm gay, Mum, and he is the best thing that has ever happened to me, and I love him, and I want to tell him I love him, but I can't because he isn't here."

His mum remained silent. Marty took her hand and held it.

"Are you happy now?" continued Tim. "Everything has changed, and I hate it. I love him and we've been on not-dates, but now I don't even know if he will ever come back home. He went away, and then I lost my job, and then the graffiti started. I don't know what to do."

She moved closer and leant her head on his shoulder. Marty took Tim's hand so they were all sat connected. "How long has this been going on?" she asked gently.

"A couple of months. Since that charity night at the snooker club a few weeks back," Tim replied.

"I am so sorry," his mum said, pulling him into a hug. "I should have known."

"No, you shouldn't," Tim replied. "I couldn't tell you."

"You could have, darling, of course you could have."

"How? I didn't even know myself at the time. I'm not sure if I do now. It's all happened so fast, and I can't seem to get thoughts out of my own head, let alone try and explain them."

"Did you know?" she asked Marty.

"Kind of," he replied. "I found out accidentally."

"Boys, listen," she said, pulling them both closer, tears on her cheeks. "I am so sorry. We can work this out together, now."

"It's not that easy," said Tim, his eyes red. "I wish I didn't have to tell you like this." Tim's breathing started becoming erratic again, struggling to find any rhythm at all. Marty let go of his mum's hand and pulled Tim close, stroking his back as his brothers' tears ran onto his shoulder.

"I love you both so much," she said eventually, wiping her face with her dirty apron, leaving white streaks of flour across her brow. "Everything about you both, I love. I wish I had known so I could have made this easier for you, Tim. The thought of you battling this alone terrifies me. I would kill for either of you. You being gay, Tim, does not change that one bit," she continued. "If I had the choice of a million boys to be mother to, I would pick you both every single time. You are my entire world, and I will do everything I can to protect you. I love you so, so much."

Tim held onto his mum's hand but said nothing.

"Does anyone else know?" she asked Tim.

"Leo, Lyds, and Callum. That's all. Well, Johann as well, of course. Oh, and Lydia's mum knows as well."

"You told her?" asked Marty.

"No, Callum did because he doesn't think before he speaks."

"Has everyone been okay about it?" asked his mum.

"Yeah, they've been great. It's me who isn't," he said.

"How so?" she asked, trying to understand.

"Just, I get so confused, and then I get angry because I'm confused, and I can't think. And all this graffiti has made it worse. I promise you it isn't me, Mum. That's kinda why I didn't stay at work today. I went to get some air, but when I got back to the desk it felt like I was suffocating. I tried my best, but I couldn't focus. I ran to try and escape my own mind, but it didn't work."

"Oh, darling, come here," she responded and pulled him in tight. "You have me now."

"And me, remember," added Marty. Their mum smiled and pulled him in, too.

"I'll speak to Jill and explain so you can try the library again, would you want that?"

Tim nodded into her shoulder.

"I love you," she said, as she sat holding him close and stroking his hair until his breathing relaxed.

"You're not mad at Johann, are you?" asked Marty.

"No. Sorry, I didn't mean what I said. Johann is family now, too, and if anyone even tries to ruin that, they will have to fight me first."

"And me," said Marty, letting out a small laugh. He then pulled Tim closer and hugged him tighter than he ever had done before.

"I think we need a family meeting," his mum said finally. She let go and headed downstairs. The boys could hear a muffled conversation from below.

"This graffiti, Tim," Marty said to fill the void. "Be completely honest with me. Is it you?"

Tim shook his head. "It's not. I don't know why it keeps appearing."

"Okay, I believe you. It's just, well there was more."

Tim sat up. "Where?"

"You remember when we were picking the fruit? After holiday?"

"Yeah."

"Well, it was there. I'll show you."

Marty took his phone out and went to the photos. "When you were sat under that tree," he started explaining as he scrolled, "I took a photo of you and asked about the face, but you just moaned and told me to stop taking your picture. Look."

Tim looked at the screen there was the picture of him sat under the tree looking miserable next to two baskets of fruit. A few feet above his head was another face, halfway up the trunk. There were no initials on this one.

"Why didn't you say this before?" he asked Marty.

"Cos, I didn't know about the graffiti until about an hour ago, did I?"

"Can you be here when the police come, please? You can say you were with me when you saw it."

"I'll show them, yeah, but I don't know if it will make it worse because you were on your own for a bit before then, so if anything, it may make it look more suspicious. I don't want them to think it was you any more than they already do. It's already complicated now Mum has found the paint in your bag."

Tim needed to show the police everything and told Marty he had to have the picture. Ignoring it would only make things worse in the long run.

"You okay?" asked Tim's dad as he came into the bedroom. Tim nodded back. He didn't question anything further.

"Tim," his mum said, "a policeman is going to come around this evening after your diving. I want you to be honest with him, okay?"

"I will," he responded.

"And you have to tell him everything you know," she added.

"But I don't know anything."

"It's best to just tell the truth to him. If there is anything you can think of, write it down and then let them know. This can be the end of it now. We will work everything else out once it's settled."

Tim sat up and nodded again. He half wanted to tell the police it had been him just to make the whole situation pass over quickly. Tim's dad pulled the desk chair into the middle of the room, his mum standing behind him with her hands on his shoulders.

"Whilst you're both here, there is something we need to say as well," his mum said. The two boys just sat side by side, not replying. "I know this has all been a lot to take in for us all in the last few minutes, but we may as well all start being honest with each other."

"What is it?" Marty asked.

Tim watched as she looked across to his dad, who nodded silently. She turned back to face her sons. "I'm pregnant."

# Fifteen

"Pregnant? Are you sure?" asked Leo as he and Tim walked from the car towards Greenwood Leisure Centre.

"Definitely pregnant," Tim reiterated to Leo. "Her and Dad sat down and told us about an hour ago. It's due in April. Everything makes sense now, I guess."

"Like what?"

"Well, the other day when we were doing the pumpkins, I found a letter from some doctor in her coat pocket."

"What did it say?"

"Well, I didn't open it obviously. Also, that's probably what they were talking to your mum about today as well. And why she has been changing her shifts around at work and wearing all those stupid kaftans."

"She wasn't drinking at Lydia's buffet, either," Leo added, which Tim hadn't even noticed. "Do you know if you'll have a brother or sister yet?"

"Not a clue. I don't mind to be honest. Like, having a brother is cool, so another will be fine. And a sister would make a change, I guess. Does your sister ever annoy you?"

"Occasionally, but if you do have a sister, they'll be much younger than you so it will be different to me and Kelis. Like, I hang around with her quite a bit when at home, looking after her and that kind of thing."

"Oh god, I am going to be roped into babysitting loads as well now, ain't I?" said Tim. "Will have to make sure Marty does some as well."

"Yeah, gotta do your fair share. It's not bad, though. And it can be quite fun."

"Mate, I'm stressed enough already just looking after a tortoise."

"Babies are easier," said Leo.

"Are they?"

"Well, no. But stop freaking out. Where are you going to put it anyway?"

"It? If you meant the baby, um, I'unno. Maybe Marty will move out and then I can have his room—"

"Cos it's bigger?"

"Because it's bigger. I'll have his room, and then the baby can have mine."

"Fair. When you said you had big news, I wasn't expecting this. I'd panic if my parents had another kid."

Tim didn't reply and walked towards the side doors of the centre. He could see Mrs Brute through the glass windows, clipboard in hand, whistle around her neck, ready to take the attendance. She stared at Tim as they walked past the double doors.

"Where are you going?" asked Leo.

Tim turned. "Follow me." The smell of chlorine was quite strong as they walked past the air vents around the back of the leisure centre. The heat spewing out was making an already warm evening even more uncomfortable. Tim took a seat on a waist-height wall, with Leo joining him. They both threw their swim bags onto the grass behind.

The situation mirrored the time they had sat on a small wall in the car park of their school during the end of year American Prom themed disco. It was at that time Leo and Tim had come out to each other. It seemed quite fitting for the situation.

"My mum being pregnant," Tim said.

"What about it?" said Leo, taking a drink of water.

"That's not the big news. The big news is Mum knows I'm gay."

"Seriously?" asked Leo. Tim nodded. "Who told her? Amy?"

"No, I did."

"Really?"

"Yeah."

"Oh. Well done, I guess. I didn't think you were gonna do that yet. And I told you to tell me before you did it."

"Yeah, sorry, it just sort of came out. We were having an argument, and I was getting angry at her, and she said some horrible things about Johann, so I ended up just blurting it out."

Leo shuffled closer to Tim and put his arm around him. "Was she alright?"

"I think so, yeah. It was all quite emotional and full on. That's when she said she was pregnant as well. As evenings go, it's been a bit mad. Johann was happier than I was when I called him before we came to get you. He was in a supermarket, and I think he freaked some people out as he screamed," laughed Tim.

"And are you okay?"

"I'm fine, I think. I don't know. It's a bit of a blur, but I am glad I am here tonight, and I am glad I am with you. The police will be coming round when I get in to talk about the library," Tim said.

"I wouldn't worry. Whilst we're here, can I talk to you about something?"

Tim shook his head. "We can chat later. I have too many problems in my head."

Leo dropped his arm, not given the chance to

respond before Tim continued.

"I mean I can't tell PC Hughes much more than I already have, except Mum found a can of paint in my rucksack. I looked through my notes again and, I dunno, something doesn't sit right with me.

"About?" asked Leo.

"I still think it's Callum," he replied.

"Tim, you've gotta stop this," Leo said, jumping onto the ground. "Just because he pissed you off this week doesn't mean you can accuse him of this, that ain't fair. You want it to be him just to make yourself feel better. I trust him."

"Do you trust him more than me, then?"

"That's not what I said, I'm just saying you're always making up this weird situation in your head again and it ain't doing you any favours."

"But what if it is him?"

"I can't be bothered with this again," said Leo, grabbing his swim bag and moving towards the leisure centre.

"Leo!" Tim called, but he just kept on going. Tim entered the building through a door that was reluctantly being held open for him. "Leo," he said again, but Leo just walked straight into the changing rooms.

"You're in the pool today," Mrs Brute said as Tim followed his friend to get undressed. He hung his bag on a hook and looked around, but Leo had gone to a cubicle to change, which was unlike him. He called out his name but got no answer. Not wanting to delay the start of the lesson, Tim got changed into his swim shorts and stood under the shower, trying to find the level on the temperature gauge between way too hot and way too cold, which were about a millimetre away from each other.

"Hey, Tim," said Jonny as he came into the shower

room. "You good?"

"Fine thanks. You?"

"Yeah, grand, grand."

Jonny was a year older than Tim, was taller and even had a hairy chest. Despite his stronger physic, they were both on the beginner's course along with six other people. The youngest was Stefan, who was only twelve. Because of their varying ages and abilities, they had all been at different stages in the gym work sessions the previous weeks. Tim was wondering if this would crossover to the pool as well. Once they had stood under the water for the required time, they headed poolside.

A loud whistle pierced through the air, and Mrs Brute appeared, like an army general. "No time to waste today," she said as she marched towards the group. "Take a seat on the edge of the pool."

Tim left a gap for Leo, but when he entered, he sat towards the far end.

Their first task was to do a pencil dive into the water, which Tim had done numerous times when swimming here. He was happy he could accomplish this but knew before long the height at which they would be entering the pool from would start increasing. He looked up to the diving boards towering high to his left, and even the one metre springboard looked frighteningly high. After two pencil dives, they were gathered into a group beside the main pool. Leo was about an arm's length away.

"Oi, Leo, what's up?" Tim asked.

"I'm fine," he replied, without looking.

"Oh, come on, you've gone weird."

"I'm fine, leave me alone."

"You're clearly not," Tim carried on, trying to force Leo to speak.

"Can you two boys be quiet and listen, please?" Mrs Brute said. Tim did as he was told.

Mrs Brute explained the lesson would involve doing a pencil dive off the one metre board (without springing), followed by a swim to the other end of the twenty-five-metre-long pool, before getting out, walking back, and repeating this. They were to do it ten times.

Each time they climbed the steps, Tim tried to go up with Leo, but was ignored, with each conversation starter rebutted by Leo asking some of his pointless questions to other people in the class instead. Tim thought he should be the one being asked. That's what they did together. He heard Stefan say he would do the beep-beep-bop teleportation thing so he could get home from school quicker, which Leo laughed at, but then agreed with. Jealously prickled Tim's wet skin.

As Tim stood on the end of the diving board, the pool looked a long way down. It was the Death Drop all over again, but with an even damper landing. The fact the board moved up and down didn't help his nerves, and the blue rubber coating was uncomfortable on the soles of his feet. He edged his way down it, knowing others were behind, eyes boring into his back. With each step forward, he was moved up and down by the board.

He wondered if it counted as seasickness if you felt sick when not actually in the water (let alone the sea). Either way, he felt seasick. He stood on the end and couldn't bring himself to move.

"Get a move on," came the murmurs from behind. As he turned, they started pressing down on the end of the board and the movement under his feet became more volatile. He counted down from three in his head and pushed himself up and outwards from the platform. As soon as he was in the air, he knew he had not got his take off correct and fell towards the water at an ever-increasing angle. He closed his eyes and stiffened every part of his body, before hitting the surface basically horizontal. He flapped for a couple of second to regain composure and started swimming away. He could hear others landing in with a controlled plop behind him as he got further towards the escape steps at the far end.

"Good start, Tim, well done," said Mrs Brute as he reached the bottom of the diving board staircase again. "Just concentrate to bend both knees together when you take off and it will all come good. Now, off you go, round two."

It took until the fourth attempt before he managed to land a dive correctly, entering the water with pointed toes, arms pushed towards the wooden slatted ceiling.

"Ten out of ten for that one, Tim," Mrs Brute said, putting her arm around him and giving him a squeeze. He realised he may have misjudged her character previously. She seemed genuinely happy he was making progress.

The end of the lesson came shortly after the usual close-down stretches, and they were told the homework was to watch the Olympic One Metre Springboard finals. Tim had seen these so much that he knew the routines, and the commentary, off by heart. In the changing rooms, he approached Leo at his locker.

"Alright?" he asked.

"Still fine. Gonna get a lift home with Stefan's mum. They live round the corner."

"Okay, whatever," said Tim as he opened his locker and pulled out his towel (he had accidentally packed a beach towel with cartoon fish on). "Want to watch the diving videos together tomorrow?"

I'm fine," Leo responded, heading back towards the changing cubicle.

"I'm not sure why you're being weird with me," Tim called across.

Leo stopped, before turning and taking a few steps

towards him. "Have a think for once, Tim," he barked. "Maybe for once the world doesn't revolve around you."

"I don't know what I've actually done here."

"And that's the problem. You don't understand. We all try to help you when things are crap, and yet you make up some conspiracy that Callum is trying to bring you down."

"Is that what this is about?"

"Not just that, no. Look, I can't be bothered, okay."

"Be like that then. I'll see you tomorrow."

Leo didn't answer, slamming the door as he disappeared from view. This was the first time Leo had been like this, and he couldn't work out why. His initial thought was Leo had developed feelings for Callum but didn't want to ask just in case he was way off the mark, which given the current situation, was probably likely. He threw on a jumper and trousers without getting fully dry and walked quickly to the waiting car.

"Where's Leo?" his mum asked as he threw his bag on to the backseats.

"Getting a lift home with someone else."

"Why? I thought he knew that I was to take him."

"I dunno, he was being weird."

She took her hands off the handbrake. "Weird how?"

"Just weird," said Tim, as he turned on the radio.

As they pulled out of the car park, his mum turned the radio off. "Are you okay?"

"I'm fine, don't worry. He will be back to normal soon, probably."

She rubbed his knee. "I meant about what happened earlier. I feel so guilty still."

"Please don't, Mum. It isn't your fault. I didn't mean to be so angry and to upset you."

"It's okay. But if you need me, just know I am here for you, okay?"

Tim smiled, his eyes spontaneously swelling with tears. He turned to watch the trees rush past the windows so she couldn't see.

"At least you have work and the fete to look forward to," she said after a few moments silence.

"I guess," Tim responded quietly.

She suddenly sat up more in the driver's seat. "That reminds me. Miriam's brother, Louis, will be there on Saturday. He's like you. I'll have to introduce you to each other."

Tim looked at her. "Mum, just because two people are gay, it doesn't mean they have to meet and get along. I appreciate you're trying to help but can you not? It's embarrassing."

"I meant he is a librarian, Tim," she said.

"Oh, sorry."

"He might be gay as well, but Miriam's never discussed his sexuality. He has just got home from a hiking holiday with his flatmate Julian."

"That doesn't mean he is gay."

"I know. I didn't say it did. Stop twisting my words. Anyway, he works at a big library in Oakshott, so he might be able to help you feel more settled in your new job."

"Thanks, Mum," Tim replied, before turning the radio up as *Saint Monique's* new single started.

***

By the Tim had showered, changed, and had some food (pie, apple), it was already past eight. PC Hughes was going to visit shortly to collect the spray can and ask for further information. Tim checked his phone to see if Leo had responded to the two messages he had sent, but there had been no reply. Even his texts to the group chat had only been answered by Lydia.

Tim walked through to the front room and called Johann on FaceTime.

"Alright," Johann said, answering after less than two rings.

"Heya. What you up to?"

"Sat here bored. No one wants to do anything." Johann squinted close to the screen. "What are you wearing?"

Tim looked down and stretched out his T-shirt. "Oh, this is an old school top. It used to be Marty's and is still way too big, but it's comfortable. Do you know if you're coming back Friday yet?"

"Not sure yet. My uncle is still in the hospital, but there is talk he is going home in the morning. If that does happen, me and Hanna can get the train back Friday lunchtime."

"Has your mum booked a flight?"

"Yeah, it's meant to take off around two on Friday afternoon, but she will cancel it if he is kept in."

"I hope he gets let out, and not in a selfish way."

Johann laughed. "Me too, I'm starting to go crazy up here."

Tim's mum came into the front room with a tray with three cups of tea. "PC Hughes will be here in a moment. Look lively," she said before adding, "Hi Johann," towards his phone.

"Hey, Katherine," he replied. "Look, Tim, you best go. Call me later and I'll try and answer. We are going to a big bowling place though with some others, so sorry in advance if I don't."

"That's cool, I'll message in a bit anyway."

*** 

It was close to nine forty-five by the time PC Hughes was sat opposite, drinking slowly from a mug with *Ain't Life Grand* written across the middle. Tim wanted to hurl it out of the window instead of answering all of his questions.

"Where were you when the criminal damage took place?"

"Do you find it strange that you discovered it?"

"Did you see anyone acting suspiciously?"

"Where did you find the spray paint?"

Question after question after question. After twenty minutes, and no real information being given, PC Hughes put his notepad to one side. "Is there anything else playing on your mind, Tim? Anything that could be making you act differently?"

A lump came to Tim's throat as he stared at the floor.

"He is perfectly fine otherwise, thank you," said Tim's mum quickly. "Everything is completely normal. He has a new job and is looking forward to starting school again."

"Understood," replied PC Hughes, as he downed the last of his tea.

"It's been a long day for him, so we will keep an ear open for anything we hear that might be related but, for now, I think it might be best if we left it there for today."

PC Hughes stood and started to pull on his hi-vis coat. "I am inclined to agree. I shall take the paint can with me, if that is okay?"

Tim's mum grabbed the can and put it into a Tesco bag for the officer.

"One can of Bristow's spray paint," he said as he jotted it down in his notebook.

Tim waited until the officer had left, before holding onto his mum. "Thank you," he whispered. He was ready for today to be over. He grabbed a further slice of pie and retreated to bed to watch something easy on Netflix, drifting off within minutes.

# Sixteen

## *Thursday*

Even before heading to Patterson's Papers, Tim had sent two further messages to Leo, however both remained unanswered. He locked his bike to a lamppost, and entered the shop, now open for the first time since Monday's incident.

Although open, Tim was sad to see the shelves bare in most places. All the birthday cards were boxed up alongside bundles of magazine returns, placed behind a small roped off area towards the back of the store. The chocolate offering was dwindling, and the cigarette cabinet remained open and empty. Mr Patterson was now only keeping the essentials as there was an abundance of milk, bread, and eggs. With less stock, the shop felt quite spacious. It looked larger than it ever had done before. Hopefully it wouldn't be big enough to be converted into a flat, however, even when the small stockroom had been included in the square footage.

Mr Patterson had seemed to be back to his old self a little as he walked towards the counter, a ring binder in his arms and whistling a jaunty tune. Tim noticed he was no longer using his cane.

"Heya, Mr Patterson, sorry I haven't been around to help this week," Tim said.

"Morning. Do not worry, young man. I know you

have had a lot going on, what with the police and your new job."

"I'm not going to let my new job come before this one," Tim promised his boss.

Mr Patterson smiled. "I don't think they will clash, however, if they do, please choose the library as a priority."

"I couldn't do that to you, sorry," said Tim.

"I'm not giving you the option. You have done so much for me so this is the least I could offer. As I say, it is unlikely to happen anyway. Now, about the paper rounds. We will be ceasing deliveries tomorrow I am afraid."

"Not Saturday?"

"I'm sorry, but with the fete, and the work we are doing there, we have decided tomorrow will be the last delivery."

Tim sighed. "I still don't want to go."

"I know. It will be strange for us both here as well. You'll soon get used to it, though, I'm sure. In a few years' time you won't be able to have any lie-ins, so make the most of them whilst you can. I don't think I have had a proper lie in for forty years," Mr Patterson laughed.

"I'll have one Saturday and see if I like them," Tim joked back. "Any updates from the police?" he added.

"Nothing yet, no. I heard about the incident at the library, and they had a couple of people of interest they were looking further into."

"Really?" asked Tim, narrowing his eyebrows.

"Yes. Why?" Mr Patterson said.

"It's just they came round to ask me more questions last night," he replied.

"Yes, but that's because you found it again I expect."

"But don't you find it strange, Mr Patterson? If you didn't know me, would you think it was weird the one person who had been next to all the graffiti so far was me?"

"Yes, I would. You'd be the first name I would give to the police. But I've told them what I always tell you. I trust you. Now don't go worrying about it as it won't do you much good. Your papers are all ready for you, over there on the ice cream fridge. Just take your time and try not to worry about anything."

"Thank you," Tim replied. He was going to miss this place, but especially Mr Patterson.

***

Tim completed his round without any incident at all. Despite his best efforts, every moment was filled with dread, as if another face would come to haunt him. He had taken his round at a slow pace for a change, so by the time he headed home the time had already gone past nine. As he got to his house, the car was parked right outside, which was strange. Maybe his parents had another hospital appointment to get to.

He couldn't imagine having another brother or sister. This house would soon be cramped. Signs of a new arrival had started to show already, and when he entered the kitchen through the backdoor there was a large cardboard box which stated it contained sixteen packs of baby wipes. Soon he imagined every spare space would be filled with nappies and children's toys. Mr Patterson was right. He best get used to having a lie in now as before long he would be woken through the night by the screams of a child. If he were to have another brother, there would be some of his old toys in the loft which could now be handed down.

"Hello?" he called out as he took a seat at the kitchen table for a few minutes. There was no reply. There still hadn't been any reply from Leo, either. Leo had updated his Instagram story, though, and it showed he was sat at home with his sister. It was the first time the two had fallen out properly. He didn't know whether to call Leo directly or speak to Lydia and ask her to sort the situation out for him. He had tried his best. He liked the update on Leo's social media regardless and hoped it would help somehow to thawing the situation a little.

The hallway was still cluttered with pumpkins, and there was also now a blue suitcase added to the end, with his mum's witch's hat on top. Maybe if he took the suitcase out to the back garden and set fire to it, it would stop her wearing the awful costume it contained. He kicked it closer to the wall and made his way upstairs.

As he reached the landing, his dad came out of the bathroom, half naked and with flecks of shaving foam in each of his ears. "Alright, son?" he said to Tim.

"Yeah, I'm okay," he replied.

"Good, good. I assume you're happy?"

"Um, same as normal, yeah. Why?"

"No reason," he added as he walked into his bedroom.

Today was meant to be the day where they would all be down at The Bell to watch the Haberdashery Menagerie debut gig, but after the fall out it was now looking like it would just be himself and his dad who would be attending. "Marty wants a word with you by the way," his dad said over the noise of the hairdryer.

"Where is he?"

"In his room."

"Makes a change for him to be home," Tim joked. He walked along the landing and tapped on his brother's bedroom door.

"Hello?" came his voice from inside.

"It's me."

Marty opened the door and told Tim to sit on the bed. "Hello. Glad you're home. I've got to tell you summat," his elder brother said.

"What have you done?" Tim replied, taking some Maltesers out of an open box on the bedside table. Marty came over and slapped his hand away, before moving the sweets onto the shelf opposite.

"I haven't done anything. Well, not deliberately anyway. But, like, you know bands have to have an image and things?"

"Like, why you're always dressed in black and stuff?" asked Tim.

"Well yes and no, but I mean like they have a band name in a particular font, and a decent symbol sometimes too. Like the way *Mirrorball* have the big MB logo on the flag waved by that soldier?"

"Ah yeah, I get you. Like *Saint Monique's* glittery microphone thing?"

"Yeah, like that but cool," said Marty as he moved over to his wardrobe and picked up a pad of paper. "Okay, so we have this gig today, and we want to make a good impression. We don't want to just turn up and look like a bunch of students who don't know what they're doing."

"But you are a bunch of students who don't know what they're doing," said Tim.

Marty glanced at him, making sure Tim said no more via eye contact alone. "Anyway," he continued. "Like, we were trying to think of something for Haberdashery Menagerie at rehearsal."

"Oh my god, what have you chosen? Is it stupid?" said Tim, already laughing.

"Um, no. Well, I didn't think so at the time anyway."

"And you want my approval, right?"

"No, definitely not. I wouldn't trust you to choose.

But I did wanna show you as soon as possible. Just remember, though, we chose this before we knew what would happen, and by the time I had found out about what had happened, it was too late."

"What is it?" asked Tim, now a bit more confused.

Marty sat on the bed. "Well, you know the picture I showed you of the graffiti on the tree where you're sat in front of it."

"The one the police have?"

"Yeah. We were sat down at the end of our practice a few days ago, trying to think of something for today, and I started scrolling through my phone. Um, I kinda suggested the face logo to the others and before I knew it, they had all agreed with me and then by the next morning they had sprayed it onto the front of the drums, and under a banner we have of our band name on."

Marty held out the pad in front of Tim and showed him the design. It was nearly identical to all the others around town, apart from this one had HM underneath, rather than TJ.

"Great," said Tim.

"I'm sorry. I wouldn't have done it if I'd have known. I wanted to show you before you turned up for the gig today. I didn't want you to freak out."

"Well, I am freaking out. Why didn't you say this yesterday?"

"Look, don't worry, I'll try and explain it to everyone."

"This is turning out to be the worst week ever," Tim said as he slumped on to Marty's chair. "How is that going to look to everyone now? Word will have got around about the graffiti, and then the next time anyone sees it, who will be sat there? Me."

"Tim, please don't panic. It will be fine. We can try and make it a show of solidarity or something."

"That won't work. At least Leo and Callum won't see it, though."

"Are they not coming now?" asked Marty, as he took a dark blue bandana out of his sock draw and started to roll it into shape.

"Nah, we sort of fell out last night," said Tim.

"That's annoying. We were hoping you'd all be there so it made us look more popular."

"Well, I'll just clap twice as loud, then. I'm not messaging them again."

Marty came and sat down next to Tim. "Dad will be with you, and there will be other kids there you know too, so you won't be on your own all afternoon. Just try and keep your chin up and when we're playing, try not to look at the face."

"That will be hard now you're plastering it in every corner."

"I know, but it's only when we are on stage."

"How many other bands are there?"

"Four like us, I think. We are all quite amateur. And then there is the headliner."

"Anyone famous?" questioned Tim.

"Not anymore, no, but he was in that band, *Level Crossing*."

"I've never heard of them."

"You know the song from the *Carpetland* advert?" Marty asked, before singing some ooh-ooh-ee-ohh type melody.

"They did that?"

"Yeah! Well, they wrote it anyway. The *Carpetland* version is a cover. But it's the guitarist Donny Mellor, I think his name is. He owns a big house now down the road. Earnt a load of money, apparently."

"He bought a house off of one song?" asked Tim. Marty nodded. "In that case, Marty, write a good song and buy me a house too, please."

"Only if you clap twice as loud," Marty responded.

"I'll clap four times as loud."

"Even better."

"Today will still be rubbish, though. I was excited to come but everything has overshadowed it."

"I can make it a bit better for you," Marty replied.

"I bet you ten pounds you can't," moaned Tim.

"Give me ten pounds now then and follow me," Marty said as he grabbed Tim's hand and started dragging him out the room.

"Where are we going?" asked Tim as he was pulled down the stairs. Marty didn't respond. Nothing more was said until Marty grabbed both of his brothers' shoulders and pushed his face towards the front room door. His nose was nearly touching the wood.

"Right. Go in there. You owe me ten pounds, don't forget," Marty said as he went to go back upstairs.

Tim looked over his shoulder as his brother skipped out of sight. He turned back, nervous at what Marty had planned. Maybe he'd bought him some new clothes or something cool. Maybe he had bought him a giant *Congrats on coming out!* cake. It would make a change from all the pie. At the least, it couldn't be something to make his week worse. He held onto the door handle nervously and pushed it open slowly. The curtains were drawn, and the room was dark and quiet. He nudged it but couldn't see anything different. He took a step forward and looked to his left, before immediately bursting into tears.

# Seventeen

"Hey you," said Johann, smiling. "Are you okay?"

Tim walked across the room and pulled him in to the tightest hug he could, still unable to speak, instead nodding into Johann's shoulder.

Johann's arms were trapped by his sides. "Come and sit down," he said, shrugging Tim off and moving him across to the sofa. Johann removed his denim jacket and tossed it onto the back of the chair opposite. "I've got something for you," he said as he opened his backpack and handed Tim a postcard. It was a skyline view of Newcastle with the words *Having a cannae time!* stamped across the middle in an oversized yellow font. "Sorry it isn't anything interesting. I didn't have enough time to get you anything better. I was gonna send it today but thought hand delivering it might be more fun."

"Thank you," said Tim eventually. He wiped his eyes. "Sorry, I'm a bit surprised to see you. I'm happy, though, obviously. Just a bit shocked. And I owe Marty ten pounds as well, now."

Johann laughed. "Why?"

"He bet me a couple of minutes ago he could cheer me up."

"Well, technically you started crying so you could use that to get out of it."

"Good point."

"Also, he knew I was here so that ain't a fair bet."

"Another good point. I have something better to spend it on anyway."

"More Wispa's?" asked Johann.

Tim shook his head. "You should see how many I have upstairs. It's a joke. You can have a load if you want."

"Please."

Tim opened the curtains to allow some natural light to come through, before sitting next to Johann, resting his head on his shoulder. "I assume everything is okay now with your uncle? And will your mum be back tomorrow?"

"Yeah, she will be getting her flight. My uncle is being released today which is great."

"Discharged. Saying released makes it sound like he has been in prison."

"That's my other uncle," Johann said.

"Really?" Tim responded. Johann nodded his head. "We need to learn way more about each other's families."

"We do. Anyway, yeah, Uncle is being discharged today, but probably not until the afternoon. I was told not to tell you I was coming but otherwise I would've, I promise. We wanted it to be a surprise."

"Who is we?"

"Your parents."

Johann took a sip of water out of a reusable bottle. It was blue with a cartoon turtle on the side. He held it up to Tim. "My sister bought me this when I was miserable the other day," Johann said, noticing Tim had been staring at it whilst he was drinking. "Think she got it from the aquarium or somewhere." He put it on the floor and held Tim's hand. "Anyway, yeah, so yesterday evening I was out for a walk as usual, and my mum phoned me up. She asked how it was all going, and if I was enjoying it up north. I told her I was in a way, but Greenwood was better."

"So, she sent you and Hanna back here?"

"No. Hanna is still in Newcastle. Just before Mum phoned me, she had a call from your mum. She didn't say anything about what you had told her but had dropped into the conversation that it might be nice if I could come back and stay here instead. Like, with everything going on with my family, your mum suggested it might be good for me to spend time with friends before school started again, and it would do you good, what with the weird graffiti and everything. Your mum asked my mum to ask me if I wanted to come and live with you for a few days instead."

"Oh my god, that's amazing," said Tim excitedly.

"I know, right! The next thing I knew, the train tickets had been booked and now here I am."

"You must be tired."

"I am," said Johann as he walked across to Barnaby's enclosure. He reached in and picked the tortoise up, carrying him to the sofa where he placed him on his lap. "I've missed you."

"Are you talking to me or Barnaby now?" asked Tim.

"You, you fool," he chuckled back. "Newcastle was alright, but the whole time I just kept thinking about you. About how we lost a week together doing all the stupid things we do."

"I've been the same. Lydia and Leo must be sick of me talking about you."

"How is Leo?"

"Still not talking. Can you speak to him for me?"

"Yeah, I'll help. Once I'm more awake, anyway."

"What time did you get up?"

"I had to get to the station for five this morning and then spent over three hours on the train. I had to change in some place called Darlington. There was nothing open apart from a supermarket, so I wandered around there for a bit and got a pastry. Once I got back, your parents picked me up and we dropped your mum off at work on the way here. It was good to see the town again. I can't believe how dusty and yellow the grass is."

"Yeah, it's been hot all week. Would rather this than cold and rain, though," said Tim.

"Same, definitely. I only arrived about ten minutes before you did. Marty told me to come and sit in here and just wait so we could surprise you. We thought you'd probably get in, grab some pie, and then come and watch television but you went upstairs instead."

"I might have kicked your suitcase, sorry. I thought it was my mum's Halloween costume."

"That's okay. It's only got clothes in it, anyway."

Tim smiled and hugged Johann again. "Did you want some breakfast?"

"I really do."

"Cool, I think we have cereal, unless you want toast? Or if you want pie, please, please have a whole one."

"Tim," said Johann.

"What?"

"Go and have a shower and then we can walk into town for breakfast."

"That sounds better. Are you showering?"

"I'm full of good ideas. Yeah, I'll jump in after you're done. I need to find some clothes out so will do that whilst you're up there."

"Cool."

"Make sure you tell Marty he ain't getting the ten pounds."

Upstairs, Tim went into his bedroom and undressed. He caught sight of himself in the mirror and shocked himself when he saw his face smiling back. It seemed a long time since he had felt truly happy, so seeing a grinning face caught him off guard. It felt as if he was wearing some kind of prosthetic 'Happy Tim Johnson' mask rather than it being his own actual face.

He poked a cheek with his finger, and then stretched his ears out just to make sure it was him. The reflection followed his actions. It was real. God, it actually was real. Johann was downstairs. His suitcase was in the hall. When he breathed in, he could still smell Johann's deodorant in his nostrils. That scent alone opened memories of the time they had spent together a few weeks ago. A sense of melancholy washed over him, wishing he was reliving that time, but this was soon replaced by gentle laughter. It didn't matter if he missed those times. He could create more. And right now, too.

He didn't know what to do first. He pulled his First Date TARDIS from under the bed, before throwing it on his sheets, deciding he should first be finding out the smartest clean clothes he had (well, the level under his formal suit anyway, which would be too much for breakfast in Greenwood).

Halfway through this he realised he was meant to be showering. His mind was suddenly all over the place. Johann had this magic effect on him, and it made him feel the need to do everything all at the same time. He looked back to the mirror. Still smiling. Good. He punched his thighs and spoke out loud to try and get himself together. "Right. Towel, shower gel, shampoo. Shower. Get money out of the jar. Get dressed. That's the plan. Oh god. Phone. Is it charged?" he picked it up and stared at the screen. "Ninety-eight per cent. That will do. Shoes. Which shoes. Converse? Yeah. C'mon Tim, sort yourself out. It's only Johann, stop panicking. Johann is downstairs. In my house. Shit. Get it together."

He sat on the bed and closed his eyes, taking a few

deep breathes to steady himself. "Johann is downstairs. Everything is fine. Act normal."

Letting the hot water in the shower pour over his body, he felt reset to an acceptable human excitement level. He had decided to open a new pack of shower accessories for the occasion. They were from a brand called Ambrosia (but not the custard people – that would be weird), and he had kept them for a special event such as this. Clean and smelling like an explosion on a citrus fruit farm, he got himself dressed swiftly and went back downstairs, throwing a towel at Johann.

"All yours," he said, as Johann pulled himself up off the sofa.

In the kitchen, he flicked on the kettle on and put a teaspoon of cheap instant coffee into a mug (one with a NASA logo on the side), almost dropping it when the kitchen door smashed open.

"Make me one, will you?" said his dad as he entered the kitchen carrying a pile of long square wooded planks.

"Coffee or tea?"

"Coffee, please."

"What are you doing with that wood?"

"Taking it to the shed," his dad said, whilst trying to open the backdoor.

Tim went over and pulled it open. "I mean what is it for?"

"A little project," came the unhelpful reply.

"What project?" Tim continued, but his dad rushed outside and threw them on the lawn. Tim stirred the mugs, watching his dad out of the window. He was now empty handed but bent forwards in a weird stretch position, as if trying to fold himself in half. He then flung his arms up and down a few times like an injured swan, before coming back towards the kitchen.

"Sorry, they were heavier than I realised. Thought I

was gonna give myself a hernia," his dad said through heavy breaths as he took his coffee off the counter.

"I haven't put sugar in that yet," Tim said, taking the cup back off him. "So, what's your project?"

"Well, we thought it might be nice to be a bit more homemade for this baby." All the time his dad had spent watching *The Great Carpentry Challenge* on Channel 4 each Wednesday evening had clearly started rubbing off on him. "I picked all this up from Derek," he said, pointing to the timber outside.

"Derek-from-the-rubbish-tip, Derek?" asked Tim.

"Yeah. I messaged him yesterday to let me know if anything suitable was dropped off, and he messaged me this morning. Went to collect it early before getting Johann and stuck it in the boot of the car."

"How did you even have time?"

"I went up before six. Derek ain't meant to give it away you see so I had to go before it opened." Tim raised his eyebrows. "Don't go telling anyone, son. Not even your boy," his dad added, pointing towards the wall separating the kitchen and front room.

*Your boy.* YOUR. BOY, Tim thought, as his excitement rose again. His dad had said it so naturally, so much so he wished he had told his parents weeks ago. They were both being cool with everything, and not in a 'try hard' kind of way. Their allyship appeared natural now they knew.

"I promise my lips are sealed, but only if you tell me what you're building," Tim said.

"Fine. As I say, we want this to be a more homemade feel, what with prices going up on everything, so I am going to attempt to build a cot from scratch."

Tim passed a coffee across. "Okay, that's actually quite cool."

"You and Johann can help if you want?"

Tim was not practical, especially in woodwork, but he wanted to do it. Not only would it be nice to play a part in creating something lasting for his new brother or sister, but it would give Johann and his dad to bond more.

Tim and Marty were lucky their dad had been around for most of their early childhood. It had only been when he was eight that his dad got promoted in the Navy, which led to many of the overseas expeditions. He hoped his dad would be there for the new sibling, too.

"When's your next time away, Dad?" he asked, wanting an answer before he could overthink it.

"Um, I have a meeting tomorrow. I'll have a clearer answer then," he replied.

"Cool, is that in Portsmouth?"

"No, gotta drive up to London. They have an office in Bloomsbury."

"Wouldn't the train be easier?"

"It would, but I will be carrying a lot of stuff. Gotta take my uniforms and all my gear."

"Can I come?" Tim asked.

"I don't know. I can't bring you in the building with me because you need the whole security clearance, and that's more hassle than it's worth, especially now Malcolm is in charge. He's useless. Well, he isn't, but he does everything by the rulebook, so a simple job takes way too long. Also, I don't want you getting lost somewhere you've never been before." Tim had expected this answer. "Anyway, aren't you back at the library tomorrow?"

"Ah, yeah, good point," Tim said, a bit dejected.

"I'll take you up some other time, okay?" his dad said, putting his arm around him.

"Promise?" asked Tim.

"I promise. I'm gonna start the cot this evening. Be

here for six if you wanna help."

"Will do. We've gotta go to Marty's gig this afternoon, remember."

"Yep, I'll drive us down."

"It's only at The Bell."

"Okay, we can walk. Right, I'm going to get the rest of this wood. Fancy giving me a hand?"

"No, sorry," said Tim. "I've just showered and me and Johann are going out to get breakfast."

"Where are you going?"

"Dunno yet. Not Freddie's."

Tim's dad reached into his pocket and pulled out a twenty-pound note. "This one's on me," he said, folding the note into his hand.

Tim stood and gave him a hug. "Thank you."

His dad ruffled his hair. "It's only twenty quid."

"I don't just mean for the money," Tim said, his head pressed against his dad's chest. "Just, thank you."

# Eighteen

"I told you you'd be too warm in that," said Johann, who was being pulled about as Tim fought to get his hoodie into his small backpack.

"I wanted to look smart."

"You do."

Johann waited for Tim to finish messing with his bag and then they continued to walk slowly along the footpath spanning the two rivers between Oak Tree Crescent and the town centre. The floodplains on either side river were damp, despite the dryness of the past week. The electric substation was singing out its usual dull humming sound, hiding the sounds of the summer morning.

"So, where do you wanna have breakfast?" asked Johann as he walked along the low wall outside of the tired looking community hall.

"Not Freddie's. We can see if there is anything up Corn Street?"

As they negotiated the crossroads, Johann suddenly stopped on the kerb.

"What are you doing?" asked Tim.

"I forgot to update Mark last week about not being able to do my paper round," he replied, refusing to walk in front of the newsagents.

"Did you want to pop in now?"

"What do I say?"

"Sorry."

"I said, what do I say?"

"No, I mean just say sorry to Mark. He probably won't care."

"Can you see if he is in there?"

"Fine," Tim said, as he walked towards the shop. "You're so lame," he added over his shoulder. The newsagents was dark, and the front door locked. A sign had been sellotaped to the window saying *Back in ten minutes*. "Johann, it's fine, he isn't here."

Johann moved gingerly forward. "I hope I don't get sacked. I'll come back later."

"We might as well wait. He will be back in ten minutes."

"He might not be."

"But it says," said Tim, pointing to the sign on the door.

"That sign means nothing. Like, when did those ten minutes start? Without having a time on there, it's pretty useless."

"Yeah, but if he put it on there five minutes ago, he will be back in five?"

"Yeah, but what if he put it on there fifteen minutes ago? Would mean he is already five minutes late."

"I guess," concluded Tim.

"I know Mark and I know he isn't as organised as Mr Patterson. Let's just go and get some food."

"You seem rushed," Tim said, as they walked back to the centre of town.

"I'm okay, I hate making people annoyed. Anyway, I have something for you when we sit down, and that's more important."

"What is it?"

"Just, come on." Johann grabbed his arm and led him

towards the high street.

They had only moved a few paces before a voice called Tim from behind.

They turned their heads.

"Shit, it's Callum," Tim said to Johann as they watched him cross the road. He was in yet another, probably gifted, football kit.

"Where you off to?" asked Callum.

"Breakfast," Tim replied. "Oh, Callum, this is Johann, by the way."

Callum stuck a hand out, which Johann reluctantly shook. "Alright, Johann?"

"Hi."

"Mind if I join you for food?" he asked.

"Sorry, I just want it to be us two," said Tim.

"Fine. Where are you going?"

"To that new place called Dixie's, down by the church," lied Johann. "Meant to do some nice pastries."

"I'll have to try it. What are you up to next weekend? It's SOCCON on the Saturday so Bryan is gonna drive me up."

"What's SOCCON?" asked Tim.

"It's the big social media convention up in Birmingham. It's gonna be mega."

Johann frowned. "I couldn't think of anything worse."

"What d'ya mean?" said Callum. "The Brewster Twins are there, and then there are rumours the Ampelmänner group are flying in from Munich."

"Never heard of them," said Tim.

Callum raised his eyebrows, before swiping open his phone and showing them a picture of four identical looking Germans on Instagram. "They're huge! How can you have not heard of them. They have over a million followers on TikTok."

Johann snorted. "If I wanted to hang around near a load of basic white twinks with no personality I'd just wait by the to the Sixth Form common room."

"What's a twink?" asked Callum.

"Google it," Johann replied. Tim started to pull at his sleeve indicating to leave as they watched Callum search his phone.

"That's gross," Callum replied, as multiple suggestive pictures appeared on his phone.

"You asked," said Johann.

Callum put his phone away and turned to walk away. "Enjoy your breakfast, dickheads," he called over his shoulder.

"Dra åt helvete," Johann called after him.

"What does that mean?" asked Tim.

"Google it," smiled Johann

They walked further through town, before Tim stopped. "Here?" he asked as he stared into the window of Huffton's Bakery. The display was stacked high with scones and homemade cakes. Johann nodded his agreement. Tim felt guilty as it was directly opposite Freddie's, and he didn't want the owner at the diner to think they had abandoned their regular visits, but it was definitely a bit more special for a breakfast not-date. He opened the door quickly and slipped inside.

The air was sweet with the scent of baking, soundtracked by conversations and the hissing of coffee machines. Tim had only ever been once before, and that was just because his mum had dragged him in to avoid a sudden rainstorm a couple of years ago. The bell above the door clanged as it closed behind them as they stood in front of the "Please Wait Here to be Seated" sign.

"This is on me," said Tim.

"Are you sure?"

"Yeah, Dad gave me some money. We better eat well

because I doubt there will be any good food at The Bell during the afternoon. We will probably only be given a bag of crisps and a pickled egg."

"British cuisine is weird," joked Johann.

"You say this like you aren't from the country which eats canned rotten fish!" Tim jibed back.

"You do know we don't always eat that, right?"

"And we don't only eat pickled eggs."

"I bet you have one later."

"Not gonna deny I won't, but still, get something decent here anyway."

The pair waited for a couple of minutes before a young blonde girl in a white shirt and dark green apron came to greet them.

"Hello Tim, just the two of you?"

Tim was taken by surprise as he had never seen this girl before. "Um, yes please, thank you."

"Follow me," she said, turning round quickly so her hair swished behind her like in a shampoo commercial.

Tim and Johann followed her through to the back room, which was also busy. Large windows filled one wall, providing a lookout into a small courtyard garden. It was a much better view than looking at traffic from the tables at the front.

"Here we go," the girl said as she went to place two menus on a square wooden table.

"Sorry, can we have the slightly larger table please?" Johann asked.

"Sure thing," came the response and they were led towards the back wall. She put the menus down, smiled, and then went to a table nearby where a rude middle-aged man with red cheeks was clicking his fingers for attention. Johann put his bag on one of the spare chairs and sat down opposite Tim.

"What was wrong with the first table?" asked Tim.

"You'll see," replied Johann. "Let's order food first, though."

They sat in silence as they studied the extensive "Breakfast and Brunch" menu. Tim wasn't sure if he wanted to have a full English breakfast, or if the environment called for something fancier. It was one of those places that made a big effort to make each item sound more upmarket than it was. For example, in Freddie's, you could order '*Eggs, Chips, Beans*' for £4.50. Not even Eggs, Chips AND Beans. Eggs. Chips. Beans. £4.50. Done. At Huffton's though, their offering was called the "Oxfordshire Brunch" and was described as such:

*"Two free range Sunnyvale farm eggs, served with triple cooked potato batons, complimented with haricot beans in a rich tomato sauce."*

And it was £2 more expensive. Tim hated pretentiousness and told Johann as much. He was struggling to decide until Johann picked up a leaflet from a wooden holder and waved it in his face. "Hey, do you fancy a full-on afternoon tea?" he asked.

"Like a scone and sandwiches?" Tim replied.

"Sandwiches, cakes, tea, scones, everything! I've always wanted to try one ever since moving across. I saw it in one of the Paddington films. It's so British!"

"But it isn't afternoon?"

"Yeah, but they serve it from eleven so it's fine. It's only twenty-five pounds as well."

Tim would normally think this was a lot for sandwiches and cakes, but with the money his dad gave him, it would technically only cost five pounds. "Go on then," he confirmed.

Johann smiled at the server, and she came back over.

"All ready to order?" she asked.

"Yes please, thank you," said Johann, suddenly

turning his accent into more of a native Brit. "We would be grateful for one Afternoon Tea for Two please," he said, whilst holding up the leaflet.

"Certainly. It shall be with you in around fifteen minutes. How is Marty?" she replied, turning to Tim.

"Yes, all good thank you." She nodded her head and wandered to the kitchen.

"Before you ask, I have no idea who she is," said Tim, anticipating Johann's question.

"Everyone knows your family," he replied.

"Does that surprise you? Anyway, talking of family, tell me about your uncle in prison."

Johann picked a sugar cube out of a small glass jar and started crunching. "We don't speak to him. He's my dad's brother, well, semi-brother."

"Half-brother," Tim replied, correcting Johann. He liked Johann's cute little word mix-ups.

"Half-brother," continued Johann. "They share the same dad, but Uncle Fredrik is about twenty years older."

"What did he do?"

"We have never been told everything, but about five years ago there was some incident involving a large Swedish Navy ship. He was in charge of it, and it ended up crashing into a harbour wall. It caused over three hundred million Swedish krona's worth of damage."

"THREE HUNDRED MILLION?"

"Hey, it's not as much as it seems." Johann replied.

"It sounds a lot. How much is that in pounds?"

"I don't know. One second." Johann stopped and pulled his phone out. Tim watched him typing away, before he put the phone back away and smiled. "Twenty-five million pounds, I guess that is quite a lot, isn't it?"

"Just a bit. And he went to jail for it?"

"Yeah. He was charged with something like naval negligence. From what we read in the papers he had lied about carrying out certain checks or something. He will be out in about four years. We don't talk to him anymore, not that we did much anyway."

"Cool story, though," said Tim.

"I guess. I think mum has the newspapers somewhere. I'll show you sometime." He took another sugar cube. The server came back over and placed cutlery and napkins on the table, alongside two China cups with saucers. They thanked her and waited for her to depart again. "So, then," said Johann, picking his bag off the floor. "I have been doing some thinking."

"About?"

"The graffiti."

"Do we have to discuss this now? I want to have a nice time," Tim replied.

"Stick with me."

Tim sat back in his chair and watched as Johann pulled out three coloured circular bits of card, each about the size of a coaster. One red, one green, one yellow. He turned them over and placed them in a line across the table. Tim noticed they had been labelled as Patterson's, Funtangutan, and The Library.

"Looks like a depressing board game," said Tim, watching as Johann went back into his bag, becoming confused when he then took four action figures out.

"So, the graffiti, right. I was drawing up a list to try and help you, and I know you think it's Callum, so I wanted to test your theory."

"Do you think it is him as well?"

"Be patient. First off, this is you," Johann said, holding up the first figure.

"Is that The Rock?"

"Yeah, I had a load of wrestling figures growing up. Now, you can stand on Patterson's Papers." Johann placed The Rock on the red circle.

"Next, shall we say Leo?"

"Who is playing him?"

"Yoda," Johann replied, putting the Star Wars character on Pattersons. "Who should represent Lydia?"

"What are the options?"

"We have either Wallace of *Wallace & Gromit* fame, or Harry Kane."

"Callum is more of a football person, so he can be Harry Kane," Tim answered, suddenly getting into it a bit more.

"Good call." Johann put Harry with the others, before taking a wide smiling Wallace to complete the group.

Johann was about to start explaining when a large pot of tea was put onto the table, along with a fancy jug of milk. The server looked at the toys, and then the boys, before raising her eyebrows and leaving again.

"Let's go from the beginning," said Johann once he had checked no one was eavesdropping. "Where were you when the newsagent incident happened?"

"Lydia's."

"Was there any time when you were alone between leaving yours and getting to hers?"

"I guess, yeah, but only a few minutes. I was sat in the park by her house for a bit."

"Good," said Johann, and moved Tim to the Funtangutan circle.

"If it's good, why am I still in the game."

"Because you were alone, it's not concrete enough for an alibi alone," replied Johann.

"But..." started Tim.

"Don't worry, I know it's not you, but just stick with me, please."

Tim sat back.

"Lydia. Where was she around the time it all

happened?"

"She was at home preparing the buffet with her mum."

"Excellent. She is safe." Johann picked up Wallace and tossed him back into his bag. "Now to Yoda."

"Leo came to Lydia's, but he was late because he had bad guts."

"A likely alibi. On to Funtangutan, Yoda!" Johann said, moving him to stand with The Rock.

"Finally, we have Callum."

"He was last to arrive."

"And he wasn't with Leo beforehand?"

"Nope."

"Straight to Funtangutan!"

"Why don't you have an action figure?" asked Tim.

"I was in Newcastle."

"Even so."

"I only picked up four."

"I'm imagining an *ABBA* action figure now," laughed Tim.

"Very funny. Anyway, all of *ABBA* are in the rucksack with Wallace."

"Tea?" asked Tim. Johann picked his cup up and moved it closer. Tim poured a cup each and watched as Johann put five sugar cubes into his brew.

"What? I like it sweet," said Johann, before taking a sip and continuing. "Okay, so Funtangutan. You discovered it, right?

"No."

"Who did?"

"Lydia."

"But Lydia is in my bag."

"But we were all sort of there at the same time," said Tim, now confused again.

"So why did people accuse you?" Johann asked.

"Because I was alone in the hut for a bit once we had completed the course," replied Tim, hands joined together in his lap. Johann picked The Rock up and put him on The Library.

"Was Leo alone at any point?"

"No. He went into the shed just behind Callum when we arrived. I was talking to Lydia's mum about being gay and he was holding the door for me when I got to the entrance."

"Excellent!" clapped Johann as he threw Yoda into the backpack.

"That leaves Callum."

"But he was with Leo."

"Did Callum enter the hut first?"

"Yes."

"Was Leo looking inside the hut at all times?"

"No."

"Well, there we go then. Callum goes to the Library with you." Johann put the cards back in his bag and left just Harry Kane and The Rock on the table, before quickly swiping them onto the floor. Tim was going to ask what happened before realising a three-tiered silver plate contraption was being carried across by a tall waiter. The boys sat back in their chairs as they watched him place it meticulously down in the centre. A second waiter then placed two plates down for each of them. They matched the cups.

"I hope you enjoy," he said in a deep voice, before retreating backwards.

"There is *so* much food here," laughed Tim. "I guess we start at the bottom and work out way up?"

"I guess any order is fine, but the cakes on top go last," said Johann.

On the large bottom tier were sixteen thin rectangular sandwiches. The handwritten card stated there were four flavours (prawn cocktail, beef and horseradish, tuna and spring onion, and egg with cress). Tim took one of each flavour and placed them neatly on his plate. The middle layer was a variety of small pastries.

"What's in these?" asked Tim, pointing at the middle tier. Johann picked up the card.

"So, we have goat's cheese tart with balsamic onion chutney in these round ones," started Johann. Tim picked up one immediately. "Then the square parcel things are…" he paused a bit. "It's in French. Petits cadeaux de jambon, apparently."

"What the hell does that mean?" questioned Tim.

"No idea. Google it."

Tim pulled out his phone. "I knew you'd say that. Anyway, it means Small Ham Presents."

"Why don't they just say that then?"

"Told you this place was pretentious. What's in the last ones?"

"Chicken and tarragon cups."

"They sound good. Which do you want?"

"We will go halves on everything. Anyway, you're already halfway through a tart."

The pair split the bottom two layers equally and sat eating for ten minutes. They discussed the walks Johann had been on in Newcastle, and Tim had explained all about the fete at the weekend, and what Johann should expect. Once conversation slowed, Johann topped up his tea and added more sugar. They'd run out at this rate. Once most of the savoury snacks had been eaten. Johann picked the toys back up.

"Do we have to?" asked Tim.

"Yes."

"Fine."

Johann put a whole sandwich in his mouth and stared at Tim as he chewed and swallowed it. "So, to the library.

You were working."

"Yes."

"And you found the graffiti."

"Yes," Tim said, now wondering why this was being acted out as nothing new was coming from it.

"Okay, you are a suspect."

"Thanks, Johann, that's made me feel great."

"But wait. Where was Callum?" pushed Johann.

"I don't know."

"Does anyone know?"

"I don't think so, no," confirmed Tim.

"So, he is also a suspect."

"That is what I have been saying all along but we don't have evidence."

"Who has the paint?" asked Johann.

"Me. Well, it was in my bag anyway."

"Hence why the police questioned you again, right?"

"Yes."

"Okay, so I need you to think."

"About?"

"Who uses paint, Tim?" he asked, holding up his left hand with fingers spread out.

"Artists," he replied dryly.

"Okay, we can rule out Picasso. Think outside the box."

"Painters and decorators," said Tim.

"Do they use spray paints?"

"I guess not."

"Okay, so not them," Johann said. He was ruling people out by putting a finger down for each guess. "Think, Tim. What might you be able to paint that isn't a house?"

"I don't knowwww," whined Tim.

"You do."

"Just tell me," said Tim, taking a custard pastry.

"I need you to get this so I don't become involved. Name some sports."

"Football."

"More."

"Rugby, hockey, basketball, diving, cricket…" Tim continued.

"What about ones you can't do at school."

"Golf?"

"Faster paced."

"BMX?"

"Getting closer. What's like BMXing, but faster."

"Superbikes?" asked Tim.

"You are so, so, close. Think of that but double the wheels."

"Formula One?"

"Yes!" said Johann. "Finally."

"How does that help? That doesn't help me at all."

"It does. What colour are Formula One cars?"

"Each team is different."

"Because they have…."

"…different paintjobs," said Tim, slowly realising. "You can paint cars."

"Exactly. And do you know anyone who paints cars?"

"I do."

"And that person is?"

"Callum's stepdad, Bryan."

Johann smiled and put The Rock back in bag, leaving just Harry Kane stood amongst the food crumbs. Johann placed a scone and a slice of Battenburg on Tim's plate and then poured a final cup of tea for them both. He used the last of the sugar cubes and took a bite of a chocolate éclair. "So, basically, I was thinking about it and my thought process was the same as yours, although with a little less guidance," he said, gently kicking Tim's foot with his own. "If Callum's stepdad repairs cars, he might have spray paint in his garage, meaning Callum has access to it, meaning Callum could be the one doing it after all, meaning you are right. We just need to prove it now."

"Is there a chance we are wrong?" asked Tim.

"Absolutely, but it's worth checking. I've text Leo."

"We aren't talking."

"I know, I haven't invited him down. I told him we were making Barnaby a new pen and needed some paint. I told him to ask if his dad has heard of a certain type of paint by a company called 'Bristow's'. As Leo's dad is practical, Leo will ask him for me. Even if his dad doesn't have it, the name will be in his head."

"Why Bristow's?"

"Because you said that was written on the side of the paint can found in your bag."

"So, he will be helping us without knowing he is helping us?"

"Exactly."

"That's genius!"

"Thank you. Now, if Leo isn't talking to you, he is probably going to hang out with Callum and go to his house, and what will he see?"

"Bristow's paint."

"Bingo!"

"You'd think the police would've worked this out," said Tim.

"They were probably too focussed on you. It's hardly their biggest investigation so probably just wanted to blame someone so they could brush it under the carpet."

Tim smiled. He wanted them to be right this time. He hoped Leo would find it and let Johann know as soon as possible. Tim wondered if they should go to the police, but as Johann said, they probably didn't care enough to want to listen to the results of a fifteen-year-olds own detective work. After finishing the last cake, Tim threw his backpack over his shoulder. "We best get home. We only have an hour before going to Marty's gig and I need to change."

The waiter brought the bill across, and Tim put thirty pounds into a small silver tray, telling them to keep the change.

# Nineteen

"Good breakfast, boys?" asked Tim's dad as they entered the house via the front door.

"All good, thanks," Johann replied.

"Is Marty in?" asked Tim.

"No, he's already left to soundcheck, why?"

"Just wanted to wish him luck."

"Why are you being nice?" asked his dad, suspiciously.

"No reason, genuinely."

He looked at Tim through squinted eyes, with Tim holding out his hands to prove his intentions were genuine.

His dad turned back towards the counter to paste a large amount of Marmite onto two pieces of white toast. "We will leave here in thirty minutes or so," he added, waving the knife over his shoulder, dropping bits of spread onto the tiled floor.

Tim and Johann headed through to the front room and sat watching daytime television, waiting to leave. "We should look for more clues," said Johann, scrolling through Callum's Instagram account.

"I'm too tired to now," replied Tim, before lying down and putting his head into Johann's lap. "Plus, I think I might have eaten too much at breakfast."

"No pickled egg for you later, then?" joked Johann, stroking Tim's hair.

"We will see."

"Have you seen Honey Latté's latest post?" asked Johann, pushing his phone in front of Tim's face as he sat up. She was wearing a gold mermaid outfit with a headdress that stood over two-feet tall.

"She looks amazing!" Tim said. "Urgh, I miss her."

"Me too," said Johann as he yawned and sunk back into the cushions. Within thirty seconds, his eyes were closed. Tim sat listening to him breathe, still unable to believe he was here. The television was running a competition to win a holiday to Malta and the over-enthusiastic presenter grated, so Tim switched it off and leant his head against Johann's. In what felt like a split second, he started to be shaken. He opened his eyes to see his dad towering above him wearing a lumberjack style shirt and a cap.

C'mon, you two," he said, as he continued to rock Tim gently by the collar.

Tim looked around, sleep causing him to lose track of what day it was. He stood up and tried to shake the grogginess from his body. His eyes snapped shut as the curtains were pulled open and bright sunlight fired directly onto him. He trudged upstairs and sprayed on some emergency deodorant before meeting Johann back in the front room. He noticed there was now a large fold out bed at the far end of the room, squeezed into the gap between the kitchen hatch and Barnaby's indoor enclosure. Tim's old Thomas the Tank Engine bedsheets laid across the top, ironed pristinely. "How long has that been there?" he asked.

His dad looked up from tying his boots to where Tim was pointing. "Oh, I set that up when you two were napping a minute ago. Thought it would save me fighting with it this evening."

"I didn't know Johann was going to be sleeping in here," Tim replied.

"Well, it was either here or the shed," he replied, laughing. Tim was secretly hoping Johann would have been allowed to camp out in his room, but he knew his parents wouldn't have permitted this just yet. They still wouldn't allow Marty to have a girl stay over, and he was nearly an actual adult.

The Bell Inn was a large mock-timber framed pub that was probably too large to be financially viable in the current climate. Every inch of the venue seemed to drip with desperation, doing anything it could to drag punters in off the street to spend some money.

Out the front stood a singular picnic table, doubling as the smoking area. It was surrounded by a collection of large, slightly faded vinyl signs, promising anyone passing they could come inside and watch over one hundred Premier League matches a season on Sky. Another sign said every match of the latest Six Nations rugby tournament would be shown. Considering the last fixtures had taken place over three months prior, Tim realised the landlords of the place didn't care too much about the upkeep of the venue.

Tim followed Johann inside, taking a seat near the windows, shivering in the shade, whilst his dad went to the bar. An old man was sat to their left, drinking slowly out of a pint glass. He was unsure how long he had been drinking, but the bubbles in his drink were no longer present.

"Have you seen this?" asked Johann, handing Tim a damp leaflet from the end of the sticky table.

"What?" replied Tim, half listening, before looking down at the advert. "Bell-Fest?" he said.

"They've called today Bell-Fest," confirmed Johann.

"God, this is going to be so bad, isn't it?"

"I'm sure it will be okay. Not sure who they got to design the poster, though. It looks like they got someone's kid to make it."

Tim squinted his eyes, trying to read the information. "Who would choose blue writing on a red background? It's so hard to read."

"Have you heard of any of the bands?"

"Only the headliner, and that's because Marty told me about him the other day. He had a hit many years ago."

"Who else is there?" asked Johann.

"Okay, so *Haberdashery Menagerie* are on at three-thirty. First, though, we have *Soul Sister Stallions*, and then *The Artichoke Hearts* after them, who play a mixture of blues and reggae, with a strong female lead."

"Can you mix blues and reggae?" asked Johann.

"We'll find out in an hour."

His dad came and joined the table, putting a glass of cola in front of each of them. He then opened three bags of crisps (Ready Salted, Cheese & Onion, Roast Beef) and spread them out across the table.

"Ain't got no pickled eggs yet," he said. "I was gonna bring one of those trays of peanuts over, but I don't know how long they have been there or who's been picking at them with their dirty hands."

"Crisps are fine, thanks," said Johann.

Tim passed the leaflet across to his dad. "Check this out."

He glanced through it, before sighing heavily. "It actually makes it sound like Haberdashery Menagerie will be the highlight."

"That's what I thought," said Tim. "What are you drinking?"

"Something called Bronze Pheasant. It's not bad."

"Don't they all taste the same?" asked Tim.

"Absolutely not. All slightly different. I can give you my top five if you want?" Luckily, he was interrupted before he could start his run down.

"Alright, Cam," came a voice. A man of about sixty was at the edge of the table, holding a golden bucket. He was dressed like someone who was on their way home from a round of golf, with a diamond patterned sensible jumper, and cream chinos. His grey hair was gelled into a neat side parting. Tim recognised him as Finlay, their old milkman from the days before supermarkets started diminishing the trade.

"Hi, Fin," his dad said. "Raffle time, is it?"

"Correct. It's a pound a strip, or six strips for five pounds," Finlay replied, holding out the bucket.

"Got any change on you, lads?" his dad asked.

Tim shook his head. "No one carries cash anymore."

"I don't think I've had a banknote on me in all the time living here," added Johann.

Finlay smiled. "Young Tim, I haven't seen you for, what is it? Must be nearly seven years."

"Probably." Tim replied. "What can we win in your raffle?"

"Oh, there is lots on offer today. Cash prizes, spa days, vouchers for places in town, or a meal at La Carbonara."

"Where's that?" asked Tim's dad.

"Some fancy Italian up in London. Michelin star and everything. The owner lives round here. There are also some chocolates, beer kegs, cakes and pies, a year supply of scampi fries, a table football game, some engraved tankards. Loads of stuff."

"Did they find all the prizes in the cellar?" asked Tim.

"Don't be rude, it's for charity," his dad whispered, as he pulled a small wallet from his pocket. "Six strips each please," he added whilst handing over fifteen pounds.

"What about Marty?"

"Four lots of six strips then Finlay, please," he said,

pulling another five pound note out. They waited for Finlay to pull out the required tickets, and he placed them down in the middle of the table. They were a mixture of colours. Tim was unsure if this gave them more chance of winning or not. He wasn't keen on any of the prizes except for the cash, so it didn't matter.

"Cheers, all," Finlay said as he moved to badger money off the rest of the sparse population of the pub, before turning and heading back to their table. "Forgot to ask, Cam, did you have success with that solicitor I gave you the number of? Can't have been worse than the first one you tried at the weekend."

Tim watched his dad get up and usher Finlay away from the table, discussing something with him quietly whilst glancing back to the table. "Why would dad need a solicitor?" he asked Johann.

"No idea."

"Do you think it's in case I go to court for the graffiti?"

"Nah, don't be stupid. It's probably nothing."

Tim sat and watched them talking, trying hard to overhear anything, but was stopped when Marty came through the pub, bounding past the pool table and dart board. He waved when he spotted them and skipped over to take a seat. He was wearing the usual bandana and the remaining black clothes he owned that hadn't faded to dark grey. "Alright?" he asked as he took a seat and shovelled a handful of crisps into his mouth.

"Why does dad need a solicitor?" Tim asked.

"What?"

"That man over there is talking to dad about a getting a solicitor. Why does he need one?"

"I dunno," Marty replied.

"I'm fifteen, Marty, you can tell me."

"I would if I knew, but I genuinely haven't got a

clue." Marty stood and readjusted his studded belt.

"Ask him when he's back, Marty" Johann said. "Anyway, how's the band sounding?" he added, trying to change the subject.

"Yeah, not bad thanks. We've done our soundcheck, so just have to hang around now. It's so busy," Marty said. Tim looked around and noticed that, aside from their group, there were now only four others in the pub, and that included the bartender. Marty noticed him mentally counting. "Well, most people are outside in the garden, obviously. Not sure why you have chosen to sit indoors. It's cold in here. You'll need to come and get a good seat for the gig. *Soul Sister Stallions* are on in ten minutes."

"The leaflet says they don't start for another forty-five minutes?" questioned Johann.

Marty shook his head whilst stealing some of Tim's drink. "Yeah, that's a misprint. What you get when you try and get them done on the cheap."

"Are the other bands any good?"

"Awful," Marty confirmed. Johann looked at Tim and forced a smile. Tim noticed Johann's hair was a lot longer than it had been when they first met. He can't have had it cut in over six weeks. He liked the way a bit of blonde fringe kept falling and covering one of his eyes. Marty sat back with his feet propped on another chair, watching some tennis on the television. The set was high up in one corner, and the poor signal kept causing the picture to vanish briefly.

All the crisps were nearly gone by the time Tim's dad returned. He licked his finger and pressed it into the crumbs, before putting it into his mouth. He realised after taking his seat his two sons were just staring at him.

"What?" he asked, before sipping more of his real ale.

"Why are you getting a solicitor?" asked Marty,

without hesitation. Their dad remained silent.

"Are you and Mum getting a divorce?" Tim followed up, before feeling Johann take his hand underneath the table.

There was silence again, but their dad put his pint down slowly, before taking out his phone and typing a quick message. "No, Tim, we are not getting a divorce," he sighed.

"So why do you need a solicitor? Have you murdered someone?"

"Look, just sit and listen for a minute," he said. All three boys put their drinks down and leant forward. "Now Tim, don't freak out."

"I wish everyone would stop telling me to not freak out. I'm fine."

"Okay, so we are having this baby."

"You don't need a solicitor for that," Tim replied.

"I know. Let me finish. Because of the baby, we are going to need more space, unless Marty moves out in the next four months, but that ain't gonna happen."

"It might," Marty interjected.

"Will it?"

"No."

"See. Anyway, we need more space, so our options are to build an extension, or move house."

"So, we are moving?" asked Marty.

Their dad nodded.

"Is it in Greenwood?" asked Tim. Johann squeezed Tim's hand harder. Tim didn't want to leave this town, even with the graffiti incidents.

"Look, boys, everything we do is to make things better for you both. With the new baby, we need to think of him as well."

"Him?" asked Johann.

"Look I'm flustered now. We were going to wait and

tell you everything once it was more finalised, but you may as well all know now. Yes, you are having a brother, and yes, we are moving."

"Where to?" asked Marty.

"Well, you might think we are insane, but it's time for a change. We have been speaking to a solicitor as we have made enquiries to move into the Patterson's house and take over the shop."

Tim raised himself up a little. "I told Mum to buy it the other day, but she said you couldn't."

"We agreed not to say anything until we had weighed everything up."

"Who's going to run it?" asked Marty. "Mum can't do it alone with a baby, and I ain't gonna be working in a shop full time."

"Me neither," confirmed Tim.

"I will," replied their dad.

"How will you have time?" asked Tim.

"Tomorrow, when I go to London for that meeting, it's to confirm my leaving date."

"This is a lot to take in," said Tim. "I'm not freaking out, though."

"I know, and I'm sorry," his dad said, rubbing Tim's shoulder. "We planned to talk through everything with you both, and we should have said something before. It will all work out, though."

"Isn't it a bit of a risk?" asked Marty.

"Yes, a huge one, but I've wanted to leave the navy for a while now, and the new baby proves now is the right time. Mr Patterson has said he thinks we are the best people to take over. You could be the new Mr Patterson in fifty years' time, Tim."

"And never leave Greenwood? No thanks."

"Understood. Look, just trust us, please, and don't moan about it in front of your mum. She is stressed enough as it is. Also, you'll get a bigger bedroom if we move too, remember."

Tim sat back. "That would be quite cool, if I'm honest."

A drumbeat started from the back garden. "Least this news took my mind off our gig a bit," said Marty. "We best head outside, though, sounds like the first band are getting ready to start."

Johann put a hand on Tim's thigh, holding him to allow the other two to leave first.

"I'm okay," Tim said, anticipating the question.

"Good," replied Johann, and gave Tim a hug. "At least you will probably have your paper round back."

"I've just got used to the idea of not having that. I don't know if I would actually want it back."

"That's fair. It'll be weird, all of this, but I think it'll be great."

"I don't know if I am ready to move soon, though."

"I know, I hated the idea too, but at least you aren't moving country like I did, and if I didn't move, then we wouldn't have met. Just think of the positives."

"I guess."

"Look, come and watch the bands and try to forget about it." Johann pulled his jacket tighter and put out his hand. Tim stood and took a hold as they walked out to the back garden together.

# Twenty

Marty had been right. It did seem like everyone was sat in the garden of The Bell Inn. A stage had been set up at the end of the garden, with the river running just behind it. Rather than a permanent structure, amplifiers and a makeshift screen had been put together on the back of a flatbed truck, with a set of ramshackle steps leading up to it on the left-hand side. The truck itself, and indeed any bits of scaffolding on it, had been draped in black curtains, but the words DJB Building Supplies could still be clearly seen through them at the bottom. The Pyramid stage it was not.

Tim's dad waved from the picnic table in the front row, and Johann walked Tim across to join. They were still holding hands, and previously this would be one thing that would have definitely made him freak out, but today was different. Something this week had seen his world shift. He didn't know if it was because his parents now knew, or if it was all the family information which had been forced upon him making him not care anymore. Whether he was expecting it, or if he wanted them to be or not, things were never going to be the same again. Here he was, walking hand in hand with a boy, in public, in a busy pub garden in Greenwood. This time last week he would've been a foot away from Johann, with his hands tucked defensively inside his sleeves, or arms folded across his chest.

He could feel the eyes of the crowd on him, watching

them in silence. He wasn't sure if he was at breaking point and paranoid, but when he sat down, he looked around and realised no one was taking a second glance. As the pair approached the table, Tim's dad stood up and thrust his arms in the air.

"Good news!" he said as he ushered them to sit down. "They have got pickled eggs!" he added and picked up a jar from the table, waving them as if he had just won the FA Cup.

Johann looked at Tim, who only responded with "you are trying one," and smiling. Marty shuffled up the table so that he was facing his younger brother once he had sat.

"Shame Mum couldn't make it," Tim said.

"Yeah. Remember to record some for her, won't you? I wonder if she knows Dad has told us everything?"

"He would've told her probably. Anyway, can we forget about it for a bit?"

Marty mimed zipping his mouth shut, before opening a pack of plain crisps, putting a pickled egg inside and shaking it as if he was making an edible cocktail for those with an acquired taste. He took a second egg from the jar and bit it in half. He held out the jar to Johann as he chewed.

"Do I have to?" Johann asked.

The Johnson boys nodded. "They're nice," said Marty.

Johann looked at everyone and sighed, before pulling one out of the jar. He gave it a quick sniff first before recoiling. "It stinks."

"They taste better than they smell," replied Tim. "Honestly, just take a bite and try not to think about it, and you'll enjoy it."

"Food shouldn't be a challenge to eat," he said, before smelling it again. He sat there being watched by the others in silence. He sniffed it a third time, before licking the white outside quickly. "It just tastes like vinegar."

"That's cos you're just licking the vinegar off it. Put it in your mouth!" said Marty, a bit more aggressively than intended.

Johann breathed deeply and bit off about three-quarters. He didn't say anything at first, instead slapping the table with his right hand, before making a face resembling a pug eating a lemon. "You eat these for fun?" Johann asked, wiping at his mouth with his sleeve.

"They're not for everyone, I guess," Tim's dad said as they waited for Johann to overcome the sharpness.

"They're disgusting!" Johann continued, before drinking half a pint of coke in three seconds. "Never again," he added definitively. "Even looking at the jar is making me feel a bit sick now."

Tim took the jar and put it on the end of the bench away from Johann. A crackle came from the amplifier behind Marty, causing his brother to jump. "Good afternoon, town!" came a voice through the speaker system, which was far too loud for the smallish garden. A tall, pale teenager was clutching a microphone tightly. They were wearing a ripped black t-shirt, and a green tartan style skirt. This wasn't as noticeable as their bright yellow Mohican haircut. Tim sat there wide-eyed.

"That's Em," said Marty. "They work behind the bar normally. They're at college with me, hence why we managed to get the gig."

Before Tim could reply, they were continuing. "Welcome to the first annual Bell-Fest music festival." There was some polite applause. Not the kind of reaction you get at a real rock gig, but more like the type you may hear after a village cricketer plays a shot to the boundary. "Would you welcome to the stage, your first act of the afternoon!SOUL! SISTER! STALIOOONNNNSSSSS."

The applause this time was slightly louder, with even a few 'woops' thrown in, but nothing that would even come close to expecting a mosh pit to start at any time soon. The band came on stage looking identical to each other in matching outfits of black trousers, blue polyester shirts, with a white tie, finished off by a trilby hat. It looked as if they had been dressed using the school lost property bin. Their image was far removed from bands like *Mirrorball*, who looked like a real band without even trying.

Having already been warned by Marty that they were awful, Tim wasn't prepared for just how bad. Halfway through the first track (an instrumental called *Summerstorm*), it was clear they could all play their instruments well, but a shame each band member seemed to be playing a different tune from everyone else on stage. Guitars squealed and the drums went at an ever-increasing tempo, like a tin can going hurtling down a cobbled hill. Tim's dad was the only one who seemed to be enjoying what he was hearing and was trying his best to tap his foot in time with the drummer.

"I gotta go backstage," Marty shouted across the table, putting in a pair of bright orange foam earplugs. Tim could see Shell and others from *Haberdashery Menagerie* stood in the ripped and stained square marquee that was doubling as the bands green room.

Johann tugged on Tim's sleeve, shaking his empty glass. "Drink?" he asked, standing from the table and moving back towards the pub as the band moved onto their second song, which sounded nearly identical to the first, but in a 3/4 time signature.

Tim felt guilty about walking out halfway through the first act, but his ears had taken as much punishment as they could handle from the rabble in the garden. He followed Johann at a distance, walking as close as he could to the large hedge in case that made him less visible to those on stage. Maybe it was the bad music outside, or some other yet to be discovered reason, but the pub had now filled up considerably since they had arrived less than an hour earlier. Finlay was still walking around with his bucket collecting as much raffle money as he could.

Johann told Tim to go and grab the last remaining table in the corner whilst he went to get more drinks. Tim's feet hung well above the floor as he jumped onto one of three tall chairs around the raised table. A song from the jukebox about a brown eyed girl flooded the air around his head, with each bass drumbeat causing a slight fuzzing noise to come from the old speakers. It took over five minutes for Johann to get served, and he walked back to the table slowly carrying two full glasses of lemonade.

"We can go out again when Marty is on," Tim said.

"What about *The Artichoke Hearts*?"

"Reggae and blues. Seriously?"

"Good point," laughed Johann.

The pub was full of older men now, decked out in leather jackets despite the outside heat, and over fifty per cent had shaved heads. Despite the intimidating crowd around them, Tim still allowed himself to hold Johann's hand under the table.

"I have to tell you something," Johann said after a few moments.

"You're not going away again, are you?" asked Tim.

"Not everything is bad news."

"Sorry."

"It's okay. But someone is coming to join us in a few minutes, and I hope you don't mind?"

"It depends on who it is."

Before he could get an answer, a popular song had

come on the jukebox, and every adult sang loudly, but strangely pretty much in tune. Wherever he looked, Tim could see grown men singing about wanting country roads to take them back to where they belong, which was apparently somewhere in West Virginia.

The ensemble went quiet for the verses, but soon picked up again by the chorus. Some were even doing mock country music style dancing along to the tune, complete with thumbs in their blue denim jean pockets. It seemed to last for ever. Eventually, the song faded out, and the following track was far less popular, so everyone went back to their conversations as if the previous few minutes hadn't happened at all. Tim wondered if he would ever get to the stage in his own life where he ended up singing in some kind of biker gang choir in an outdated pub. He couldn't picture himself doing so.

"So, who is coming?" asked Tim again. "And before you say it, I won't be freaking out."

"Okay, but don't be mad, alright?."

"Promise."

"It's Leo."

Tim sat back in his chair and put his hands on his head. "Why? We aren't talking."

"You will be."

"Is that a threat?" Tim half joked.

"No, trust me, it'll be fine. You miss him deep down."

Tim forced a smile. "I guess I do miss that idiot."

"See. Maybe don't call him an idiot, though," Johann replied. "He will be here in about two minutes. He wants to see Marty's band, and he has something of interest."

Tim was leant forward and drinking through a straw without using his hands to hold the glass. He almost spat out his drink when he saw his dad re-enter the pub, followed closely by PC Hughes, who was instantly recognisable despite lacking his work uniform. Tim slapped Johann on the arm whilst trying to look casual and pointed with his eyes and head in the officer's direction. "That's PC Hughes," Tim said out of the corner of his mouth. "What is he doing here? And why is he with my dad? Should we go? What if he sees the graffiti image Marty has used for the band? I'm going to be in so much trouble," Tim rattled off quickly. Johann grabbed at his hand again.

"It'll be okay. He's probably just here to enjoy the music like us. You haven't done anything wrong so stop panicking."

To his horror, the pair approached the table.

"Hello, Tim," said PC Hughes.

"Hi," he responded, nervously.

PC Hughes noticed this. "Don't be worried. I am off duty."

"I've already told him about the *Haberdashery Menagerie* logo," his dad said, knowing Tim too well to not guess what he was concerned about.

"Can happen to anyone. Just bad luck," PC Hughes said. "Would you like a pint, Cameron?" he asked.

"Yeah, go on then," he replied, before turning to the boys. "The raffle is just starting by the way. Well, the first half of it. The rest is before Marty's lot get on stage. Are you coming out or do you want me to check the tickets?"

"Um, can you check them please?" asked Tim.

His dad nodded, before both adults turned and walked to the bar.

"Should we tell him your theory?" asked Tim.

"Theory?"

"Yeah, the one where you think it was Callum as well."

"Not yet."

"Please? It would make me feel so much better. I

want to clear my name."

"Later," said Johann.

"Why not now?" begged Tim.

"Because of this." Johann stood up on the footrest of his chair and waved towards the front doors. Leo stood there smiling, carrier bag in hand.

Johann walked across and gave him a fist bump, and they had a moment talking to each other away from the table. Johann then approached alone whilst Leo queued to get a drink. "I'm going outside for the raffle," he said.

"Don't leave me with him yet," Tim said desperately.

"No, I am going to. I'll be back in a few minutes, and you two need to have a chat."

"You invited him down and said he could help the investigation?"

"He can, but we will sort that once you two have made up," Johann replied, putting his finger vertically on Tim's lips until he was sat dead still, before he took his drink and headed outside.

A few minutes later, Leo approached and put a new drink in front of Tim. "Hi," he said quietly as he put the carrier bag on the floor.

"Hello," Tim replied.

At first, they didn't know what to say to each other, and sat silently sipping lemonade over an awkward silence. "I'm sorry," Tim said eventually. Leo smiled back at him. "I mean, I don't know exactly what I did, but I'm sorry for whatever it was that upset you. I was saying to Johann I have kinda missed you."

"Only kinda?" questioned Leo.

"Figure of speech. You good?"

"I am, thanks. And I'm sorry too, for what it's worth."

"You haven't done anything, though?" said Tim.

"I shouldn't have got angry. It was just everything,"

he replied, waving his hands to gesture at all the metaphorical problems flying around his head. "Maybe I was just too excited to be near Callum, thinking that sticking with him would make me popular. I should have just stayed with you if you had concerns."

"It's okay, honestly," said Tim. "Can't change it now and you did what you thought was right at the time, so it's cool."

"Thanks. I'll still feel guilty, though. It's just all become a bit too much. Maybe Lydia's mum finding out I was bi pushed me over the edge without me realising. I was feeling down earlier this week, well, all this week. Even when I seemed okay on the outside, inside I was tearing myself apart. I tried talking to you about it, but I should have made myself clearer so you understood."

"I thought I did understand, sorry," said Tim.

"Yeah. It's okay. The thing is you are going through so much more than I am—"

"No, we both are," interjected Tim.

"Well, yeah, true, but maybe it was too much for me to expect you to take on my problems as well. Not that I don't think you would, or that you don't care, but there's sometimes too much going on in your own head there simply isn't any room for other people's problems to be stored as well. When we were on the way back from seeing Mr Patterson's shop after it was damaged, I raised it and you said you would be there for me, but I think in your head you were thinking about your name being on the shop. I tried calling you a few times like you said I could if I was feeling low, but each time you never answered. It's not your fault before you apologise again. I woulda been the same."

Leo took a sip of his drink before continuing. "I also wanted to chat to you about it before diving when we were sat around the side of the leisure centre. I had gone through what I wanted to say in my head about a million times on the way down, but then you told me your mum was pregnant and you had come out. I was trying to find the right time to change the subject, but then you accused Callum of the graffiti. I wanted to tell you, and I was angry I had listened to your problems all week, but you never asked how I was doing. I understand now this might be too much for us to sort out ourselves."

"I didn't even notice I hadn't asked you how you were, sorry. I didn't mean to ignore you like that."

"I know now you didn't. At the time, not so much."

"I promise I will ask more in future. If I ever don't ask and you need me to, you have permission to tell me."

"Me too," said Leo.

"Perhaps we should go and speak to someone together about it. I mean, Mr Barakat at school might be a good one but we ain't back there for a bit yet."

"There will be places online who can support maybe. If you want, you can come to the summerhouse at the weekend, and we can look into getting help. Mr Barakat might be at the fete, too."

"Ah yeah, probably. Shall we try and talk to him?"

Leo nodded. "I think we have to."

Tim gave a half-smile, before he held up his glass and pushed it in Leo's direction. "Friends?" he asked.

"Friends," replied Leo, and dinked his glass onto the other. "So then, what have I missed?"

"I don't even know where to start. What do you wanna hear first? That I am having a brother? How about we are moving house? Or I could tell you that Dad is retiring and we are taking over Patterson's Papers."

"All of this has happened in the last half a day?" asked Leo. Tim nodded. "Okay, let's start with your baby brother, because at least I know a bit of that already."

Tim started explaining how Johann had noticed his

dad's language slip up earlier in the afternoon when the Swede ran into the pub excitedly.

"Tim! Tim! Tim!" He said loudly, causing a few of the bikers to turn around.

"What? What? What?" mocked Tim.

"Hi, Leo. Put your hands on your ears," Johann requested.

"Why?" he replied.

"Just do it," Tim said, rolling his eyes. Leo sighed, and reluctantly put his fingers in his ears.

Johann looked at Leo. "That's fine, I guess. Tim, can I ask you something?"

"Is it going to be 'can we go home because the bands are rubbish?' or something similar?"

"No. Even though they are. But I was wondering if you wanted to go on a proper date with me?"

"You made me cover my ears for that?" said Leo. The other two looked at him until he put his fingers back in.

"So, will you?"

"Um, yeah, of course."

"Good. Tomorrow afternoon as soon as you finish work."

"Okay, great," said Tim, smiling widely. "Will I be able to come home and get changed first? I don't wanna go in my library clothes."

"Yes, but you need to dress smart."

"Where are we going?"

"Guess who won first prize in the raffle?" said Johann, waving a slip of paper around.

"Oh my god, you won the cash? That's amazing."

"Um, not quite. Cash was the second prize. But I did win the meal at La Carbonara. Look!" he said, thrusting the voucher for a meal for two into Tim's hand.

Tim looked at it and sat back. "But it's in London,

Johann," he said sadly.

"Your dad is gonna drive us. He is going to phone the Navy office in a moment and rearrange the meeting. He will drop us off, and then collect us a bit later. Turns out the restaurant is only a few streets from his work in Bloomsbury."

"That's lucky," said Tim. "Amazing, though, thank you."

"What's lucky is having you in my life," said Johann, before hugging him.

"Jeez, stop it you two," said Leo, hands now holding his drink.

"Sorry," said Tim. "I can't believe you actually won something!"

"So did your dad."

"The cash?" asked Tim.

Johann laughed. "Not quite. He won a homemade pie."

"As if we don't have enough of those at home," joked Tim.

"What makes it worse is it's one your mum donated. We should go out in a bit and sit with your dad to get ready for Marty's lot. First, though, I wanna show you something. Leo, you got the goods?"

Leo picked the carrier bag off from the floor. "I think calling it 'goods' makes it seem a bit more mafia than it is, but yeah, I have them."

Tim sat forward in his chair and watched as Leo made a display about reaching in and pulling out the object. After confirming he gwas ready, Leo pulled out a can and put it in the middle of the table.

"One can of Bristow's spray paint," said Johann, clapping his hands together.

"Where did you get it from?" asked Tim, hoping the answer was what he was expecting.

"I saw it at Callum's. Johann was asking me about it for some school project he is doing over the summer," Leo confirmed. Tim looked at Johann outside of Leo's eyeline. "So yeah, I was round Callum's house, and I was helping him film one of his football videos on his drive, using his garage doors as a goal. Anyway, the ball went into the garage, and I went to get it and saw this paint."

"So, you stole it to give to Johann for his project?"

"I'm not an idiot, Tim. But yes and no. I stole it on my way home after I knew the coast was clear. It took a bit of time to click before I did. though. We had gone to Callum's room to play on his Switch, and it suddenly hit me why Johann had been asking. So yeah, I stole it."

"Good work," said Tim.

Leo nodded. "For what it's worth, I think it is Callum now, too."

"That makes three of us," confirmed Johann. "You might want to put it away now, though, Leo. PC Hughes is here."

Leo put the can back in the bag and hid it in less than a second, knocking some lemonade across the table as he did so. Once he had completed this, Tim caught Leo up with everything that had happened.

***

*Haberdashery Menagerie* entered the stage to a loud round of applause from Tim and the others, the now empty jar of pickled eggs standing at the edge of the table. Tim was shocked to find out Marty's band were quite good live. The song formally known as *Checkout Check Out* still needed some work, but they looked like a band, and sounded like a band. If the graffiti logo wasn't present, Tim would have enjoyed it fully. A few locals got up and danced near the stage when they played a song he thought was called *Bear Bones*, but the lyrics didn't mention anything about animals (he later found out it was actually called *Bare Bones* and was written about losing your identity).

Despite cringing at the thought of the gig all week, Tim and Johann both found themselves tapping their feet along. Tim watched as his dad filmed some clips to show his mum. "Dad, you need to turn the phone so it is in landscape." Despite this, he still filmed in portrait until Marty explained it to him from the stage.

After *Insomnia*, their final song, parts of the crowd called for an encore. Tim looked at those cheering, guessing they must have been college friends, judging purely on their age and their slightly abnormal dress sense. In the centre was the waitress from Huffton's who had served them earlier that morning. She was staring longingly at Marty. As the crowd's chant for an encore grew louder, Haberdashery Menagerie obliged and finished with a cover by a band called *Status Quo* that Tim recognised from being played in the car on many journeys he had taken with his dad when younger.

Five minutes later, Marty was back at the table, his fringe sticking to his forehead with sweat. "So?" he asked them all collectively.

"It was surprisingly good," Tim replied, and gave his brother a hug, which was shaken off by an embarrassed Marty.

"Nice one," said their dad, shaking his eldest son's hand.

Marty blushed and said his thanks, before going off to bask in the post-gig glory with his bandmates and the waitress. As he left, Tim noticed the band banners being removed from the stage and hoped this would be the last time he would ever see the stupid smiling face grinning back at him. Sadly, he was soon proven wrong.

"Mind if I sit?" asked PC Hughes, a glass of water in his hand. Tim's dad gestured for him to continue. "So, about the graffiti."

"I thought you were off duty?" said Tim.

"I am." He left a pregnant pause. "You see, I have just been informed there is more."

"We've all been here this afternoon," Leo said, voice shaking.

Tim thought about the can of spray paint hidden by his feet and decided to act. "We've discovered something. We have a friend called Callum. He was at Funtangutan when you first came. His dad fixes cars and he has spray paint in his garage."

PC Hughes pulled out his notebook. "Are you sure?"

Tim nodded. "Leo took some when he was there earlier. Show him, Leo."

Leo reached under the table and pulled the carrier bag with the can up onto the table. "Where was the new graffiti?"

"On the side of the scout hut, down by the church."

"I've not been there all week," said Tim.

"He was with me," added Johann.

"Did it have my initials?"

PC Hughes nodded. "Were you with them, Leo?"

"I was at home all morning. Well, I went to Callum's but wasn't there for long. I can prove it." Leo opened his phone and showed PC Hughes the video of the football he filmed with Callum earlier in the day.

The officer took the paint can and put it back into the plastic bag. "Thank you. Now is not the right time to be asking questions, but I will be in touch later."

"Please check where Callum was," said Tim.

"Please leave us to do our job, Tim," PC Hughes responded.

Johann suddenly sat up. "Me and Tim bumped into

Callum this morning. I told him we were going to have breakfast at Dixies. That's next to the church. He's obviously trying to set Tim up."

PC Hughes shook his head. "Here and now is not the best place to speculate. As I say, I will be in touch, probably tomorrow rather than today. I actually want to enjoy my day off."

Tim's dad thanked the officer. "How do you lot fancy going to the cinema?" he asked. "I am not sure I can face any more of these bands."

"Can we go to the big one out of town and see *Beans on Ghost 2*?" asked Tim.

"If you want."

"Wanna come, Leo?" asked Johann.

Leo nodded, before finishing his remaining lemonade. At least they would be safe from trouble there.

# Twenty-One

## *Friday*

Sunlight burst through the kitchen windows as Tim poured himself a bowl of cornflakes, shielding his sleepy eyes from the light.

"Morning," said Johann croakily as he leant against the doorframe. His hair was unkempt, and he was still dressed in the clothes he had slept in. He rubbed at his face with his palms.

"Heya. Coffee?" asked Tim.

"Please." Johann moved and took a seat at the table. "I forgot to go to Mark's and ask about my paper round yesterday," he said. "I should go and see him today."

"If you're missing it, you can help me on mine if you want?"

"Nah, you're okay thanks. Anyway, I said I would help your dad with building the cot."

"I thought we were all going to do that together?" Tim said, with a tinge of sadness in his voice at the thought of missing out.

"We will," Johann responded as he walked across the room and hugged Tim. "It's just the wood needs cleaning up first, and I didn't think you'd want to help with that. I know what you're like around spiders."

Tim breathed in so he could fill his nose with Johann's scent. He didn't smell of anything specific, but it was one hundred percent a Johann aroma. Despite him having not been at his own house for a few days, Johann still smelled the same as his home had done when Tim had visited it previously. "I'll leave the cleaning to you and Dad. You two can clear the mud and all the evil beasts from it for me."

"It's not in that bad a condition. Your dad just said we need to sand it down a bit so there aren't any splinters."

"Fair." Tim moved towards the fridge, dragging Johann with him who was in a clingy mood. "If you want your coffee, you'll need to let go a minute, sorry," he added. Johann obliged.

Tim took out a four-pint carton of semi-skimmed and filled up the remainder of both mugs to the brim. "I have to head off in about ten minutes to Mr Patterson's. I'll have my phone on me if you get bored of sandpapering and want to come and join. Marty's new bike is behind the shed so feel free to take that."

"Okay, I will do. I need to unpack my suitcase properly, though, as I can't keep pulling it apart every time I want fresh clothes."

"If you find that more exciting than hanging out with me, then go ahead," joked Tim. "Did you sleep okay?" Tim's eyes were drawn immediately to the small section of stomach that appeared below Johann's pyjama top as he stretched his linked hands into the air.

"I woke a few times. Probably being in another new bed. I might have another thirty minutes before I get started. I don't want to be overtired before the fete tomorrow."

"The fete is not that exciting,"

"It is for me!" Johann said enthusiastically. "It will be my first."

"Just don't get your hopes up too high," joked Tim.

"I'll try not to. Will you be back here before going to the library today?"

"Yeah, I have about an hour in between jobs. Why?"

"Cool. I will walk to town with you. I need to get something for Hanna's birthday."

"When is it?"

"Monday. Hopefully she'll be back."

"I'm sure she will be."

Tim took his mug and sat at the table, with Johann staying by the counter and opening every cupboard. "What are you looking for?" he asked.

"Sugar," Johann grunted as he bent down to look on the lowest shelves.

"Cupboard above the microwave in the blue pot," Tim replied. He watched as Johann put four teaspoons into his coffee. "Don't your teeth feel funny having so much sugar?"

"Nope. The sweeter the better."

"Like me," Tim smiled.

"Cheesy. Are you any good at wrapping by the way?" Johann asked.

"Not really no. I sort of know some of the words to the latest *MC Baesic* song, but it's not my kinda thing."

Johann stopped and stared at him. "As in wrapping presents, not rapping music, you idiot."

"Oh," Tim replied. "Still no. Sorry."

"No worries, I'll ask your mum for help."

"How old is your sister by the way?"

"She'll be nineteen."

"Did she not want to stay in Sweden? If I was eighteen, I would have done. It would be weird to move as soon as you are an adult."

"Nah, she hated our town," Johann said as he joined Tim at the table. "Hanna is more ambitious than I am, and she wanted to settle somewhere new, have a fresh start. She is looking into doing a college course from September. It might be too late to apply so she is waiting to see what course will accept her. She wants to do some sort of computer coding."

"That's quite cool. Can't believe she'd want to swap Sweden for Greenwood, though. Nothing happens here."

"It's a change, though. And anyway, her ex-girlfriend lived down the road and it was quite a horrendous break-up, and she never wants to see her again."

"Hang on, Hanna is gay, too?"

"Bisexual," Johann said, before taking a long sip of coffee.

"Why have you not mentioned this before?"

Johann shrugged. "I've never seen it as a big deal."

"I know that, and that isn't what I mean. She could help Leo out."

"How?"

"Don't tell him I told you this, but he's struggling with it. He feels as if he isn't valid. Did Hanna feel that way, too?"

"I don't know to be honest. Her and her girlfriend were together for two years, so it might be completely different circumstances. I'll ask her though and then we can try and sort something out between them?"

"I think we should. Make a note in your phone so you won't forget."

"I won't forget," Johann said, before noting Tim was staring at him. Reluctantly, he pulled out his phone and typed a reminder on his calendar. Tim watched Johann as he started flicking through a lifestyle magazine that had been discarded on the table. There was something about seeing him in a just-woken-up state which stirred something inside. He couldn't shake it away and kept stealing glances when he knew Johann wasn't looking.

Johann drained the rest of his drink and went to wash up. Tim passed him his mug, continuing to watch as Johann splash water over the counter, before he heard him mutter something in Swedish under his breath. After drying his hands quickly on the tea towel, Johann ran his hands through Tim's greasy hair. "You've been quiet," he said. "Something is on your mind."

"It's nothing."

"Tell me," Johann replied, poking Tim on the shoulder.

"I want to kiss you," Tim said quickly. He let the words fall out of his mouth before he was able to talk himself out of it.

Johann smiled widely. "Where did that come from?"

"I honestly don't know."

"Well, I want to kiss you too, but not here."

"No one is about."

"I know, but I want it to be special. Being in your kitchen in my pyjamas doesn't feel special enough," Johann reasoned.

"I guess I can wait a little bit longer."

***

The thought of kissing Johann continued to occupy Tim's mind during the morning. This feeling had been bubbling away for a few weeks, but over the past two hours it had risen to the surface and swamped every other thought he had. He was thinking about it so much he barely remembered completing his penultimate paper round. He knew he had spoken to Mr Patterson inside the shop but couldn't remember what they had discussed. He hoped he hadn't come across as rude or distant.

He was now approaching the library doors and was praying for a more successful shift than the one on Wednesday. He looked around the edges of the building and was glad to see there was no further graffiti present. He prayed it stayed that way.

On the walk across the rivers the pair had held hands again briefly, but this was broken when Tim spotted Pat and Pet in the distance walking towards him. Town had been too busy for Tim to feel comfortable to retake Johann's hand, instead he just waved him off towards the bookshop to find a present for Hanna. In just over four hours, he would meet him back at home and prepare for their adventure to London.

Charlotte was stood on the other side of the library doors waving at him. He waved back, but she continued her movements. It was only when he got to about three metres away that he realised she had a cloth and was wiping the inside of the pane. She soon spotted him though and opened the door to allow him to enter.

"Morning, Charlotte," he said as he slipped his rucksack off into his hand.

"Hi, Tim, how are you feeling today?" she replied warmly.

"I'm well, thank you. I'm sorry about Wednesday."

She stroked his arm. "Oh, don't worry about that. Things happen. Today is a fresh start. Think of it as a first shift do-over if you like."

"I will, thanks. Do you want a coffee?"

"I am fine, thank you. Jill is already in the backroom. We have some stickering to do today you can help with when on the desk if you like?"

"Sounds great, thank you," Tim replied, even though the task sounded anything but fun. He was here to give the job a chance though and knew he had to do whatever was asked of him after letting them both down earlier in the week.

Ten minutes later he was at the counter with a large roll of green stickers. Jill had explained the library was taking part in a nationwide initiative to help get more Year Six children using their services, and they had been emailed a spreadsheet with over seven hundred books listed that were recommended for people within that age category.

When the library had opened there was a pile of books on the floor by Tim's chair which had been selected the day before, and he had been asked to put a green label around the top of the spine of each. As he was doing so, Jill would be darting around the shelves selecting more to bring to him.

Mrs Whataday was the first customer in as always. Once again, she asked who Tim was, and then requested information on a book about the history of the Aztec Empire. Tim searched the system and found it's number (972) and showed her across to the correct area.

"Mary isn't happy today," Mrs Whataday said.

"Who?" asked Tim confused.

"The ghost. She is rocking in her chair again, look," she replied, pointing to the children's corner.

He looked across and saw the chair moving slowly forward and back amongst the beanbags. A shiver ran up his spine despite him not believing in the paranormal.

As he sat back at the desk Jill noticed he had gone a bit white. "The ghost?" she asked.

"Yeah," Tim replied quietly.

"Ignore her, honestly. There is an aircon unit on the ceiling above the rocking chair that is a bit too powerful. I don't think it has worked properly ever since the library was opened."

For the next hour he helped sticker every book he had been given, sporadically taking phone calls, and greeting the odd visitor in between. Jill had headed off to lunch, whilst Charlotte hid in the office replying to emails. Alone, he wasted some quiet time reading a young adult book about an American walking some forest trail in Montana, but soon grew bored. His mind wandered again towards Johann as he stared out of the window towards the passing traffic. He didn't want to overthink it in case the first kiss was an anti-climax when it finally happened, but nothing could shift it from his thoughts. The metronome-like ticking of the clock on the wall caused him to go into a semi-trance. Tim was suddenly woken from his daydream by the library phone ringing. He sat up and picked up the receiver.

"Good afternoon, Greenwood Library, Tim speaking, how can I assist you today?" he answered, trying to come back to reality.

"Oh, good afternoon," came a weirdly husky male voice on the other end. "I am looking for a book and wondered if you may check to see if it is in stock, if you would be so kind."

"Yes certainly, Sir," Tim replied. "Do you have the name to hand, please?"

"One second." Tim heard the phone being put to one side, with the voice muttering in the background incoherently. A moment later it was back. "I am sorry about that young man, I needed to find my reading glasses to understand my own handwriting."

"That's okay," Tim answered. There was something about the voice which seemed familiar, but he couldn't quite place it. He mentally listed all the older people he knew but it didn't help. "Can I take the name of the book please?"

"Yes. It is *The Wonderful World of Britain's Sealife Centres.*"

"One moment, please," said Tim, before turning to the library computer and typing the title in. Nothing showed up in the search results, so he tried again using the keywords *Sealife* and *Wonderful.* Still no results. He picked the phone back up. "Sorry, I don't seem to have a record of that on our system. Do you have the authors name, please?"

"Certainly. It is a Mister Cecil Lion."

Tim searched the author's name but still nothing showed on his screen as a potential match. "I'm sorry, it still isn't showing on our system. Are the author and title definitely correct?"

"Oh, I am certain. It was in the Gazette yesterday. Is there anyone else who could check please?"

Tim felt a bit aggrieved he wasn't being believed, but Charlotte re-entered the library with perfect timing. She put her meal deal on a low shelf as Tim relayed the title and author to her whilst he remained on the phone, reassuring the customer it was being looked into.

"Is that definitely the title?" Charlotte asked.

"He's certain," Tim replied, covering the mouthpiece with his hand.

"And what was the author's name again?" she asked back. "Surname will do as usually the first name is just listed by the initial."

"Cecil Lion," Tim said confidently. Charlotte typed about four letters before looking back at him with a blank stare. Tim raised his eyebrows. She took a pink post-it note and passed it back to Tim waiting for it to click. He looked down at it and was none the wiser.

"Mr C Lion," she said. "A book on Sealife centres by a C Lion. I think it's a wind up, kid," she added before wandering off. At the other end of the phone Tim could hear laughing.

"Alright, mate?" asked Leo, still chuckling to himself.

"You're a knob," Tim replied. "You made me look a right twat."

"Sorry, I was bored," Leo replied. "How's work?"

"Let's just say Mr Sealion is the most interesting thing to happen today. Anyway, you shouldn't be bothering me here. I don't wanna get sacked."

"It was just this once, I promise. Ready for London?"

"I think so. I'm quite excited for the meal and to have a proper date finally."

"Are you nervous?" asked Leo.

"Nope," Tim replied confidently.

"Really?"

"Should I be?"

"No!"

"Well now you've made me think I should. Look, I'll update you later. I've got a customer in, so I best go."

"Before you go, do you have a copy of the gazette with you?"

Tim looked around, spotting a copy by the photocopier. "Yeah."

"Page three."

Tim turned over the front page, immediately drawn to the picture in the centre. A woman was stood, arms folded. Behind her was the wall of the scout hut, complete with the latest graffiti face. POLICE HUNT FOR THE GREENWOOD BANKSY screamed the headline. "The Greenwood Banksy is overselling it a little."

"Just a bit," replied Leo. "It doesn't mention you though, so that's good."

"True. I wonder if PC Hughes has seen this?"

"Probably. Anyway, just thought you should know."

"Cheers." Tim had started sweating. He didn't want today to be overshadowed by the incidents that had occurred. "Look, I have to go Leo, we have some customers. Speak laters, okay?"

"Sure. Message me."

"Bye," Tim replied hanging up. There were no customers, but he needed an excuse to get rid of his friend so he could focus, realising after he probably could have somehow mentioned Johann's sister.

After stickering books for two more hours, he took

two bourbon creams as he threw his bag on, agreeing with Charlotte he would be back on the following Wednesday. It was time for him to head to London for the first time.

# Twenty-Two

Tim blinked as he came out of Russell Square underground station and caught his first glimpse of the capital. His thighs were burning after having climbed the one hundred and seventy-five steps to the street level from the platform. It had just past four o'clock and, although the tall buildings were shading any direct sunlight, the heat was stifling. It was as if the air in London had not moved for hours. Johann exited the station shortly afterwards, clanking one of Tim's dads large suitcase up every step. They were filled with the uniform and equipment he would no longer need now his sea days were coming to an end.

"How far is it to your office?" Johann asked between deep breaths, as he sat on the case.

"Literally five minutes," he replied. "It's on Handel Street, which is just on the right up there," he added, pointing to a road directly opposite their position.

Tim was leaning back against the red tiles of the station walls. They had been driven to Uxbridge, before parking up and getting on the Piccadilly Line into central London. His ears were still ringing from the unbearable noise inside the carriages, and he was sweating through his blue cotton shirt from the humidity of the tunnels. He would have worn shorts instead of his school trousers if he was sure there would be a space to change into his date clothes.

Johann had booked at table at La Carbonara for five

thirty to allow them time to explore the local area before they needed to be seated. The plan was to drag the suitcases to his dad's offices, and then walk to a café somewhere to relax before their booking. Tim assumed there must be many cafés on every street here, unlike back in Greenwood. He wanted to try a locally run one rather than a generic chain, like he had seen in family films set in the capital.

Despite his aching legs, Tim took the suitcase from Johann and set off alongside his dad down a quiet street before they cut through a community garden leading directly to the outside of the imposing Naval offices. Not having the required security clearance meant this was as far as Tim and Johann could go.

Tim's dad relived the boys of the luggage. "I'll stay local after the meeting," he said. "When you are ready, or if you need me, give me a call, okay?"

"Shall do," said Tim, giving a wave towards him as he showed his ID to a security guard near the entrance.

"London is exciting!" Johann said excitedly as he grabbed Tim's arm and started walking down a tree lined road, black bricked town houses flanking them on both sides.

"It's crazy," Tim replied. "Everything is just so big here. And there's a lot more traffic. In fact, there are more tourist buses here than there are cars in Greenwood," said Tim, as they watched the top deck of another pass above the bushes on the edge of the gardens. "I don't think I would want to live here."

"You've only been here five minutes, give it a chance."

"Nah, it's way too busy for me."

"I've always liked the idea of city living myself," said Johann. "In a different universe I might be living in Stockholm or Gothenburg."

"Well, I am glad you aren't still in Sweden," Tim replied.

"Me too," said Johann, taking Tim's hand. Tim felt more comfortable knowing there was no chance of them seeing anyone they knew. His shoulders relaxed immediately.

"Do you believe in all that? Like, the universe?" asked Johann.

"It depends on what you mean. If you are asking if I believe in stars and galaxies, then yes, obviously. If you mean do I believe the universe decides our life for us, then I'm not so sure. Horoscopes are a load of nonsense if you ask me, though. Do you?"

"Not horoscopes, no," said Johann. "It is weird though how things sometimes work out. Do you ever think back to how you ended up in a certain time and place?"

"Not really."

"Think about it. We are right here, right now. We only came here because we have a meal booked."

Tim furrowed his eyebrows. "Right."

"Let me explain," replied Johann, spinning so he was facing Tim, taking hold of both of his hands. "We are here for a meal. We have the meal because I won the raffle. I won the raffle because we went to The Bell to watch *Haberdashery Menagerie*. *Haberdashery Menagerie* started because Marty went to college and met Shell in the canteen. Shell might have only been in the canteen because she had decided not to take any lunch with her from home. If you think about it, we are on this street because someone completely unconnected didn't make a sandwich three months ago."

"When you put it like that, it does sound quite crazy," said Tim. "But if that didn't happen, then something equally as good might have happened?"

"Maybe, maybe not. It works with any situation as well. Every situation you are in can be traced back to a completely unrelated event in the past. This is why you should never blame yourself if you feel as if you have done something stupid. Blame the universe for putting you in that place instead."

Tim smiled. Weirdly Johann's viewpoint made sense, and he now believed he had a reason for why he always ended up in embarrassing situations, as well as feeling extremely thankful for Shell and her laziness to prepare lunch. "It is a nice way of looking at life, I guess," he concluded.

Johann retook his hand, and started to set off, stopping to read every blue plaque he saw.

"We should probably look at a map before we get lost," Tim said as he dug around his pockets for his phone.

"It is okay. I know where we are going," Johann replied, pulling him further along the street, tripping over the broom of a street cleaner, who mumbled something as he picked it up off the paving slabs.

"Are you sure you know where you're going?" Tim said after apologising to the cleaner.

"I have a surprise for you," Johann said, attempting to drag Tim along faster. "You don't have to be so nervous," he added, noticing Tim was looking at him with narrowed eyes. "Follow me, it is only a few minutes' walk."

Tim allowed himself to be led, wondering where he was being taken to. They reached a street named Lamb's Conduit, which he thought was a strange name for somewhere. It was a narrow semi-pedestrianised street but remained quiet from both traffic and people. He stared through the ground floor windows, catching glimpses of grand fireplaces and well stocked bookshelves. Many even had chandeliers that probably cost as much as the Johnson house alone.

"Here we are!" Johann exclaimed as he stopped on the edge of a quiet junction. A small independent coffee shop was sat straddling the corner. The tables outside were occupied by well-dressed people, sat in the shade under its yellow awning.

"Is the coffee shop the surprise?" asked Tim.

"No. Inside is your surprise. Come."

Tim followed Johann into the café, decorated with wooden furniture and a large selection of house plants. There were only three tables, with a raised bar area along the right-hand wall. The place was quiet, with only one customer indoors, a balding person that Tim would place in their mid-thirties. Tim caught their eye as the door clicked shut and was shocked when the customer waved enthusiastically at him. He had no idea who they were. As Tim stood trying to work it out, Johann had already moved across and was giving them a hug.

"Come sit down, Tim," said the unknown figure.

Tim shuffled across and took a seat next to Johann. A puzzled look remained on his face.

"Come dear, it looks like you have seen a ghost," they laughed. "I suppose I do look slightly different out of my drag outfit, though."

The penny dropped. "Honey Latté?" asked Tim.

"The very same, the very same. Although this is my 'Daniel' outfit. I am unsure if my full dress and heels combination would be suitable on those cobbles outside. I heard a rumour you would be here today," Honey said.

"How?" asked Tim.

"This one here messaged me," Honey replied, pointing towards Johann.

"I didn't know you had each other's number?" Tim questioned.

"Oh, we don't," replied Johann.

"He contacted me via my agent through my Instagram," confirmed Honey. "Well, I say agent. It's actually just my flatmate, Vittoria, but he's far more organised than I am so I allow him to sort my diary. He is much more accustomed to sniffing out bullshit too, if you pardon my Français. But yes, I got the message, and as I don't have to be down the Royal Vauxhall Tavern until seven, seeing you both seemed like too good of an opportunity to miss."

"It's good to see you, genuinely," said Tim. "I enjoyed meeting you in Greenwood. I think things are getting better for me because of seeing you perform. It made me feel better about myself."

"I am glad to hear. That is my purpose in life." Honey took out a black fan, the words *Bitch, please* emblazoned across it when fully extended, and started to fan their face. "So, what's new? Are you two…." they tailed off, as they waved their finger back and forth between the boys.

"Together? No!" said Tim quickly, before remembering this was a safe audience. "Sorry, what I mean is we aren't but, we sort of are a little bit." He felt himself blush as he stumbled over his words.

"Unofficially official," added Johann, as he looked up from the paper drinks menu.

"I see," said Honey as they took a long sip of an iced coffee through a straw. When Johann was back studying the menu, Tim watched as they mouthed "He isn't your boyfriend yet?" in his direction. Tim shook his head. "What have I missed, then?" they added out loud.

Tim filled Honey in on all the events that had happened since their cabaret night at the Greenwood Snooker Club in July. Johann had stood to order drinks as he allowed Tim to explain.

Honey sat back and listened intently, nodding in all the right places. "You seem much more comfortable with yourself," they concluded.

"I am, I think," said Tim.

"And how does that make you feel?"

Tim realised this was starting to sound like a therapy session, or at least a subtle intervention. Maybe Johann had planned this to get him to speak his mind a bit more. "I guess I feel okay about everything. Things have moved on so fast, though, and I've not spent time to think or take it all in. I am worried more people finding out I am gay could be a bad thing. There's this kid called Campbell in my year who is homophobic, and I'm scared others will be the same."

"Remember one thing, Tim. Campbell does not own you. He has no power over you anymore. No one has power over you."

"It feels like they do sometimes, though. I wish I could just go back to when things were easier."

Honey let out a large *ha!* noise. "Don't ever wish yourself to regress, darling. Things move on, and you must move on with them, even if you don't feel as if you are ready. Longing for the past, though, can be common. You are experiencing grief," said Honey.

"Am I? It's not like anyone has died," replied Tim.

"Grief isn't an emotion reserved solely for the death of someone you love, Tim. You can grieve for the loss of anything."

"But I don't want to feel grief. It feels wrong when there are people with more serious problems than I have myself, real problems, you know?"

"Even so," said Honey, between noisy slurps as they finished their drink. "Grief isn't an emotion that can have gatekeepers. Same as any other emotion. That's like saying you can't be happy because other people are happier, isn't it? Also, you can't control it. You have done so much growing up this summer, and part of you may be grieving your past self, even if that past was only a matter of weeks ago. Since we last met, you have had big changes in terms of your work and your family, and all this graffiti nonsense has been thrown in on top. You have been made to grow up quickly, and none of what has happened can be put back into a box and hidden under your bed."

"I guess. I do feel guilty, though, maybe a bit selfish too?"

"Why? It is no different to joy, or sadness. Even envy and jealousy, too. Emotions are messed up. They sneak up on you unexpectedly, sometimes when you are feeling completely different seconds before. Whether you want to feel a particular emotion is an entirely different story. You are like a pebble on the beach, with the waves representing every known human emotion there is. You sit there, often in the sunshine, and a wave comes at you quickly and overwhelms you. The important thing to remember is this wave will retreat, and a new wave will wash over you."

"Did you ever feel like this?" asked Tim.

Honey nodded as they played with their straw, swirling amongst the ice in the bottom of their plastic cup. "Too many times. I will in the future too, no doubt."

"Is there a way to stop feeling guilty?" Tim asked, as Johann returned with two Strawberry Frappuccino's.

"Everyone's different but try to think of the positives. You may no longer be the old Tim, but the new Tim has so much to look forward to." Honey sat forward, leaning closer to Tim, so close he could smell the fruit on their breath. "For a start, this wonderful boy is in your life," they said, pointing at Johann, who smiled widely in return. "Also, everyone else in your school year will be battling their own emotions as well, so they probably feel the same as you do about moving on. At the end of the day, no one cares as much as you think they do. Just treat people kindly like you always do, and they will support you in return. The ones who criticise are likely to be those who are the most scared of change. They hold themselves back and try to bring everyone back to where they are stood. They fear seeing people blossom."

Johann passed the drink across, before weighing in. "There's this kid called Callum. We think he is the one who has been doing the graffiti, but he's so well liked everyone will probably take his side. We aren't as popular as he is."

Honey held one hand of each of the boys. "Please excuse my directness, but what you just said was a load of crap."

"It's true," Tim replied.

"Not a chance," they said, shaking their head. "All social media followings are fake. No matter who you are, when you open Instagram and those apps, you will always see someone displaying something you long for. There will always be someone younger, someone better looking, someone with a better body, someone going on better holidays. The pictures are just a front for all the loneliness and grief they have themselves but are too afraid to show. We all want to be richer and better looking, every one of us. It's why so many beautiful celebrities end up botoxed up to the bollocks. The real person is hidden."

Johann nodded, stroking Tim's thigh with his free hand.

"When I hit thirty," Honey continued, "I used to wish the world was so connected when I was a teenager.

Social media opens you up to a world where you can find likeminded people, helping you to discover yourself and not feel so alone at the times you need it. On the other side of the coin, though, I am now thankful smartphones were not around when I was your age. It used to be that school was where the popularity contests took place, but once the final bell went, you could escape. These days, though? Never. You no longer have to try and fake your popularity between nine and three, Monday to Friday. You are pressured into keeping up appearances twenty-four seven. Its knackering for me and I've been dealing with hecklers for twenty years, but at least I can see them. For kids these days it must be downright exhausting. My simple advice is, if you ever look at someone online and wish you had what they had, be thankful you have something they don't, whatever that may be. Also, if anyone tries to tell you otherwise, promise me you will stand up for yourself, okay?"

Tim squeezed their hand. "I promise." He found himself wishing Honey Latté lived closer so they could guide him through life, providing snippets of advice whenever he needed them, like his own personal guardian angel. "Is it okay if I take your number, please?" he asked.

"As long as this one doesn't get jealous," they replied, ruffling Johann's hair, before handing a glittery business card across from inside their denim shirt pocket.

When Tim returned to the table after a quick toilet break, Honey was stuffing a large collection of make-up back into a holdall.

"Have you had a busy summer?" Johann asked Honey.

"Very. It's better to be busy than sat on your backside at home, though. Me and the girls who I perform with were on a float for the pride parade. It was great fun, but it did leave me with a sunburn line where my wig had rested."

"I'd love to go to a pride one day," said Tim.

"Oh, you should," Honey replied. "They are great fun. All likeminded people together in one place. You should come to the one in London next year. There will be lots of events you can enjoy."

"Sounds amazing," said Johann.

"It's a shame Greenwood doesn't have a Pride," said Tim.

"It needs someone like you two to organise one," Honey said.

"Maybe next year," replied Tim. He would think about it for sure.

"Look, I have to shoot off in a moment," Honey added as they poured the contents of a small silver bag onto the table. "Phew, I nearly had a panic attack thinking I had left my housekeys somewhere. It's all good, though. You can see why I let Vittoria organise my life for me. How long until your Italiano?"

"About half an hour. We will start walking across shortly," said Johann.

"Do you know where it is?" asked Tim.

"Not too far. A few streets at most," he confirmed.

"In that case I shall leave you two lovebirds to it," Honey said as they slipped on a light golden jacket. "Have fun, and let me know how it goes," they added, speaking directly to Johann. "Right, until next time!" Honey stood from the table and heaved their bag over their shoulder. and gave Johann a hug. As they hugged Tim, Honey whispered into his ear. "Remember, no one has power over you."

"Walk and drink?" Johann asked once they were alone.

"Let's do it," replied Tim, feeling as if his perspective

on life had been reset.

# Twenty-Three

La Carbonara was only a ten-minute walk away from the café. Tim and Johann had wandered in the direction of the Italian restaurant slowly, finishing their drinks en route. They took some time to sit on a bench along a quiet backroad, away from the heavy traffic of the main roads in the Bloomsbury area discussing the fete whilst they watched an elderly lady feed pigeons with crumbs from the bottom of a bag of bread.

"Thanks for asking Honey to meet us," Tim said. He meant it, too. Honey Latté had experience of all the confusion that comes your way when you are a gay teenager in a conservative area. Their outlook on life always seemed to be positive, and Tim felt a lot calmer having spoken to them this afternoon. One thing was certain: He needed Johann. He couldn't picture life without Johann in it, and never wanted to repeat the time he was alone earlier in the week.

He would always have Lydia and Leo, but life would pull their friendship apart at times. In the next few years, it would be likely one or all of them could be attending university, based in different towns or cities across the country.

The moment this time came would be the final page in the current volume of his life. There was no doubt they would always remain friends, but new relationships would form with a new circle of people at their universities, so it would become rarer for it to just be the three of them. Tim guessed he was the catalyst of this shift in dynamic, though. He had brought Johann into the group, and now they were becoming closer, the change had already started. Callum was proof that new people did not always mean positive outcomes.

At the beginning of the week, when he had learnt Mr Patterson would be closing the newsagents, Tim had been fearful of change. Sometimes, though, he now realised change was often a risk worth embracing.

"Here we are," said Johann as they approached a junction. La Carbonara sat opposite on the edge of the quiet backroad. It was a small corner building with a deep blue exterior. Fake red, white, and green flowers adorned the entrance. As they opened the door from the street, a waiter in a dark waistcoat was already holding the interior door wide open, a small white towel draped over his left forearm. His black hair was styled slickly back, with the ends curling out slightly at the back of his head. He smiled warmly and looked at Tim and Johann with bright white eyes.

"Good evening," he said in a strong Welsh accent, which shocked Tim. He had assumed he would be Italian. He allowed Johann to take control.

"Hello. We have a booking for two, under the name Johannson," Johann said calmly.

"Not a problem at all," the waiter replied, sliding his finger down the page of a reservation book. He made a few clicking sounds with his tongue, before jabbing at the page. "Ah, yes, right. Here we are now!" he said. "You are the lucky winners of a voucher, I hear."

"That's correct, yes," confirmed Johann.

"Marvellous. We have your table ready for you. Please do follow me."

They stepped inside to the main restaurant. The air was filled with the scent of tomato and herbs, and it was accompanied by the clatter of pans and a wave of heat flowing out of the open kitchen, which sat in the centre of the restaurant. Tim was transfixed watching multiple chefs stirring dishes and shaping dough. An open fire pizza oven stood to the side, its chimney heading up through a pipe into the ceiling. Even though it was barely early evening, most tables were full. There were many other couples dining, but also larger groups of people sat celebrating various events. Tim eyed them all up as they passed them by, certain he recognised one rotund man as the presenter of an early evening BBC food programme.

The waiter led them to another door which sat at the foot of a staircase that was seemingly too large to be located in an establishment of this size. The waiter looked back and smiled as he pulled the gold door handle. It opened into a small room.

"Please," the waiter said as he opened the door, revealing a small room furnished with just a single table in the centre. Johann walked first, with Tim just behind, feeling his mobile vibrate in his trouser pocket. He fumbled and declined the call without looking. He repeated this twice more before taking a seat. Light jazz music played over the speakers, hidden amongst the decoration of the softly lit room.

The waiter pulled a box of matches from his pocket, striking one to light the tall white candle in the middle of the table, doubling the illumination of the room. "Welcome to La Carbonara," he said, as he placed an envelope in front of them. "We are a family run restaurant and have been in these premises since nineteen fifty-four. My name is Francesco, and I shall be looking after you this evening. Before the inevitable question, I was born in a town named Sapri, which is in southern Italy, but I was schooled in Swansea, Wales. The restaurant was founded by my great uncle Niccola. He moved to London with his British wife, however before doing so, he had run our sister restaurant in our hometown for a decade. They live close to you both in Greenwood now."

Tim was impressed. The service here was already above and beyond all the times he had visited Freddie's Diner combined.

"As for your meal today, we have the handpicked six-course tasting menu for you to try. Some of the items will be familiar, no doubt, but we hope others may push you out of your comfort zone, allowing you to try authentic Italian cuisine that you may not stumble across ordinarily. The envelope contains all of the information you will need. Please refer to the postcard designed for each course. I shall bring you some lemon water, along with the first course. I, and my whole family, wish you a pleasant evening dining with us. I will be back now, in a minute," he said grinning as he backed out of the room slowly, in a semi-bow.

"This is fancy," Tim said to Johann once they were alone.

"Very," Johann agreed, looking at their surroundings. A bookcase containing leather-bound books stood on one side, with a large (now disused) fireplace on the opposite wall. A bay window gave a view to the outside world.

"Have you ever eaten anywhere like this before?" Tim asked.

"I have been to places with my family, but nothing on this scale."

"I feel I should have dressed a bit smarter," said Tim, wiping at a small stain on his sleeve.

"You look great, honestly," said Johann, holding out his hand across the table. Tim leant across and took hold of it, rubbing Johann's fingers with his own. "In fact,"

Johann continued, before being interrupted by Francesco wheeling a trolley into the room backwards.

"Course one," he said, as he placed two covered silver dishes onto the table. "Water?"

The pair nodded and waited silently as their glasses were filled halfway. "I shall be back in five minutes with your second course."

"They don't give you much time to eat, do they?" said Tim once the waiter had departed. He took a large gulp of water, almost choking when he realised too late it was sparkling. The bubbles bounced down his throat as he tried to regain his breath.

"We best start then," said Johann, pulling at the envelope and pulling out a postcard. "So, this is Pane Pugliese. It's a type of bread that originated in Turkey and is served with salted butter."

The boys removed the plate coverings and saw two slices of bread on their plate, with a heart-shaped lump of butter on the side. Tim felt his mobile ringing again, so repeated the earlier action and stopped it. Johann then had to follow suit.

"I am not letting the next hour get ruined by someone talking rubbish down the phone," said Johann, as he placed his phone under his chair.

"Agreed," Tim concurred.

They were halfway through their second slice of bread when the next course was brought through. "Your turn to read," said Johann, pushing the envelope towards Tim.

He picked it up and chuckled. "Italian Wedding Soup," he said. "They are going with the romantic theme here, aren't they?" he added. Before Johann could answer, he continued with the description. "This isn't served at weddings, traditionally. It contains meatballs which are wedded to herbs, vegetables, and small bits of pasta. Sounds good." Tim dipped his remaining bread in, not realising how warm the soup was. Johann had started saying something, but Tim was too busy flapping at his mouth to listen. He downed three large gulps of water to cool himself, trying his best not to burp in Johann's face. He felt his phone ringing again. This time he left it to ring out, before feeling a buzz a few seconds after, which he assumed to be a message. Whatever, and whoever, it was, was not urgent enough for him to want to answer during the date.

After a third course of a green bean salad, the pair were brought creamy chicken with tagliatelle, topped with herbs. The sauce was so rich, much nicer than the value tinned variety his mum always bought.

"How is your mum's dance routine coming along?" asked Johann.

Tim shook his head. "I have tried not to think about that. I hope no one sees it."

"I'll be watching," confirmed Johann.

"As long as you promise never to tell anyone about it, ever," Tim replied whilst waving a silver spoon in his direction.

"I won't. Anyway, are you enjoying your chicken?" questioned Johann.

Tim nodded as he chewed and swallowed. "It's actually incredible."

"It is, isn't it?" replied Johann as he cut another slice of breast off. "Back home, there is this film called *Tillsammans*, I am assuming you haven't heard of it?" Tim shook his head. Johann put his cutlery down. "It is about these two strangers who are thrown together because of a massive rainstorm. A ship is unable to leave port, so the main character is forced to spend time in a small town where he doesn't know anyone. There is a strange chain of events, and he ends up having to hide from the rain in a doorway, trapped with another man. They only could meet because of them being in the same place at the same time when the storm started. The two men get talking, and realise they have a lot in common, like being shunned by their families, and being on a mission to discover their true selves. From that moment, they realise they were destined for each other, and a romance develops between them. It was like the universe decided to bring them together."

"Sounds cute," Tim replied.

"It is. I watched it every day for like two weeks last Christmas when the snow was bad back home. I will show it you one day but would need to find a copy with English subtitles."

"That would be quicker than me learning Swedish," said Tim.

"Definitely. Anyway, there is a scene where they are eating a chicken and pasta dish in a restaurant, and the main character has this speech prepared. It's about how fate picks you up and puts you in the perfect place at the perfect time."

"If only life was that simple," said Tim as he scrapped the last of the sauce from his plate.

"Tim, listen," Johann continued, before the buzzing of Tim's mobile restarted.

"I won't answer," Tim said as he took the phone out his pocket. Four missed calls from Leo. One from Lydia. He swiped it onto 'Do Not Disturb' mode and put it on the floor. "Sorry," he said as he sat back upright. "What were you saying?"

"I'll tell you in a bit," said Johann, topping up their glasses.

The penultimate course was Tuscan Chicken Liver Crostini and was Tim's least favourite of the five dishes so far. He ate a quarter of it but moved the rest around so it looked like he had eaten more than he actually had. Johann only managed slightly more. Tim had never been a fan of any paté, but the thick coarse offering in front of him was somehow the worst he had tasted, like eating slightly damp meaty mud. Luckily, the dessert of homemade ice cream balanced this out.

"I was asked when booking what flavour ice cream I would prefer," said Johann. "I went with chocolate. I thought I would play it safe."

"A very good choice," replied Tim. "It's so creamy." It genuinely was one of the best ice creams Tim had ever had and was gone in no time.

Francesco came back to the room and cleared the plates away, putting complimentary mints on the table for them both. "How did you find your courses?" he asked.

"It might have been the best thing I have ever eaten," said Johann.

"I wish your restaurant was closer so we could come all the time," added Tim, to which the waiter laughed.

"Seriously," Johann reiterated. "It was incredible."

"Thank you very much, from both me and my entire family. Please do leave us a favourable review."

"We will for sure," said Tim.

Once Francesco had removed the glasses, Tim and Johann were walked back to the front door. They thanked him again and stepped out into the street. Warm summer rain had started to fall. It was slow, but the droplets heavy. Johann pulled his jacket over his head and started jogging down a side street. "Come on!" he shouted as he spun around, water marks splattering his coat.

Tim was about to follow him, but his mobile rang as soon as he had taken it off from Do Not Disturb. It was Leo again. "Hey Leo, sorry, I can't talk now. I have been at the meal with Johann. It was so good, honestly, like—"

"Tim, stop and listen," Leo said.

"What is it? Is everything okay?"

"It's all over."

"What is?" asked Tim.

"The graffiti. We were right. You were right."

"Callum?" asked Tim cautiously.

"I am sorry I ever doubted you. I will fill you in when you're back home. Just know, though, it has all been sorted. Enjoy London."

"I could cry," said Tim.

"Well don't, you'll worry Johann."

"I'll try not to," said Tim, laughing with relief. "Look, I'll be back late tonight. Wanna come on my final paper round tomorrow morning and tell me about it?"

"Sorry, can't. Been told I'm helping unload stuff at the fete. I'll meet you on the school field before it starts, though. I'll buy you a choc ice to celebrate or something."

"Awesome and thank you. I'll message later."

"In a bit."

"Laters, Leo."

Tim put his phone back in his pocket, trying to take the news in fully. He wanted to know what had happened to make Leo so sure the ordeal had come to an end. The relief he felt meant he hadn't realised the rain had got heavier and the patter of water hitting the leafy trees around him was growing louder. He could see Johann further down the street, hiding from the weather in a small alcove, so skipped to join him. As he dived under the cover near a fire exit door, he turned to Johann. "Guess what!" he said.

"Lydia sent me a message. I am so glad it's over."

"Me too," said Tim.

"And I am glad you might never have to pretend to like Callum again."

"Not as glad as I am," Tim replied. "I can't wait to tell Dad. Let's hope this rain stops soon, though. I will call him in a bit to let him know we are on our way."

"Wait for a minute," said Johann, holding Tim still, before turning him so they were face to face. "Tillsammans," he added.

"The film?" asked Tim.

"Yes. Kind of. Look, I need to tell you something," said Johann. Tim looked at him, not blinking. "I know everyone says this to you, but don't freak out. And before you ask, no I am not going anywhere this time." He moved so he was holding both of Tim's hands. "I've been needing to tell you something all week. Like, I was trying to tell you at the gig, but it was too busy, and then I tried again in the restaurant, but things kept happening just at the wrong moment, so I am going to say it all now quickly because you need to know." He took a deep breath and looked directly into Tim's eyes.

"Tim, I love you. I love everything about you. I have wanted to tell you so for ages but needed to wait for the perfect moment. When I phoned La Carbonara to make the booking, I chose the menu, except for the paté, that one wasn't me. But I wanted you to feel you were cared for. I know how this summer has been, what with the graffiti, the paper round, and both of us having to do things with our families that kept us apart from each other. The butter in the shape of a heart? That was my request. The Wedding Soup, also me."

Johann wiped a tear away from Tim's eyes, who for once was not nervously answering or saying anything. Tim stood waiting to hear everything Johann was telling him.

"I wanted it to be the most romantic meal you had ever had, and I think I did quite well." Tim nodded, still silent. "I mentioned the film because a thought struck me when I was watching it last week. Those characters are us. They were bought together by fate, and I think we have been too, even if neither of us believe in that fully. All those small moments we spoke about before have led towards me and you sharing the same space and I am so glad we are here, both of us, sharing these moments. Just like the film, we are now stuck in a doorway because of bad weather. It is almost too perfect. I don't know what the future will hold for us both going forward, but whatever has been behind everything until now has done a pretty good job so far, so I am throwing all my trust onto it to do the same in our future. I just need you to know leaving Sweden was hard, but now I know I was forced to leave my home country just to make sure I met you, leaving was the best thing that could have happened. You're the best thing that could have happened. I love you Tim, and I genuinely believe I always will."

Tim couldn't find the words to respond. He just held onto Johann's hands tightly, choking back the tears that were on the edge of bursting out.

"Tillsammans," Johann said again. "Do you know what that means?" Tim shook his head. "It means together." Johann moved his hands up and held both of Tim's cheeks. "I love you, Tim Johnson."

Tim took some deep breaths, unable to believe this moment was happening to an awkward kid like him. He held onto Johann's waist. "I love you too, Johann. I always have loved you. I wish fate had brought you to me sooner, so I didn't have to wait to love you."

Johann burst into a wide smile and Tim watched as a tear ran down his left cheek. "Can I kiss you now?" Tim asked. Johann smiled and nodded silently.

Everything around them melted away as their lips touched for the first time. They could have been stood anywhere, at any time, and in any weather. All that was important was they were right here, right now, together.

# Twenty-Four

## *Saturday*

Even after spending some time to reflect, Tim did not feel the sadness he had expected as he entered Patterson's Papers as a paper boy for the last time. "Hello?" he called out to the empty shop as he looked at all the bare fixtures and fittings.

Leo's dad had once said time is like a river, and you can't stop it from flowing forward from your own personal boat. Tim realised now he was travelling much faster than he had ever realised but getting closer to the sea meant getting closer to the freedom of being an adult. He would do his best to slow it where he could so he could enjoy the view.

He thought back to when he was younger, to the time where he told his dad he never wanted to grow up. At that time, he would have been happy staying in his class in the Lower Juniors, before going home to watch cartoons and play on his PS4 every single day.

"Heya," came a voice from behind. Tim turned and saw Johann enter the newsagents. "How are you feeling?" Johann asked as he came and gave Tim a hug.

"This feels so weird, but good weird," Tim replied close to his ear. "Thanks for coming."

"That's alright," replied Johann, before adding, "I went to see Mark today about my round."

"What did he say?" asked Tim.

"My days of being a paper boy are also done. He

replaced me whilst I was away."

"That sucks."

"Not at all. I'm quite glad," replied Johann. "Anyway, this means we can start hanging out earlier each day for the rest of summer."

"Tillsammans," said Tim, finding himself smiling again.

"Tillsammans. When we get home we have something to show you."

"What is it?"

"It is a surprise. But—"

"Don't freak out?"

"I won't."

"Good. Hey, Mr Patterson."

Tim turned and saw his boss walking from the backroom carrying a box.

"Hi Tim, hi Johann," Mr Patterson said as he put the box next to Tim, offering a handshake, which he immediately accepted. "So, this is it, then."

Tim nodded. "This feels weird."

"Life must go on. One day this could all be yours."

"Mum and Dad won't tell me anything yet. Can you?"

Mr Patterson laughed. "These things take time. We will get there, though. Now, before you go, I want you to have this." He picked the box up and handed it across.

Tim slowly lifted the lid open, pulling out a wad of tissue paper. There was a clanging on the floor. Tim looked down to see a long bronze key on the tiles. "What is this?" he asked as he picked it up.

"Follow me," Mr Patterson said, locking the front door before leading them through the cold brick corridor towards the back of the property. He opened the stiff wooden door at the end, and sunlight flooded in from the garden. "See that there?" he said, pointing to a small square white bricked building. "That is my old workshop."

"What do you use it for?"

"Oh, just when I have to fix things," Mr Patterson said, as he strolled down the garden path. "I haven't used it for a while now, and never will need to ever again. It used to be a place where I could switch off from all the stress. My own little private sanctuary. That key you have will open the door."

"Is this in case you lose yours?" asked Tim.

Mr Patterson shook his head. "This is yours now." He watched Tim as his mouth dropped open. "Honestly. I don't need it any longer and, after all that has happened, I think you should be the next person to inherit it."

"Thank you so much!" Tim shouted, as he slipped the key into the lock. The hinges squeaked as he pulled it open. It was empty inside, aside from two sets of shelves on either side wall, but he could already imagine how he would utilise the space. He could use it as a hangout with the others, maybe seeing if he could get hold of an old sofa and a kettle. He picked up a cloth and swiped some cobwebs from the window, before turning back to Mr Patterson. "What happens when you move out, though?"

"If everything goes to plan, it will be your family moving here, so there is no point worrying about that for now. I will tell your parents I want you to have this space as your own little sanctuary before they have any ideas to turn it into a playroom for your new brother."

"Or before Marty sees it and wants it for band rehearsals," added Johann.

"Indeed," Mr Patterson agreed. "It isn't soundproof anyway so I don't think Mrs Huggins next door would be too happy with a band in here."

"Thank you again," Tim said. "And not just for this, but for everything you have done for me these last three years."

Mr Patterson walked across and pulled Tim into a hug. "Just always remember me won't you?"

"I will," Tim said. There would never be a chance he would forget him.

***

Tim entered the front room carrying a slice of pie whilst Johann showered upstairs. He took a seat and played with the key that was now attached to his string necklace. He had not got fully comfortable before his dad entered, walking up to a bedsheet covered object with an electronic screwdriver in his hands.

"Heya," his dad said whilst picking up bits of dirt from the frayed white rug behind the armchair. "We are heading to the school at about ten if you want a lift?"

"I might walk if that's okay. We are gonna catch up with Leo so will leave a little earlier."

"No problem. I'll text when we arrive so you can help unload all the pumpkins."

"Can't wait," Tim replied whilst chewing.

"The quicker we unload the quicker we can forget about them. Have you spoke to PC Hughes at all by the way?"

"No. Has he been round?"

His dad shook his head. "All we have heard is it has come to a conclusion. I guess we will have to wait to find out exactly what happened."

"I'm just glad it's all over. Where's Mum, by the way?"

"Upstairs. She's probably trying on a hat, getting ahead of herself thinking her son is getting married."

Tim sat up. "We've only been dating for like twelve hours."

"Who has?" asked his dad as he stood with his hands

on his hips.

"Me and Johann."

His dad smiled. "That's great news. I was on about Marty and Rebecca, though."

"Who the hell is Rebecca?" asked Tim as he put his half-empty pie bowl on the coffee table.

"Your brothers' new girlfriend. I think it must have been that blonde girl who was with him at the gig on Thursday. When I tell your mum you and Johann are also dating she will probably start bringing home Mother of the Bride magazines, knowing her."

Tim sat back and resumed eating. "I think we have plenty of time before reaching the wedding stage, both me and Marty. Anyway, what's under the sheet?" he asked, pointing at the object with a custard covered spoon.

"Me and your boy have been working hard."

"You finished the cot already?"

"We sure have," his dad replied proudly, before pulling the cover back like the unveiling of a high-powered sports car.

Tim was impressed with the sight before him. Even though he had supported the idea of making a homemade cot for his soon-to-be brother, he had to admit deep down he thought it may have been a bit rough around the edges. Seeing the result made him realise he had to give his dad more credit. "It looks great, Dad," he said as he stood and walked around it to take it in from all angles.

"Thanks."

"Genuinely. I'm impressed."

It stood about three foot high, and all the scrap wood he had seen earlier in the week formed a slatted structure, complete with a side which moved up and down with ease. Nothing looked out of place, and the wood shined like an ice-covered lake with the heavy layers of varnish they had applied.

"There is still a fair bit of wood out in the shed," said his dad as he wiped his hands on a stained tea towel. "Thought it might be nice to keep it for another project."

"Such as?" asked Tim.

"Well, me and Johann were chatting this morning whilst we were finishing it off, and we thought it might be nice if the three of us built a new house for Barnaby."

"He'd love that," replied Tim.

"It will be the most deluxe tortoise home in the world," his dad laughed. "Plus, I enjoyed working with Johann on this, and would love to do more with you involved too now I've got more free time."

Tim stood next to his dad. "It's going to be good having you here all the time," he said.

"We will make up for lost time," he responded. "Also," he added a few moments later, "Johann told me all about your meal last night."

"It was so good," Tim said. He wanted to give a mouthful by mouthful run down of everything, but his dad spoke first.

"I'm proud of you. You're growing into a wonderful man. If you'd have told me at the start of the year I would be spending the summer at home with Marty, you, and your boyfriend, I wouldn't have believed it."

Despite their heartfelt chat the evening before, neither Tim nor Johann had used the word boyfriend yet, but they didn't need to use it to make it official. It was only a short word, but those nine letters held so much weight. He had a boyfriend. An actual boyfriend and not a make believe one from a sports magazine. He felt prickles of heat bound through his veins, hoping this was just the final part of the old Tim leaving his conscience. He had no reason to hide anymore.

# Twenty-Five

Tim entered the school grounds, navigating his way past the gazebos and pop-up tables that now covered most of the school hockey pitches. A line of classic cars were lined up near the hedge, and at the far end he could see small fairground stalls. He reluctantly approached the area where the stage had been set up. Much like at The Bell, it was the back of a flatbed truck, decorated with yellow and green bunting, the seemingly vomit-inspired school colours.

A square area in front had been roped off, and his mouth became dry at the thought of The Dolly Mixtures performing in this space in a few hours' time. he could already see the boxes of pumpkins stacked next to one of the wheels.

"Tim!" came a shout from near the sixth form common room. He swung his head and saw Leo approaching with a Tesco carrier bag. He waved, and Leo bounded across to meet him.

"Choc ice?" he asked as he pulled two out of his bag.

"I'm good, thanks," replied Tim.

"Ah, come on, I can't eat them all and I don't want them to melt."

"I'm too nervous to eat," he replied, gesturing at the pumpkins.

"Fair enough. How was your meal last night?" Tim simply grinned back at him. "What?" Why are you looking like that?" he questioned.

"No reason," Tim answered. "Just thought I might wait for my boyfriend to come back before I tell you everything."

Leo jumped up immediately, dropping his food on to the floor where it started to melt immediately in the burning sun. He grabbed Tim and squeezed his shoulders hard. "No waaaaaaay," he said, dragging out the syllables for as long as possible. "Why didn't you tell me last night? I need ALL the details now."

"Get off," Tim replied, pushing him away and before putting his hands inside his pockets, embarrassed. "I'll tell you later."

"Nah, come on, this is huge news!" Leo begged.

"What's huge news?" asked Leo's mum as she came across with two carrier bags.

"It's nothing, Mrs Gardner," Tim said, before sarcastically grinning at Leo.

"As you wish. Now, you two can make yourselves useful and help me blow these up," she said, handing across two packs of balloons. "These have to be tied to each of the fence posts."

"Do we have to?" asked Leo.

"Yes," she replied, tossing him a solitary balloon pump before walking away.

Tim joined him on the steps. "Is there much more to prepare?"

"Nah, the tables are all set up, Dad has done the wellywanging markings and the dance area is all good to go now. We still have over an hour until it all starts anyway."

"Heya," said Johann as he crunched along the gravel path to join them.

"Leo knows about us," said Tim, passing him a handful of deflated balloons.

Johann rolled his eyes and laughed. "Him and Lydia

knew before we decided, I think."

After five minutes, a total of four balloons had been inflated. Most had zoomed off into the sky before they could tie a knot. They were further set back when Campbell walked past with Callum, popping the three that were attached to the fence behind them. Tim stared at them as they headed towards the fields.

"My mum phoned on my way here," Johann said as he fought to tie another knot.

"She alright?" asked Tim.

"Yeah. My uncle is back at home, so she is going to fly back this afternoon."

"That's great news!" said Leo.

"It is," added Tim. "I guess this means we won't be housemates for much longer, though."

"Yeah, I'll have to head back to my house this evening I think," said Johann, looking at Tim and noticing his disappointment. "I'm still gonna be round all the time, though." He kissed Tim and grabbed another balloon.

"Jeez, get a room you two," laughed Leo before Tim kicked his foot gently.

From the far end of the grounds, a loud large squeal of feedback echoed through the sky. Once faded, a few gentle taps of a microphone appeared. "One, two, one, two," came the voice of Mr Patterson.

Tim looked around at the small trailer that housed the announcement microphone. He thought it was loud enough for sure.

"One, two, one, two," came the voice again through the old speakers on trailer roof. Tim stood up and climbed on the first rung of the fence, waving in the direction of Mr Patterson.

"Can you hear me, Tim?" Mr Patterson asked. Tim responded by putting both his thumbs up. Mr Patterson thanked him before the sound of the speakers crackled off.

Once the balloons were complete, they tied them badly to the fence and went for a walk around the field. Tim was amazed on how you could improve an area with some banners and a bit of colour. Being back in the schoolgrounds made him feel a bit nervous about Year Eleven again. He hoped he was able to cope with it all.

He was mostly worried he would be subject to direct homophobic bullying now more people would know he was gay. Even though he had not officially come out to everyone, it would be extremely obvious to anyone attending the fete that him and Johann were now a couple. Campbell's behaviour had already made him believe he would be targeted directly. Every time someone looked in his direction, he would drop Johann's hand and feel his cheeks burn red.

Tim had taken on board all Honey Latté had told him and was trying his absolute best to not hide who he was in order to make other people happy. His family supported him, and so did the people around him who mattered. Everyone else would just have to get used to it. It was not his problem to solve anymore. He would follow the advice Leo had given earlier in the week and speak to Mr Barakat as soon as he could, though. Having the headteacher fully briefed with the situation would hopefully mean any bullying could be dealt with quickly and properly. He had heard rumours of people older than him who had been forced from the school due to being verbally abused and not receiving sufficient support. He was not going to be another statistic.

As the group of friends walked down the far end of the playing field, Tim's mum appeared and summoned them into the small marquee acting as the refreshments stall. They slipped in through the back entrance and were met with the sight of nearly every cake imaginable. Tim noticed his mum's pies were front and centre. Lydia was at the far end putting clingfilm on various desserts, whilst her mum stood nearby with a clipboard alongside a lady he didn't recognise.

"Got your pies here in one piece then?" Tim asked his mum.

"Just about," she responded. "I'll be honest, I don't think we are going to win. Some of these others are incredible, look," she added, pointing to a large cake in the shape of a waterfall in a forest.

"It's okay, Mum, you tried your best. I'm oddly proud of you," Tim said, trying to sound reassuring. She smiled back at him. "Where's Dad?" he asked.

"I'm not sure. He was helping me unload the car, but I haven't seen him for about ten minutes."

"Maybe he is doing some last-minute alterations to your dance outfit."

"No, we have already made sure both me and my bump still fit into it. I bet he is at the Foxborough Brewery stand already."

"I'll go and have a look in a minute," he said.

"Cheers. Now, don't be late for the dance off later, will you?"

"If I have to be there, I will," Tim responded.

"You do. It's all such a kerfuffle anyway now. One of Elaine's kids has come down with something, so we are a skeleton short."

"I'm not doing it," Tim said, anticipating he would be dragged into performing.

"I wasn't going to ask you. Just some moral support, though. I'm a bit nervous now I am here."

"I'm sure you'll be fine."

"Hey, Lyds," he heard Leo say.

Tim turned around as she approached, a half-eaten

muffin in her hand. "Alright?" she asked. The others nodded. "I think the food tent is all done now if you wanna come for a coffee in the canteen with me?"

"Yeah, can do," said Tim. "Who is your mum with?"

"Oh, that's Sheila Jenkins. She's the head of the PTA. Her daughter, Penelope, is Head Girl. She definitely got given that role because of her mum."

"You should apply to be Head Girl next year, Lydia," said Leo.

"No way. I don't care enough to do that."

"We'd vote for you," said Tim.

"Cheers, but still no."

"I don't think we have head boys or girls at my school," added Johann. "It's odd if you think about it. If we do then there is no way I'd apply for head boy. The jokes would write themselves."

"You're not nerdy enough to be Head Boy," Tim replied.

"How do you know?"

"Because you're too normal. Especially in a Greenwood sense."

"I guess. Tim, can you show me your form room whilst we wait for this fete to open."

"Why d'ya wanna see that?"

"Because I'm nosey. And I want to see if it's better than mine will be."

"Your school is way better," said Leo. "Ours will look like it's falling down in comparison. Your school is older, and the buildings were built to last more than twenty years."

"I still wanna see, though."

"Come on then," said Tim.

The four friends had only made it halfway across the school field when Mr Patterson's voice sputtered through the speakers again.

"Is this thing on?" said Mr Patterson before a muffled conversation was played out to everyone. "Yes, of course I have pressed the red button," he could hear Mr Patterson say in the background, before he coughed and came back loud and clear. "Sorry everyone, I have just been passed a piece of paper." A few more taps on the microphone came before the first official announcement of the day blasted out. "Could Timothy Johnson, Leo Gardner, and Lydia Flanagan please report to room D234. That's Tim, Leo and Lydia to room D234."

***

Tim, Leo, Lydia, and Johann sat on a row of chairs outside of the office belonging to the Head of English, which was located on the second floor of the Lower School form block.

"What do you think this is about?" asked Leo as they sat waiting.

Tim shrugged. "I always feel nervous when I get called up here, not that it happens often. Plus, we can't get detention outside of term, can we?"

"I doubt it. It's probably just checking we are all okay as they've definitely heard about the graffiti," said Lydia.

"But that wasn't us," said Leo.

"I know, but still."

"What are all those trophies for?" asked Johann, pointing to a dark and dusty cabinet on the wall opposite.

"They're all old ones," said Leo. "I don't think this school has won anything of note for years now."

Tim nodded. "Yeah, these are the old sports trophies. There are some team photos in there as well. My dad is in one of them, come and have a look."

Johann followed Tim across to the framed photos of

various sport teams. He watched as Tim studied the wall to find the right one.

"This one," Tim said, jabbing a finger to a faded photo of the Greenwood Secondary First XI Football Squad that had been taken in the early nineties. He watched as Johann studied it.

"I don't even need to ask which one is your dad," Johann said eventually, smiling.

"Has he not changed?"

"Yeah, he looks a lot different now, it's just he looks identical to you in it."

"Nah, no way does he."

"He absolutely does," continued Johann. "In fact, if you gave yourself a centre parting with a curtain fringe then you would practically look like twins."

"I wish I hadn't shown you now," Tim joked, taking Johann's hand and sitting back down again. "I think it's safe to say I haven't inherited his footballing ability, that's for sure."

"I don't think any of us will ever be in one of those team photos," added Lydia.

"Definitely not," said Leo.

They sat in silence for two minutes before the door to the office opened a fraction. They sat forward waiting for whoever it had been who had asked them up. A moment later, Tim's dad exited the office.

"Ah, you're all here, good," he said.

"What's happened?" asked Tim.

"We will explain, come through. You too Johann, if you want."

Tim entered first. The room was warm, with no ventilation. The bookshelves immediately on the right were cluttered and used coffee mugs were resting on the top of a filing cabinet, seemingly uncleaned since the end of summer term. As he turned towards the large desk, he saw their headteacher, Mr Barakat, sat facing him. It was odd not to see him in his usual brown suit. Instead, he was in a garish summer shirt, unbuttoned to reveal a shell necklace. To his right, PC Hughes was perched on a stool in his uniform. On a lone chair in the corner was Callum. His mum stood just behind.

"Please, take a seat," Mr Barakat said, gesturing to the extra chairs that had been brought through to the usually spacious room. The four children did as they were told, with a look of confusion coming over his face as they shuffled about. "I don't believe we have met," he said to Johann, as he stood slightly and offered his hand.

"Sorry," said Tim's dad. "This is Johann. He is Tim's boyfriend. He knows about this situation also."

"Nice to meet you, Johann. Unfortunately, it may be best if he waits outside, if that is okay? Without him being a pupil at this school or a parent present, I believe we would be in the wrong to include him."

"Agreed," added PC Hughes.

Tim's worries lifted slightly when he realised Mr Barakat had not raised his eyebrows at the use of the 'B' word. He made a mental note to tell him the full story as soon as possible.

Johann stroked Tim on the shoulder. "I'll be outside by the announcement van," he said, before departing.

"We are just waiting on the others, and then we can start," said Mr Barakat. "Please, help yourself to coffees."

The large clock on the mantelpiece chimed for eleven o'clock as Katherine Johnson, Flo and John Gardner, and Amy Flanagan entered the now cramped office. Mr Barakat waited for them to be settled before passing to PC Hughes.

"Many thanks for taking the time to come here this morning. I will keep this brief as I know the fete is due to start any moment now and we don't want to miss that, do we?" He waited for a moment, before continuing. "As you may have heard now, we have got to the bottom of the criminal damage situation that has plagued the town this week."

Callum shifted in his chair as Tim stared at him.

PC Hughes cleared his throat and continued. "We were going to see you all individually this afternoon, however, doing things this way will make things much quicker."

"Will he be going to prison?" asked Leo.

"Leo, please allow PC Hughes to speak," said Flo, before gesturing at the officer to continue.

"There will be no prison and there was never likely to be. All parties involved have confirmed they do not wish to press charges, so today is just to draw a line under the matter. I can confirm, however, the individual involved will not be attending Greenwood Secondary as planned this coming term, instead the family have agreed for the culprit to return to an address in London."

He was speaking as if Callum wasn't in the room.

"Why did you do it?" Tim asked. Callum didn't make eye contact, instead shrugging.

"Remember what we discussed, Callum," said PC Hughes.

"Sorry," muttered Callum.

"Is that it?" said Leo.

"I wanted to go back to London, you know that," Callum added.

"Why did you pick on me, though?" asked Tim.

"You were an easy target. And my cousin said you were bullying him."

"I don't even know your cousin."

"Yeah, you do, it's Campbell. He said you kept saying stuff to him all through school."

"He was the one being homophobic, not me," argued

Tim.

"Boys, let's try and keep this civil," Mr Barakat said, intervening.

"Sod that. I hate him."

"Tim, please," Mr Barakat replied, voice a few decibels higher. "Look, I don't want to be in here as much as anyone else, so the quicker we get this sorted, the quicker we can try and get on with our lives."

"I'd rather not have to look at him," said Tim. "At least he will be happier in London so he won't do it to anyone else."

"London will be much better," Callum confirmed.

"Yeah, for everyone." Tim didn't want to forgive him but didn't want to sit in the room any longer.

"Are you allowed to tell us how you were sure it was him?" asked Leo.

"I am unable to give full details, mainly due to the individual being a minor, however, let's just say we had evidence that placed Callum in the location of each piece of damage around the times they took place. In the end he decided admitting his guilt would be for the best."

"So, is that it?" asked Tim. "Is it really all over?"

"It is," confirmed PC Hughes.

"Now," started Mr Barakat, "I appreciate this may have been quite a tough week for you all, especially yourself, Tim. I know all parents are aware, however I understand you may feel worried in the future because of the situation, so if you ever need to speak to someone neutral, my door will always be open for you."

"Will do, thanks," Tim replied. He wanted to ask more questions, but PC Hughes was already slipping his coat on.

Tim took one final look as Callum was taken from the room by his mum, as the others started to depart.

"Tim, are you sure you are okay?" asked PC Hughes.

"I'm fine, I think. Thank you. Nobody still thinks it's me, do they?"

"No. All the businesses are aware. With any chain of events, the perpetrator will always make a mistake."

"What was Callum's?" asked Tim.

"Let's just say, if you are going to get caught on CCTV, try not to wear the same brand of clothing you are trying to promote on Instagram." PC Hughes winked, and then told them all to go and enjoy the activities out on the field.

The trio of friends had thanked Mr Barakat and PC Hughes, before being led back downstairs to the field by their parents. The hockey pitches had already started to fill with people, and pop music was playing over the sound system. They picked up four ice lollies from their physics teacher Mr Stephenson, who had been roped into running the ice cream stall, before they headed to meet Johann.

"I've got something to show you," said Johann as he pulled the wrapper off his Calippo. "Follow me." He led them up the slope and onto the sports field. "Now, you know when we did our research, Tim, we tried working out where Callum was each time didn't we?"

"Yeah but had no evidence."

"I think I've worked it out."

"How?"

"So, at the party, he was the last to arrive so he could have done the graffiti on his way."

"Yeah, we knew that," Tim said.

"He also knew you would be at the library on Wednesday lunchtime."

"Did I tell him?"

"Not directly, no, but when we were carving pumpkins, you spoke about it."

"Yeah, cos I complained about you not telling me,"

said Leo.

"It all makes sense," says Tim.

"Everything except why he did it," said Johann.

"It was because of his cousin, Campbell. He's the homophobe in our year I told you about. He said I was the bully, so Callum must have done this as some kind of revenge."

"Hopefully his cousin isn't at the fete," said Johann.

"He is. He is the one who popped our balloons."

"I guess being a knobhead runs in their family," said Johann.

"The only thing I don't understand is how you ended up with the paint, Tim," said Leo.

"He must have slipped it into my rucksack somehow," said Tim. "But what about Funtangutan? How did he manage to draw it without us seeing?"

"That's what I want to show you," said Johann. "Look."

As they had been talking, they had moved across the field and were now stood on the edge of the Children's Fun Zone. Alongside the various fairground stalls stood a large bouncy castle. A ginger haired man was wiping dirt from the inflatable base and complaining to parents about letting their children use it with their shoes still on. In large letters across the base of the inflatable was the word SPITFIRE.

"The Death Drop!" said Tim.

"Exactly," responded Johann.

"Explain for those not quite on the ball, please," said Leo.

"When I spoke to Tim about Funtangutan he told me how he felt sick at the end of the assault course because of him being shit scared of heights. He said the word Spitfire gave him flashbacks because it was written on the landing mat."

"It was yeah, I remember that, too," said Lydia.

"So," continued Johann, "if it's the same inflatable company, then Callum's stepdad could have been at Funtangutan."

"But how can we be sure Callum had been there too?" asked Tim.

"Remember he told us he had helped his stepdad with some faulty equipment? He must have been at Funtangutan the evening before we went. He had already done the graffiti on the shop, so could have easily done more in the entrance hut so it was ready for when we got there. He had everything planned out all along."

"I hate Callum," said Tim.

"I think we all do," said Johann.

"You were right though, Leo, his stepdad does look like Ed Sheeran," said Lydia.

"Told you!"

Tim felt Johann take his hand again and he was led away. "Come on you lot. Let's try and have some fun and forget about all this now."

*** 

Tim sat on the grass as Johann walked towards him with Pat and Pet's Jack Russell, Archie, who was being louder and more yappy than normal. Everyone had been watching a dog display when the balloons the group had blown up earlier started popping in the midday sun. With each bang, more chaos came to the display arena.

Dogs were running in every direction, all being chased by their owners, the show was eventually called off by a despairing man with a clipboard, looking like he was on the verge of a complete breakdown. There was a Dalmatian hiding in a material tunnel and a Miniature Schnauzer stood rigid on top of a wooden climbing obstacle. Archie had run in a straight line when the first bang occurred and picked up its pace with each further explosion. Johann had gone to retrieve it from its final position behind the small school pond, where it had also taken an unexpected dip.

"Thank you," said Pat as she took the damp dog from Johann and led it away, giving it a talking to as she did so. As the four laid back on the grass, Leo's phone buzzed.

"Here, it's a text from Callum," he said.

"I don't care," replied Tim, as he laid his head back across Johann's chest.

Leo ignored the brush off and read it out to the group. "Hi all. Just wanted to say sorry again for what I did. I'm being sent back to London tomorrow to live with Dad. Won't be at the fete now as have been grounded by Mum. Was good meeting you. Hope we can still be friends."

"We are never being his friend," said Lydia.

"I told you ages ago he was dodgy," said Tim. "Who else would choose invisibility as a superpower?"

"I guess."

"Has he posted anything on Instagram?" asked Johann.

Leo found his profile and checked his latest post. "He posted a pic this morning of some boxer."

"What's the caption?" asked Tim.

"When you get knocked down, it's not about how quickly you get back up, but how strong you are when you rise. #EyeOfTheTiger #RiseUp #FightOrFlight #NeverGonnaKeepMeDown."

"What an absolute knobhead," said Tim. "How can he say you can never keep him down when he's been grounded."

"It's already got over a thousand likes," added Leo.

"Good for him," said Tim. "I've already blocked him."

"Anyone want to have a go on some of the stalls?" asked Johann.

They walked along a row of tables, playing a few games on their way. Johann was the only one who was successful, winning a bottle of Ranch Dressing on the vicar's tombola. As they walked across the playground, Tim's mum ran over dressed in her witch outfit and grabbed him.

"We need your help, Tim, over the field, follow me," she said, before rushing away from him. He grabbed Johann's hand and followed her towards the dance arena. As he approached, he saw the pumpkins had all been rearranged into a pyramid. Behind a small screen made from a bedsheet tied to two javelins, he saw the Dolly Mixtures in costume waiting to take to the stage. The previous group, dressed as sunflowers, were removing their make-up and throwing outfits back into their bags. Tim approached his mum who was pulling items out of a black bin bag at pace.

"What do you need?" he asked.

She turned round and threw a skeleton onesie at him. "Put this on!"

"What? No way!" he replied, before turning away.

"Johann, help me out here," she begged.

"There's no way I am doing that," Tim said. "I've told you this already."

"We have lost both our skeletons, Tim. We will never win."

"I'll do it," said Johann. He walked forward and took an outfit from Tim's mum, before stripping off his shirt and trousers and forcing his legs into the relevant holes. It was two or three sizes too small.

"You don't have to do this, y'know," said Tim as he

watched his boyfriend hop about.

"I know, but it'll be fun."

"I might die of embarrassment."

"You need a sense of adventure," Johann added. He was clearly not yet up to date with just what it was to be a member of the Johnson family. Tim and Marty had both learned agreeing to anything their mum planned would see them ridiculed down the line. Tim decided to let it go this time so Johann could learn the hard way.

"I'll get some photos," Tim said as he stroked Johann's arm.

"Thanks. Before you go, help me zip the hood."

Tim obliged and gave him a hug before heading to take a seat out the front. He would watch through his fingers. As he passed the main dance area, he noticed it was the busiest part of the fete. Everyone was invested in this for some reason. He saw Lydia wave at him from the front row on the far side, so he made his way through the seated crowd to join them. As he was walking, he was tripped, and he stumbled to the floor. As he got to his feet, he heard laughter from the side.

"Watch where you're going, gay boy," sniggered Campbell. Tim decided to ignore him and moved forward, heart pounding in his chest. He had moved one step when his ankles were kicked again. He turned round and Campbell was now stood up and in his face. "I said, watch where you're going, gay boy," he sneered, dragging out the final words to emphasise the insult.

"Leave me alone," Tim said.

"Why? You're the one who has just got my cousin kicked out of school. I told him he shouldn't hang out with you losers, but he wouldn't listen."

"It's his own fault for putting graffiti everywhere. Maybe it's your family who are the losers," Tim argued.

Campbell went to take another step towards to him,

but Tim pushed him down onto his seat hard before rushing away to join Leo and Lydia.

"What was that about?" asked Lydia as Tim took a seat next to her.

"Nothing," mumbled Tim

"It didn't look like nothing."

"It's just Campbell being a dick as usual."

"Want me to sort him out?" asked Leo.

"No, I'm fine."

"You look pale," said Lydia.

"I'm fine."

"Want some yoghurt banana chip thing?" Leo asked, handing Tim a brown paper bag. "They've started melting together, sorry."

Tim ignored the offer, instead sitting firmly back in his chair and crossing his arms. He couldn't concentrate fully on his surroundings after the argument and wanted to be anywhere else, but there was no way of avoiding the upcoming nightmare that was about to be played out. At least Johann being in the display would make it more bearable.

His geography teacher, Ms Bellingham, came out to the front as the intro to the Grease Megamix started playing in the background. "Please welcome to the stage, The Dolly Mixtures!"

There was a round of applause and some people started to stand as Tim sank as low into his chair as possible. As the vocals began, his mum's dance group entered the arena. It started off at an acceptable level, but by the time the change into the second song of the mash-up came, Frankenstein's Monster was already well out of time. Johann was at the back moving his arms slightly, but generally keeping out of the limelight. Tim could tell the realisation of what he was doing had dawned on him.

His mum was now front and centre, encouraging the

crowd to clap along. He could see Jill just behind, picking her vampire fangs up off of the grass. Tim reluctantly joined in the clapping until he felt a shiver down his spine. This was not from fear, though, and he felt cold liquid run down his back and onto the chair. He stood up and saw Campbell behind him.

"No one pushes me, gay boy," he scoffed as he flicked the remainder of his drink into Tim's face. Leo stood and started pushing Campbell as Tim fled from the scene. The music faded out inside his head as he focussed on putting one foot in front of the other. He found himself backstage and was worried Campbell would be close behind. He pulled off his wet t-shirt and shorts and dug around the bin bag for the spare skeleton costume. He jumped into it in record time and headed out into the arena with the back still unzipped.

Johann was still at the back as Tim joined him, rocking about slightly as he scanned the crowd. He could see Leo with fists clenched, looking bemused. Campbell had moved back towards the left-hand side. The music was still playing, and the finale was approaching. Johann handed a water pistol across to Tim.

"When they hit the final note, we have to fire this fake blood over the dancers," Johann shouted as he got into position. Tim walked to the opposite side and took his spot. He could hear Campbell sat less than a metre beside him still jeering and throwing insults. The climax of the song came, and Johann sprayed the fake blood over The Dolly Mixtures as planned.

As Tim went to follow suit, a wave of anger came over him. He thought of Honey Latté and how he had promised to stand up for himself more. He turned and towered over Campbell's seat, before emptying the thick red contents of his water pistol all over Campbell's white shirt, before picking up the refill bucket and throwing that over him also.

Campbell stood, dripping red liquid onto his trainers. Tim remained rooted to the spot, finally confident to stand his ground.

"You are going to pay for this," Campbell shouted as he took a step forward, his facing turning the same shade as his clothes. As he clenched his fist and pulled his arm back, Marty flew in from the side and rugby tackled him to the floor, sitting on him as he laid face down on the grass.

Mr Barakat arrived on the scene and tried to drag Campbell away. Despite the headteachers best efforts to silence him, Campbell continued his tirade. "You are going to pay for this, Tim," he spat.

Tim picked up the empty bucket and moved his face inches away from Campbell's. "You have no power over me," Tim said, before walking away smiling.

## Acknowledgements

Thank you to Stuart at SRL Publishing for taking a chance on Tim and Johann. It has been a pleasure to work with you and I have learnt so much about the publishing world through our conversations.

A big thanks to Emily for the amazing cover and for decoding the ideas I sent across. It looks just how I had pictured in my mind.

Thanks also to those who have taken the time to read through my writing in all its various stages, especially David for reading it about ten times, also to Jam for your continued help and support.

I wouldn't have completed this without a massive support network, so in no particular order (and with fingers crossed I haven't missed anyone): Mum, Dad, Katherine, Chris, Jamie, Howi, Hewer, Banko, Rob, Eddy, Matt, Conroy, Sara, Lauren, Tor, Adam, Joe G, Perks, Andy, Rougie, Lynden, Grant, Ryder, Anna-L, Sam, Hannah, Jenni, Mads, Mickey, Ollie, Sammy, Zoe, Bradley, Katie, William, Paggy, Fran, Bournemouth EBC & Talbot crews, and anyone who has supported and shared on social media.

Finally, thank you to all the cool authors who have chatted and helped support, including but not limited to: Anna Britton, Ian Eagleton, L. D. Lapinski, Julia Hien, and all the amazing writers in the querying Discord group who you won't know… yet.

*SRL Publishing don't just publish books, we also do our best in keeping this world sustainable. In the UK alone, over 77 million books are destroyed each year, unsold and unread, due to overproduction and bigger profit margins.*

*Our business model is inherently sustainable by only printing what we sell. While this means our cost price is much higher, it means we have minimum waste and zero returns. We made a public promise in 2020 to never overprint our books for the sake of profit.*

*We give back to our planet by calculating the number of trees used for our products so we can then replace them. We also calculate our carbon emissions and support projects which reduce C02. These same projects also support the United Nations Sustainable Development Goals.*

*The way we operate means we knowingly waive our profit margins for the sake of the environment. Every book sold via the SRL website plants at least one tree.*

*To find out more, please visit www.srlpublishing.co.uk/responsibility*